SPEAK
FOR
YOURSELF

SPEAK FOR YOURSELF

LANA WOOD JOHNSON

Scholastic Press / New York

Library of Congress Cataloging-in-Publication Data

Names: Johnson, Lana Wood, author.

Title: Speak for yourself / Lana Wood Johnson.

Description: First edition. | New York: Scholastic Press, an imprint of Scholastic Inc., 2021. | Audience: Ages 12 and up. | Audience: Grades 7–9. | Summary: Skylar Collins of Lovelace Academy intends to win at the Scholastic Exposition, (an extremely nerdy academic competition) using her latest app, which she considers a brilliant piece of coding; but first she has to assemble a team, and she will do anything to accomplish that, even if it means playing Cupid for teammates Joey and Zane—but her people skills are not as good as her coding, and when she starts to feel attracted to Zane things get even more complicated.

Identifiers: LCCN 2020047457 | ISBN 9781338660401 (hardcover) | ISBN 9781338660418 (ebook)

Subjects: LCSH: Academic achievement—Competitions—Juvenile fiction. | Competition (Psychology)—Juvenile fiction. | Application software—Juvenile fiction. | Mobile apps—Juvenile fiction. | High school students—Juvenile fiction. | Dating (Social customs)—Juvenile fiction. | Interpersonal relations—Juvenile fiction. | Friendship—Juvenile fiction. | CYAC: High schools—Fiction. | Schools—Fiction. | Contests—Fiction. | Competition (Psychology) —Fiction. | Mobile apps—Fiction. | Dating (Social customs)—Fiction. | Interpersonal relations—Fiction. | Friendship—Fiction.

Classification: LCC PZ7.1.J6285 Sp 2021 | DDC 813.6 [Fic]—dc23

1 2021

Printed in the U.S.A.   23

First edition, June 2021

Book design by Baily Crawford

For the '93-'94
TRHS and Lincoln
Academic Decathlon teams

The theme for this year is: The Second Industrial Revolution (1870–1914).

Lovelace Academy's captain is: Skylar Collins.

Each Scholastic Exposition is made up of two parts: the Quizposition and the Booth Expo. Together they are meant to display your understanding of this year's theme.

Quizposition is the exciting speed knowledge event ScholEx is known for. Teams must have enough scholars in two challenging rounds:

Achiever (three or four students with a GPA above 3.0)

Pathfinder (three or four students with a GPA below 3.0)

In each round, participating scholars will accumulate points for their team. All questions are based on information provided in the attached packet covering the areas of art, music, history, science, and literature. Get those buzzer thumbs limber!

The Booth Expo brings Achiever and Pathfinder scholars together to demonstrate an applied understanding of the knowledge they gained in studying for the Quizposition. At the competitions, six to eight participants will set up and present an interactive booth that uses multimedia to display a variety of aspects of the year's theme. Every member of the team should be able to share their knowledge by presenting different elements of the booth through conversations with the Expo judges.

We will be meeting Thursdays after school in room 204.

Our first meet will be December 12 and will include a qualifying Quizposition. There you will have the opportunity to see prior State- and National-level booths. This will inspire us for our own booth, which we'll present at Regionals in late January. Where we go from there depends on you!

CLICK HERE TO ACCEPT THE INVITATION

CHAPTER ONE

"I NEED YOU to accept Mrs. James's invite so I can configure the GroupHub before practice tonight," I say, loudly dropping my tray of salad onto my usual spot at the farthest table in the cafeteria. To make it seem like an excessively dramatic gesture, the sugar cookie decorated like a pumpkin jumps off and lands a foot away.

My best friend, Mads, looks up from her all-consuming conversation with Kaden on the other side of her and hooks her thin black bangs behind her ears. "You need what?"

Her mom finally let her dye her hair black this summer, and even though it's November, I'm still not used to it. Her equally darkened brows are furrowed at me. Her clothes match her hair, all blackness and lace—on which she spends every penny she makes doing art commissions as the goth queen LeBrat. One of her pieces sold for almost a hundred dollars last month.

The Mads in my brain has mousy-brown hair, a squeaky voice, and ink stains on her hands and usually the corner of her lip, too.

The Mads in my brain doesn't wear lace at school.

The Mads in my brain isn't dating Kaden.

I should be grateful they're not making out or something. Kaden used to be *our* friend. It's been the three of us at this same table since freshman year. But the two of them started dating last spring break—making me a third wheel in my own best friendship.

But while Mads has changed physically, Kaden is still Kaden: T-shirt, jeans, boots more suitable for a construction site than a school cafeteria. Like Mads and me and most of the school, Kaden is white, but unlike any of us, their hair has been buzzed out of existence. A choice made in ninth grade not long after they started sitting with us at the lunch table. But they're not just Kaden. Not anymore. Now Mads and Kaden are a defined object.

"I convinced Mrs. James we're going to need a private group on HubBub, which I can't get ready until there's more people in the GroupHub. So . . . I need you to confirm your invitations," I explain, sitting on the bench that is either too small or too big, but definitely digs into my legs in all the wrong ways.

"You're still active on that cesspool?" Kaden asks, judgment thick in their voice.

"Oh, come off it, you're still there, too," I say, settling into an argument that predates even their dating. HubBub may not be the only social platform out there, but it's by far the biggest. Nowhere else has apps, chats, and groups. It's definitely the only one that makes it easy for individual coders to create or publish at the level of a development company.

Which, I guess, is a thing I'm the only one in the whole school cares about. But still.

"Only because this bourgeoisie manufacturing facility known as our high school has sold out to the corporate overlords of the so-called social media site that's neither social nor media or even merely a site at this point," they say for like the fiftieth time.

"Corporations pay HubBub millions for access to the extra services our school gets for free," I say. "It would be ridiculous not to take advantage of all that the HubBub platform has to offer." Ever since Kaden discovered socialism they've become a real snob.

"Platform, like they're trying to lift us up. They only do it to turn us into drones, so addicted to their mind-numbing content that by the time we graduate we assume they're the answer for everything," Kaden says, leaning past Mads to glare at me. "Wake up, Skylar, this is the real world."

"We'll accept later, all right, Sky?" Mads says, laying a black-gloved hand on Kaden's arm.

I bite back comments that, intellectually, I know would lead to a shouting match on whether capitalism has any merits in the first place. Because that's how all our conversations go now. Instead I decide to focus on what really matters. "Please? I need at least three members to confirm before they'll let me install my app."

"Of course this is about the app," Kaden says under their breath.

"Does this mean we're good to go for Study Buddy?" Mads asks, perking up a little bit.

Ever since HubBub opened up their Young Developers' track to our school, Mads and I have been making apps. I handle the coding, and she makes the graphics. It started with a kitty puzzle game in seventh grade that used a basic template. It got five hundred downloads, which is no small feat for middle schoolers. But Study Buddy is on a whole different level. It turns class notes into flash cards for better group studying. People actually need it, and I'll be the one who brings it to them.

"Yeah. I got the last of the bugs worked out Friday, and your new buttons finally loaded in this weekend. The HubBub team that approves education apps is normally slow—we're talking weeks. But since I was just addressing the edits they sent me, they put me into the priority testing queue, so it's already live." I know I'm talking nerd at them, but they're the only ones in the whole school who have half a chance of understanding what I'm saying. If I try to talk to my dad, he starts going on about what he's working on, and my mom gets maybe half of it. She wants me to use smaller words and less detail, but the details are important.

Plus, I got into the priority testing queue!

Normally if you want to get an app on their site, you have to build tests into it and have it pass some quality checks. The priority queue is for big software companies with whole departments that do just testing. Before now I had to go to the "Young Developers Queue" so HubBub's people could do quality checks for me and then give me a list of things that didn't work so I could fix them.

At first they just sent me instructions, but as I progressed, they began to guide me through how they do the checks so I can do them myself. The better I get, the more areas of development they open to me. Study Buddy was so good I can now develop social apps—which aren't hard to create, they just require a new level of customer support and give me access to marketing training and a whole nightmare of unreadable reports.

"So the bigger size did work for the buttons?" Mads asks, her lips curling into the smile that only appears when she's been proven right, entirely missing the important part of what I just said.

"I still prefer the original ones," I mutter, not ready to concede the point in what is now a months-old argument.

"I told you they were way too small, but you never listen."

"I can't help that I have a lot of content to fit on a single screen."

"You can," Kaden weighs in while snagging one of Mads's Tater Tots and her attention, "since you're the developer." I honestly don't know how either of them can eat the poorly fried nonsense that comes out of that cafeteria. The salad bar has the only halfway edible stuff in this place. Don't get me wrong, I like a good Tot, but there's nothing good about these.

"Hey, that's mine!" She scowls, taking one of Kaden's grapes in revenge.

"Can you just accept the request? I want to have every-thing installed before our meeting this afternoon so I can show everyone how it works."

"Uhhh, that's not today," Kaden says.

"It's every Thursday so it doesn't conflict with debate prep," I say.

Kaden, a member of said debate team, grins at me sheepishly.

"No!" I shout, turning in my chair. "No!" Most of the rest of the debate team is roosted two tables over like they nor-mally are. And as usual they're surrounded by more scraps of paper, laptops, school-issued tablets, and assorted accordion files than actual food. "You said I could have Thursdays!"

Mads says, under her breath, "Teachers can hear you."

Kaden says, "The entire school can hear her."

But I'm already off my seat, not willing to be ignored by the one person who needs to hear me. "*Every* includes this Thursday!"

Before I reach my target, my older brother, Logan, puts himself between me and the rest of his team like a particu-larly annoying wall. If everyone didn't already know we're related, they could tell by looking at us. He keeps his light brown hair short, while I keep mine in a ponytail. We also share the physique that made our dad a great offensive line-man in college, but only looks right on Logan despite neither of us being remotely good at any sport that doesn't involve a controller. He's one growth spurt short of six feet, while I'm still a few inches shorter. But currently he has his giant finger pressed against the middle of my forehead in a way that both Mom and Dad would definitely have a problem with if they ever saw him doing it.

"Back to earth, nerdling."

"Stop it, you beast. I'm really going to kill him this time."

"Who's she killing now?" Zane asks from behind the wall of jerk.

My brother grins. "You, Captain, who else?"

"What'd I do now?" The russet mop of Zane's hair is visible just above my brother's shoulder. The captain of the debate team sounds perfectly innocent even though I know he's not.

"He doesn't deserve to be called a captain. He's just a jerk who breaks promises." I grab Logan's finger and grin. He knows I'm strong enough now to pull it backward in a way that super hurts. But he also knows I won't risk getting in real trouble at school. So instead he kind of twists and wraps his arm around my shoulder so we're both facing Zane. No doubt everyone thinks we're just particularly close family based on his big grin. No one suspects that charming, lovable Logan has me trapped in some big-brother-side-hug thing.

"What promises?" Zane asks, eyes sparkling. He knows what I'm talking about. He always knows. He never does anything accidentally. Not breaking my beaker in our chemistry class freshman year and not scheduling his practice session on top of ours. He's on the ScholEx team; he got the email.

"Today is ScholEx practice."

"Today," he corrects in his superior tone, "is our last chance to prep cards before the invitational."

"You're going back on your promise because you're behind on copying Google down in your notepad?"

"There's more to it than that," Zane says defensively.

"Oh, right, there's also summarizing Wikipedia. I forgot."

"No need to get snippy."

"You did promise her Thursdays," Dom says from somewhere down the table. Dom, one of the only Black kids on the debate team, is always far more rational than his best friend, Zane. I can only see the top of his fade through the sea of paper, but I still flash my most winning smile in his direction. He's a good person despite his terrible taste in friends.

"See!" I say, trying once more to tug away from my brother, but he has me tight.

"You can have next Thursday," Zane says with a sigh. "Today is too important."

"I need this one."

"ScholEx doesn't even have an event for weeks," he says, as if he's entirely forgotten that Thanksgiving is in the middle of that.

"ScholEx has a grand total of one Pathfinder scholar. We need three . . . minimum," I say.

"Can't you just call them C-level students instead of Pathfinder scholars?" Zane asks. "That's what they are."

"Some of the most creative ScholEx students don't achieve academically," I say, as my captain's handbook told me to.

"No one will want to join if you scream about their grades in front of everyone, Zane." I don't mention that I have utterly failed to find anyone who fits in Pathfinder except Mads, and she only joined for the obvious reasons.

"If I get you a 'Pathfinder,' will you back off today?" Zane asks, putting air quotes around *Pathfinder* with his fingers and continuing to be a really big snot about it.

"No."

"Okay, how about two?"

"You don't know two Pathfinder scholars."

"Logan," Zane says, his voice suddenly dripping with honey, "will you join another club for your sister?"

My brother jostles me. "Will she ask nicely?"

I squint up at him. "No, you oaf, I need people who will actually study to prove my app works."

"I'll study. It'll be fun."

"You don't need the extracurriculars! Why would you join?"

"I do so."

"You're not even applying to any worthwhile colleges!"

While Logan's been annoying, so far he hasn't actually hurt me, but the college jab hurts him. He lets go of my shoulder and steps away. "Ouch, dude."

"I'm sorry," I say, and I mean it. Mom has been riding him about applying early decision. She's not wrong, but it's not his fault he's never had the clear vision of the future that I've had.

"I mean, it's fair, but ouch, dude."

"I didn't mean it like that."

"Then you'll let me on your nerd team?"

"You don't want to be in ScholEx. It's literally all studying."

"But that's why you spent all summer making your super-study instant-knowledge app, right, nerdling?"

I roll my eyes. "It's still work."

He winks at me. "I'm joining your team, if only to keep you and Zane away from each other."

"I haven't hurt him yet."

"Because I'm always around."

"Okay, fair."

We both look back at Zane, who is wearing his smuggest smile.

"Deal?"

"No," I say. "I also need to do an orientation for my app."

"Monday," Zane says.

"Mrs. James won't be around on Monday," I say.

"Not here, in the GroupHub we're going to join. You've heard of it, right? It's this magical place where you can make anything happen?"

"You'll accept the invite?"

He picks up his phone. "Already done." Then, as he unlocks his screen, he says over his shoulder, "Right, Dom?"

I can feel my phone vibrating in my pocket and know he's actually done it. Incredible. "One more Pathfinder, you twit."

"Oh, I can find you someone."

"You're not perfect, you know."

"You have a card for that?" Zane says, clearly making some sort of hilarious debate reference because his table full of nerds laughs right on cue.

"I hate you."

"You wish you hated me," Zane says.

"We good?" Logan asks me.

"Only if you make up for slowing me down by winning your event this weekend."

"Trust me, I will," Zane says.

"I wasn't talking to you." I turn sharply on my heel and take a really deep breath, heading back to the table with Mads and Kaden, who are very specifically not looking at me.

"Doesn't mean I won't win," Zane calls after me.

 Study Buddy

Study Buddy allows you to divide and conquer.
Difficult subjects are made easier by divvying up the coaching among students based on their familiarity with the topic and skill level. Using BubbleViews, the weakest students create review materials for the strongest students to verify. HubBub APIs allow students to interact with BVs by converting notes into scoreable flash cards.

Developer: SkyLessLimits

CLICK HERE TO INSTALL LOVELACE ACADEMY SCHOLASTIC EXPOSITION TEAM

CHAPTER TWO

IT'S FINALLY MONDAY. The night I actually get real users for my app. It took some serious negotiating to get everyone to meet, and I had to get all my homework done so I'd have time to get everything set up. As I walk into the kitchen for supper, I say, "Logan and I have a meeting at seven." But the words come out so fast I'm not sure they're even words. Mom is putting the finishing touches on supper, and Dad isn't home from work, so at least I'm not late.

"Well, who scheduled that?" my mom asks as if I made perfect sense. She pulls a big pot of pasta off the heat and drops a handful of spinach and parsley into it.

"Who do you think?" Logan asks, reaching over her to steal one of the shrimp she's about to put in a bowl only to have Mom swat his hand away with the wooden spoon. She's been the shortest of us since this summer, but somehow she doesn't take up any less space.

"Ow," he says, pulling his hand back.

"Skylar, you know Monday night is family night." She goes back to stirring. "It's hard enough getting us all together with your dad's hours and all your after-school stuff. Logan, get the salad dressing out of the fridge."

"This is an after-school thing, Mom. It's ScholEx. Plus, it's not for another hour. We can eat a good healthy dinner and converse like civilized people, I promise."

Dad walks in from the garage carrying the messenger bag with his laptop. "I have a call at seven," he says, and I cover a smile under my hand.

Mom gives him a face. "You two, I swear."

Logan dances past with the dressing on his way to the dining room table, singing, "I'm the good one."

"I wouldn't go that far," Mom says, following him into the dining room with the bowl full of pasta. "Forks, Sky. It's the least you could do."

Dad stands awkwardly in the middle of the kitchen for a second with no assignment. "Do you think she got the cheese?"

"Probably not," I say, grabbing forks from the drawer.

He opens the fridge door and digs around, finally pulling out a green container of what is at least labeled cheese. "I don't know what she has against it."

"I have the cheese," Mom shouts from the other room, and we both laugh.

I follow him to the dining room, where Mom is grating fresh Parmesan over her pasta. "Put that back, it's three-quarters plastic shavings."

"Delicious, delicious plastic shavings," Dad says, putting the cheese product firmly on the table in front of him.

She glares at it and keeps grating cheese onto her pasta. "So what are you up to that's more important than family time?" Mom asks, handing me the forked spoon thing so I can serve myself a plate of pasta.

"We have a call with China," my dad says, passing Logan the cheese under the table.

Mom glares at Logan pouring cheese product onto his fresh pasta, the grater directly in front of him remaining unused by anyone but her. "Stop encouraging your children to villainy."

Dad looks up from his phone, where he's dialing down the intensity on the lights to the point it feels more like a restaurant than a dining room. "I don't want to be accused of not being a good provider."

"I swear you've managed to make this house smarter than you are," she mutters, putting a dollop of dressing on her salad.

"That reminds me," he says. "Sky, can you help me this weekend? The new thermostat came in."

Mom puts her fork down with a clatter. "What was wrong with the old one?"

"It's first gen," I say through a forkful of pasta. "It was losing efficiency."

"Why don't you ever ask me to help, Dad?" Logan asks before shoving a shrimp in his mouth sans pasta.

Dad just looks at Logan, and Mom is doing the same.

Logan breaks first, laughing. "Sorry, worth a shot."

Dad looks relieved, but Mom says, "You probably should help them—learn a few things."

"I am learning plenty. But I can't this weekend. It's the all-around."

"You just had a tournament last weekend," she says.

"It's the season. And we're basically booked now through December thanks to ScholEx." He gives me a look, and my parents glance between us.

"You joined ScholEx?" Mom asks, shocked, looking to me for confirmation.

I just shrug.

Dad asks, "What'd you bribe him with, sunshine?"

"It wasn't me," I say, quickly shoving salad in my mouth so I don't have to explain.

"Please say this means you're actually starting to take your college admissions seriously. Though doesn't that season go kind of late for applications?" Mom asks.

"It's a favor to Zane, if you must know. Extra time messing with Sky is just a bonus."

"And how is your latest little project coming along?" Dad asks.

"It's fine," I say, but I want to remind him that it's not little. I put as much time into this as one of his developers would into his stuff. It's The One. But I don't say that. I just chew my salad.

"Don't denigrate her like that, Charles," Mom says. "You're sure this is the one, right, Sky?"

"I didn't mean that. I'm sure you did an excellent job," Dad says.

"I got through the second round of approvals in the priority queue." I grab another forkful and hope the conversation will move on.

"That's great, sunshine!" Dad says, because he can never sound like a CEO when he says it. He has to sound like a dad. He started a small data-management company about seven years ago after working for another tech start-up that kind of went under. Now he has his own staff, who create app-like things on other people's platforms . . . just like I do. He jokes he's going to hire me and pass the company on, but his dreams are too small for me. He's happy with a few big contracts for other people's work.

I'm going to make my own platform one day.

"Did you get your tests figured out?" Mom asks. She's not a programmer—she's a project manager for massive projects working with a lot of nerds like Dad and me. They do stuff with big data and analytics. This means she always knows what to ask even if she doesn't actually know how to do any of it. And she's usually trying to use our conversations as practice for "speaking to laypeople."

Dad tried to hire her away, but even he can't afford her.

"Yeah, turned out I was overthinking it, and they were actually pretty straightforward."

"Story of your life," Logan says, the black sheep of the family with his social skills and public-speaking abilities but none of the logic.

"Speaking of applications," Mom says, looking at him.

"There's still time." It's his turn to shove a forkful in his mouth.

"Have you given any more thought to Dartmouth?" she asks, and I laugh through my own bite, almost choking on the powdered cheese.

Logan just glares at me, and Mom says, "It's got a very prestigious debate program."

When he finishes chewing, Logan says, "A prestigious policy program, Mom. I do extemporaneous speaking." He's clarifying this for about the hundredth time. "I explain things so people understand. I don't argue at high speeds."

"Then what are you thinking?" Mom asks, her fork going back down to her plate. "Business school?"

"I'm thinking Iowa State. We've discussed this." He's said it before, but it's like a hush goes through the room. State is fine if you want to study to be an engineer, which he clearly doesn't.

"Logan, son," Dad says after Mom gives him a look. "At least consider Grinnell College." I don't laugh at this; I would never. Mom went there. But even though I have totally behaved, I'm pulled in all the same when Dad adds, "You've got to keep your sights high. Just look at your sister."

"Skylar's going to Stanford, Dad." Logan puts his own fork down with a clatter. "Other parents would want me to save a few bucks on gen ed while figuring things out."

"I'm just concerned you're not applying yourself," Mom says for about the five billionth time, and goes on about how she's worried about him. It's almost one of Logan's extemporaneous speeches at this point, with a framework and a persuasive point. It even lasts a solid seven minutes.

"Well"—Logan stands up—"good thing I'm joining ScholEx with the genius child. Right?"

"Sit down, Logan," Dad says.

"You haven't been excused," Mom says.

Logan looks at them and then at his plate, which is actually reasonably clean.

"No, we have to go," I say, standing up, too. Maybe in solidarity, but probably just so I don't get dragged into all this even further. Mom has an equally practiced speech about how I should be taking better care of myself and not push so hard. Half of it undermines everything in her Logan speech.

Dad frowns at his watch, which has clearly just vibrated at him. "They're right. I have to get set up."

"Who is going to help me with all of these?" Mom asks, still with a half-full plate.

"I'll come down and clean when we're done," Logan says. "I'm at least good for that much."

"Logan, that's not what I . . ." But she trails off with a sigh and then starts up again with questions about what he wants. Questions he's never been interested in answering.

I wish they cared half as much about my future as they do about Logan's, or at least acknowledged I had a future. My parents keep trying to slow me down, get me to smell the roses. They keep reminding me that the stress isn't good for my migraines. Mom thinks I need to pace myself as I figure out these meds, or that diet, or some new treatment. They both think there will be more time when I'm older.

They say that, but there's always an imaginary ticking clock somewhere off to the side. Like there isn't as much time as we think, even though the doctors say this is just how it'll be for me from now on. Family nights have this frantic quality to them, like Mom's using them to hit milestones on a project she never shares with us. A secret project she started after one of my headaches got bad enough to land me in the hospital last January.

Since this whole thing is my fault, it's not fair of me to let them dig into Logan, but today I've got bigger stuff to worry about. I'm about to launch my app to its first real users. I carry my plate to the kitchen just so I don't get yelled at by either Logan or Mom later. As I sneak through the back hall upstairs, I can still hear Mom making a case for applying to Dartmouth and Logan, yet again, explaining the difference between his speech event and what Zane does.

I don't help this time. I can't. I need to get on before anyone else so I can make sure the chat's set up properly.

Lovelace Academy Scholastic Exposition Team's GroupHub
Admin: Skylar Collins

ADMIN: Before proceeding to your GroupHub, please confirm
your content filter:
(Required for all SchoolHubs)
___ ASCII
_X_ Bleep
___ Smash

Since this is your first time logging in, here's a reminder of how
GroupHubs work:
Starting text with " adds dialogue tags as if you are having a
conversation.
Starting text with ; adds the text after your name without
dialogue tags.
For more commands type @HELP.

Welcome, Skylar.

You created the LAScholEx channel.

This channel closes and conversation is archived when
all participants have left or been idle for more than
an hour.

Your meeting starts in 5 minutes.

Zane has joined LAScholEx.

Skylar says, "Why are you here so early?"

Zane says, "Why are YOU here so early?"

Skylar says, "I'm team captain."

Zane says, "I'm~team~captain."

Skylar says, "Real mature."

Zane says, "You know I'm kidding."

Zane says, "But for real. We just got done with our policy prep session, and I logged in here too."

Skylar says, "On the internet? Is that allowed? I thought all you did was kill trees."

Zane laughs, but ironically.

Zane says, "Is that really what you want to run against me? Debate BAD on environment GOOD."

Skylar rolls her eyes.

Skylar says, "You know I don't speak debate."

Skylar says, "Why don't you go try to impress whoever your partner is now that Sal graduated?"

Zane says, "Sky, it's November."

Skylar says, "What?"

Zane says, "Joey and I have been partners for over a month."

Skylar says, "Who is Joey? The wormy looking freshman?"

Zane says, "That's Geoff. Joey is one of the homeschool kids who does extracurriculars through Lovelace. She's really quick. SUPER nice. Amazing breath control. She can spread like no one's business."

Skylar says, "Well, congratulations on finding a speed reader."

Dominic has joined LAScholEx.

Mads has joined LAScholEx.

Kaden has joined LAScholEx.

Mads says, "Who left you unchaperoned????<??"

Dominic bows.

Dominic says, "Nice, you've got full actions."

Dominic says, "Bleep that."

Dominic laughs. "Really, Sky?"

Zane says, "Trust Dom to immediately test the filters."

Your meeting has started.
Dominic has changed his name to Dom.

Kaden says, "You two haven't killed each other yet"

Skylar rolls her eyes, again.

Dom says, "She's using the bleep filter. The worst she can do to him is call him a goofy pants."

Mads says, "Dominic!!@!! LANGUAGE!!!"

Dom laughs.

Zane laughs.

Skylar says, "You all are hilarious."

Logan has joined LAScholEx.

Logan says, "Never fear, Logan's here!"

Logan says, "Bleep."

Logan laughs.

Skylar says, "Seriously? Are you twelve?"

Dom laughs.

Kaden says, "Twelve is generous"

Mads says, "It's vital to know one's filters."

Kaden rolls their eyes.

Mads says, "I've left you around Sky too long."

Skylar says, "What's that supposed to mean?"

Kaden says, "What's that supposed to mean?"

Zane laughs.

Dom laughs.

Logan says, ";laughs."

Skylar says, "Who is missing?"

Mads says, "The Pathfinder we need to be able to participate at the local meet."

Skylar looks at Zane.

Zane looks behind himself.

Skylar says, "Haha. Where are we with that, Mr. Liar?"

Zane says, "At least you're putting some respect on the name."

Zane says, "I have an idea. Trust me."

Skylar says, "An idea isn't going to get us to Nationals."

Kaden says, "Nationals"

Skylar says, "Yes, Nationals."

Kaden says, "Isn't that a bit ambitious"

Logan laughs.

Logan says, "Hello, Kaden, this is my sister Skylar, have you met?"

Mads simply sighs.

Skylar says, "I've installed Study Buddy to the group. We'll use it to divvy up some of the responsibilities for studying the materials."

Skylar says, "It's not enough to know the answer, you need to know it faster than anyone on any of the other teams."

Skylar says, "Since all the questions come from the packet Mrs. J sent about the Second Industrial Revolution, we should be able to use it to prove my app works."

Kaden says, "WHEE rampant colonialism"

Skylar says, "Kaden, obviously, will be taking lead on history."

Zane says, "Is that how it goes? Folks take the lead on subjects?"

Kaden says, "What makes you think I know anything about the rise of labor in the face of monopolistic robber barons?"

Logan says, "Well, for one, you use words like monopolistic robber barons?"

Kaden says, "Fair . . ."

Mads says, "I'm art."

Skylar says, "Obviously!"

Zane says, "What do you want the leads to do, Captain?"

Skylar says, "Didn't you read the app intro?"

Zane says, "Of course I did."

Zane says, "It was a bit . . . opaque."

Dom totally did.

Logan says, "Explain it, sis, we don't all speak nerd."

Kaden says, "I did coding and even I don't know what you mean about APIs and BVs"

Skylar rolls her eyes.

Skylar says, "APIs are how I connect my code to HubBub's existing tools."

Skylar says, "BV is HubBub's API that I'm using to make the flash cards."

Kaden says, "So your app turns our notes into flash cards"

Logan says, "Why don't you just say that?"

Skylar says, "I did."

Logan says, "No, you really didn't."

Mads says, "Sky, why don't you just tell us what we need to do?"

Skylar says, "OK, so basically, using Mrs. J's packet we each read through it and take notes in the app."

Skylar says, "The system will turn the notes into flash cards with various point values."

Logan says, "Which packet?"

Skylar says, "The one from ScholEx that Mrs. J sent us all on Thursday with the stuff we need to know for each topic area."

Logan says, "Can't you just load THAT into your system?"

Skylar says, "No, the whole point is that we take notes."

Zane says, "How does it know what to turn into a card?"

Skylar says, "The leads review all our notes to make sure we're on track. If something's wrong or weird, they mark it and put in the right answer. Then the system increases the point score for that batch of questions."

Kaden says, "How does it know the lead is right?"

Zane says, "Excellent question!"

Skylar says, "It doesn't."

Dom says, "So the lead has to study, too?"

Skylar says, "Everyone has to study! You don't get to Nationals coasting!"

Logan says, "How do we figure out these leads?"

Skylar says, "We play to everyone's strengths."

Skylar says, "Zane, instead of a subject, do you want to take point on coaching us on demonstrations for the booth?"

Zane says, "No."

Skylar says, "Why not?"

Zane says, "Why would you ask me when Logan is right there?"

Logan says, "Yeah, why would you ask Zane when I'm right here?"

Skylar says, "Because you're the captain of the debate team and he's very much not."

Zane says, "GOOD captains know their members' skills. If you want research spewed at you fast, you ask me. You want someone to explain something in a way that makes it sound interesting, ask Logan."

Zane says, "Why do you think I volunteered him for this team?"

Skylar says, "Some sort of personal torment for me."

Zane says, "That's just an extra bonus."

Logan says, "What are these demonstrations?"

Skylar says, "For Regionals we have to set up a booth. Judges will walk around and ask us about various pieces of it, and we need to be able to explain anything they ask about."

Logan says, "A booth like at a con where they demo games and stuff?"

Zane says, "You see why you're here?"

Skylar says, "Only we're demonstrating our understanding of the Second Industrial Revolution."

Skylar says, "The point is to show that we didn't just memorize facts but can present the information in a more subjective way."

Logan says, "Don't worry, team, I got you all. We'll dominate these demonstrations."

Dom dominates everything he does.

Skylar says, "Including teaching my brother the basics of the internal combustion engine?"

Dom says, "Uhh."

Skylar says, "But you WILL handle science, right?"

Dom looks around the room in a way that indicates he'd like anyone at all to challenge him in this.

Logan says, "Gas goes BOOOOOOOOOMMMMMMMM!!!"

Dom says, "Very basics done!!!"

Logan says, "I'm great at science, don't let Skylar tell you otherwise."

Skylar says, "Just don't let him actually combust anything."

Logan says, "No promises."

Skylar rolls her eyes yet again.

Skylar says, "So, Zane, what ARE you taking?"

Zane says, "I've got lit."

Skylar says, "Really?"

Zane says, "Yes, why?"

Logan says, "She doesn't think you can handle it."

Logan says, "She still thinks you eat mud on dares."

Kaden says, "He does still eat mud on dares"

Zane says, "WHAT HAPPENS AT INVITATIONALS STAYS AT INVITATIONALS."

Mads snickers.

Zane says, "Snitches get stitches, Kaden."

Kaden says, "Girlfriends don't count"

Zane says, "Everyone counts, Commander Spyglass."

Kaden says, "I was in fifth grade"

Zane says, "I have a loooong memory."

Mads says, "Your secrets are quite safe with me . . ."

Skylar says, "If you're done being cooler than us for having more than one extracurricular, then I'll be taking music I guess."

Zane says, "You need someone for that?"

Skylar says, "You don't think I can handle it?"

Zane says, "That's not what I said."

Logan says, "You think she'd do it?"

Zane says, "If we're going to Nationals, who else is going to get us there?"

Skylar says, "You don't think I can handle it."

Logan says, "Yeah, but, dude."

Zane says, "She's cool."

Dom says, "She'll need convincing."

Skylar says, "Who are you talking about?"

Zane says, "There's someone we know who might work."

Logan says, "She'll do it if you ask, Zane."

Zane says, "I don't know about that."

Dom says, "I do."

Skylar says, "WHAT ARE YOU TALKING ABOUT?!@!?@"

Kaden says, "Zane's new debate partner"

Logan says, "She's like a music nerd or some bleep."

Mads says, "You think she won't join???"

Dom says, "She's homeschooled, so she doesn't really like doing clubs."

Zane says, "Exactly, she's homeschooled, so her school GPA is nonexistent. Pathfinder perfection."

Dom says, "She only does debate because her mom makes her."

Zane says, "It'll be fine."

Skylar says, "Fine, whatever. We need a Pathfinder. Just get someone."

Zane grins.

Zane says, "Aye, aye, Captain."

Dom says, "So, is that it? Zane's going to try to convince Joey to do another after-school activity and we're splitting up the duties for your little app?"

Skylar says, "For now. Does anybody NOT see the link to Study Buddy in the lower left corner?

Logan says, "Which one's left?"

Skylar says, "You have it."

Logan says, "How do you know?"

Skylar says, "Shut up."

Skylar says, "I'll assign you the subjects you just claimed tonight."

Skylar says, "We don't have to worry about the booth yet. Just focus on learning the material for Quizposition first."

Skylar says, "You'll see your topic in blue and all the other topics in green."

Kaden says, "You went with green and blue"

Mads says, "Red was searing my eyes."

Skylar says, "As you start looking through Mrs. J's packet put each new thing you learn into ONE box."

Logan says, "Even for the subjects that are ours?"

Skylar says, "No, there you'll check everyone else's work."

Logan says, "I got all the topics."

Skylar says, "Not in Study Buddy."

Skylar says, "We'll do most of the booth stuff with Mrs. James on Thursdays after winter break."

Skylar says, "So I'm assuming you all understand what I'm saying."

Dom nods.

Logan says, "No, but I know where you sleep."

Zane says, "It's pretty clear."

Mads says, "I helped create it . . . so . . ."

Skylar says, "If you have questions, just send me a message. I'm basically always on."

Kaden says, "Skylar sold her soul to the machine"

Skylar says, "OR, if you're a luddite, you can see me at lunch."

Skylar says, "And if there are no more questions, that's it for tonight! Thanks for taking the time!!!!@!!@"

Kaden has left.

Logan has left.

Mads says, "Message me later???? We need to talk."

Dom has left.

Skylar says, "After nine."

Mads says, "Excellent."

Mads has left.

Zane says, "I'll let you know what happens with Joey."

Skylar says, "I just need a Pathfinder."

Zane says, "The app is a cool idea."

Skylar says, "So long as it gets us to Nationals."

You have left.

CHAPTER THREE

AN HOUR LATER I am still relishing putting real data into Study Buddy. Finally. I could be doing this on my tablet, but that would entirely defeat the purpose of spending my precious savings on a thirty-two-inch, curved, 4K monitor. I even mounted it so it doesn't take up space on the tabletop desk my dad and I put in freshman year. Mom suggested it when she found a board that was exactly the same size as the back wall of my room. It took longer to find the right chair: wide, black, and extra cushioned, with arms that don't dig into my hips. Perfect for spinning around as I think.

Not that there's much thinking to do right now. I get into the rhythm pretty quickly, but by the time I'm starting the music module, I have the best idea on how to improve this page. Without thinking, I open the app I use for coding. Only my code isn't sitting in another window waiting for me to make it better like it has been since this summer. Because I submitted the version for people to use and now it's locked. If I want to make a change, I have to start a whole new file.

Then actually do all the coding, which would involve days of writing and testing and fixing and improving everything I touched until I was sure it worked perfectly.

Not to mention the time it would take to build tests so they can confirm all my changes actually worked.

Then I'd submit the whole thing for the HubBub Education team to test for themselves, which—if I screwed up—could take weeks.

And a screw-up would mean a giant list of fixes to things I didn't think to test or improvements I never even considered and possibly losing access to the new modules they enabled.

It's not like this summer, when I could just throw in a feature because I thought about it. I have to be careful. Intentional.

I grab my tablet and the pencil stylus off my bed nearby and open up my digital planner so I can scribble in notes on how I'd fix this when I have enough good ideas to make the whole process worthwhile.

As my notes grow and grow, I realize it's probably better I have to wait. Even this small idea will be a lot of programming just for a mild convenience at the beginning. But the beginning matters more than any other part. If people find it awkward, they'll uninstall. Too many people uninstall right away and the algorithms will turn against me. Worse, if they downrate me, nearly four months of my life are just gone, wasted on a project that no one even knows exists.

I'm adding notes on how we can color-code some of the bulk functions when a message from Mads appears in a bubble at the top of my tablet's screen.

You never messaged me.

I pull the HubBub message app into a parallel window so I don't lose my place in my notes.

Sorry, I'm configuring.

You can't change the code, she sends as I'm drawing her a rough little picture of what I think the bulk upload page should look like and writing notes to myself on how it'll hook into the database. There's a lot more to it than I originally thought.

I know, I send, then add, I'm thinking we should have a way to color-code each subject.

Because this is how our conversations go. We talk code and design and functionality, not rumors and clothes. And that's how it's always been, but also . . . not. There was more before. Before my headaches got worse and Mads started dating Kaden. Definitely before Study Buddy. Or maybe it's why I started Study Buddy. Because I felt like Mads was so far away, and I didn't know how to tell her that. Or say that it feels like I lost two friends at once. Not without sounding childish or selfish. It got even worse as the months passed, until all we had to talk about was the homework I was missing and the code I was working on. So instead of making myself the third wheel, I threw myself into the code. Unlike people, there's never a wrong time to fix code, so long as I can figure out exactly where it went wrong.

We do!!@!#@&! she replies.

What? OH! Why didn't we put them on here?

I go back to Study Buddy in my computer's browser window to see what she's talking about and realize a nearly invisible square is clickable. I tap it and some preset color options appear.

We should have added a label, I type.

It was YOU who felt it would throw off the balance of the page!!@!!

I didn't.

Did.

No way.

I did not cut interface corners. It's not a thing I would do. Study Buddy isn't just my whole summer, it's my entire future. Study Buddy gets us to ScholEx Nationals. ScholEx Nationals gets the publicity I need to get recruited into a prestigious early developer program. They love coders who get media attention, especially the really good ones at MIT and Stanford. The buzz from a ScholEx Nationals win will definitely be enough to get me into their summer programs. I'll pick Stanford, obviously. MIT is great—amazing, really—but Stanford is for networking. A year or two at Stanford and I'll have the investors I need to start my own platform.

Tiny mistakes can derail big plans. And big plans are necessary to get big places. Even now I can hear Mom giving Logan yet another lecture on his lack of goals as he helps her do the dishes just like he said he would.

But that's not what I want to talk about . . . , . , . , . Mads sends.

What's up?

K said there was an . . . incident at the invitational this weekend. Zane may have a new archnemesis.

I frown at my screen. Of all the things we've ever done, it hasn't been gossiping about Zane.

And why should I care?

The little dots pop up to indicate Mads is composing a masterpiece of punctuation and explanation. In the time I'm waiting I finish adding the music module and turn it a cheerful blue.

You have to promise not to freak out . . . But I guess Nate and his partner had the bad luck to go against Zane and Joey and they did NOT hold back!!@! Kaden says it was a true thing of beauty!!#! Z and Joey crushed them with nearly perfect scores. There was an argument in the hall afterward between Nate and Z. Kaden doesn't think anyone said anything about you, but we thought maybe you should know. They seriously doubted anyone would know to say anything, but I didn't want you to hear from someone else. Not even Logan . . . not that he knows about Nate . . . right?????!!!??

I read the whole thing, not quite sure what to do with it all. I definitely don't want to think about the boy I wasted this past summer on. No, Study Buddy was this past summer. That's all that matters. Nate doesn't exist anymore in my world. He's not a real person. Just a memory. Not worth the time or energy to even think about.

He was just a short-term side effect of my really bad headache. Unlike family night, he went away.

I send back, Huh, because I need to send something and those are the only letters I can put together for Mads. Because even though she knows about Nate, she doesn't really know. Not all of it, because we don't talk crushes, we talk code.

Which is how she ended up dating Kaden without me even knowing she liked them. And how I could think I was maybe kind of dating someone who was just playing with me.

I hate that he can still throw me off like this. I was configuring Study Buddy for actual users; now I'm wasting energy on someone who doesn't even care I exist.

Are you all right?

I laugh at the screen. No, I'm not. I had a crush on a boy who thinks nothing of me at all. I don't even know what I was thinking. We barely saw each other. It was mostly online. If he hadn't been dropping his mom's car off at that terrible neurologist's office when I had my appointment, we never would have even met.

I definitely never would have had all those conversations with him. I wouldn't have thought he was interested in me. I wouldn't have interpreted the stuff he was saying so wrongly that I thought we were sort of going out. I certainly wouldn't have taken Mads to see him at the restaurant where he works so she knew he even existed. I absolutely wouldn't have been devastated when he started posting pictures of himself with his actual girlfriend.

And it's too late to tell her all of this because it doesn't matter. He doesn't matter.

Sky?><??<>??><?

I have to finish setting up Study Buddy, I send her.

I really don't think anyone knows, she sends.

How does Kaden know? I send, feeling a rush of anxiety. It's a simple question.

44

. . . , . , ... ; ; ; ; ; ; . . . . . . she sends. You're friends with Kaden, too.

Sure.

I click the save button four times and then shove my mouse away. Of course I'm friends with Kaden, but that doesn't mean I want them to find out about this. There was a time I was allowed to tell Kaden things myself. But that was before the two of them started dating and the whole world outside of them ceased to exist.

I'm sorry . . . Mads sends finally.

This is ridiculous. It's in the past. Like that awful neurologist Nate's mom worked for and all the ridiculous tests he put me through that basically did nothing. I escaped the doctor and I escaped Nate. Mads and I are talking more. Sort of. My new doctor listens to me. I haven't even had a really bad headache in a while. My migraines are under control and so is my future.

Thanks for telling me, I send back, but I'm not actually thankful. Kaden knows. Mads knows. Zane knows Nate exists on this planet.

I could kill him for you if you want, she sends, and I can't help but smile.

I'm not ready to help you bury any bodies yet, I send back, an old joke. A familiar one. Logan used to say we're ride or die. I'm ride, she's die.

Who says there'd be a whole body????????:"??

I smile even wider at the message window, her words tiny against the massive screen but full of Mads's massive personality.

I have to finish this, I send.

Just remember you're on code lock until at least December.

And we're back to talking code.

She sounds like an actual tech nerd when she says that. *Code lock* is the business way of saying no one in the company is allowed to make any changes. It's something we'll do when we're a for-real business. Or maybe we're already just coworkers.

Who says?

Me. I am tired of your panicked messages about curly brackets.

It's not my fault they kept disappearing!!!

Your code . . , . . your fault.

You just don't get code.

You're right. I'm the artiste! I swan in, beautify things, and then swan back out, letting you deal with both the nitty and the gritty.

Which is why I may need a new base.

WINTER BREAK! Give me half a semester of a friend with only one obsession.

Or maybe we're not just coworkers.

I'll see what I can do.

Night, Sky.

Night.

I close the window, somehow feeling better despite everything. Maybe because my app, even with its imperfections, is totally ready for its first users to start studying.

NotThatZane

Joey has questions about ScholEx.

Well, then, answer them.

She wants to know if she has to be at the Thursday afternoon stuff.

I mean, it'd be nice.

She has orchestra practice on Thursdays through the end of the year.

Can she do the online stuff?

Yeah, and she can study she says.

But she's being cagey.

I thought you were friends.

We're debate partners. Not the same thing.

Tell her the first thing she HAS to be at is the local meet December 12.

I think that should work.

She says she has Saturdays clear for debate anyway and we don't have a tournament that weekend.

This is like pulling teeth. She's not normally like this.

Does she not want to do it?

No, I think she does.

Maybe she's busy.

Maybe you need to find someone else.

Where are we going to find anyone who knows music?

I told you I could do music.

I'm trying.

Try harder.

Do you want to do this?

She's YOUR debate partner.

OK, she's thinking about it.

You said you could do this, Zane.

She wants to talk to you.

Me? Why?

She said something about a favor.

Just talk to her, OK?
For me?

You're the one who's supposed to be doing this for ME. Remember?

OK, fine. Do it for ScholEx.

What could she possibly want from me?

I don't know.

She wouldn't say.

This is weird.

You're weird.

You're weirder.

I got you someone who knows music.

What else do you want from me?

We don't have her yet.

You can convince her.

I know you.

Do we really need music? I can probably handle it.

Fine, handle it then.

This is all on you now.

You promised me a Pathfinder.

And I have delivered one on a silver platter.

All you have to do is talk to her.

Ugh.

Don't be a scaredy-cat.

I'm NOT a scaredy-cat.

Right, you're not.

But do it.

She's the one.

For real.

Fine.

I'll message her later or something.

I'm giving her your handle.

Then she can message me.

Do it, Sky.

Scaredy-cat.

You're the scaredy-cat.

Your kritiks are the worst.

You're the worst.

And I still don't speak debate.

I'll give you that.

Look, we can talk about this at practice tomorrow. OK?

Fine.

See you tomorrow, Sky.

CHAPTER FOUR

THURSDAY AFTER SCHOOL, room 205 is still in a massive circle from the discussion our AP US History class just had about Martin Van Buren's reaction to the Petticoat Affair. It was an epic battle between the three people who did the readings and the two who listened long enough that the whole thing got them mad so they joined in. The rest of us pretended to pay attention while doing other things, like making lists about what we needed to handle during our first actual ScholEx meeting. Mrs. James just wants us all to participate in these debates, so I made sure to answer something I knew and went back to my real work.

Logan walks in with Dom close behind, and they both stop at the destruction. "Did a bomb hit this place?" Logan asks.

"An in-class discussion that went all the way to the last bell. They all fled before fixing the desks," I say as I shove one back into place.

"Wait," Dom says. "We can use this."

"What for?" I say, stopping immediately because I'm really not excited about lugging these desks around, even with Logan, who has started helping.

"It's something my old French teacher used to do. The plan was to run drills, right?" he says, putting his backpack down at a desk in the front of the circle.

"Yeah," I say, indicating he should go on with a wave of my hands.

"So, we'll have Mrs. James read the practice questions and pick one of us—if that person gets it right, they get a point."

I'm about to explain that I have the whole meeting planned out already when Mrs. James walks in behind Dom and says, "Most points gets a pencil!"

My eyes go wide. "Really?"

Dom laughs. "A pencil?"

"You've never had Mrs. James?" I ask.

Dom shakes his head. "Timing never worked out."

Mrs. James says, "Are you in Mr. Cornelius's AP Calculus BC?"

Dom nods. "So what's the deal with the pencil?"

From the doorway, Zane says, "Wait, there's a pencil up for grabs?"

I glare at him. "Don't even think about it, that's my pencil."

"You wish," Zane says. "I'm not letting Sky have my pencil."

Dom nudges his elbow in greeting.

"Usually," Mrs. James says, derailing my response, "the person with the most pencils by the AP test gets to pick the special pizza toppings for the survival pizza party in the next class."

Dom says, "I feel like I should have heard about this before now."

"It's not normally a thing people care about. Because most people know to get a supreme like rational humans." Logan braces himself against the desk next to Dom.

Zane and I turn on him. "Lies," I say, while Zane just gasps.

Logan laughs. "I'm tired of being a victim of you nerds and your terrible taste in pizza. I get it from both ends."

"Pepperoni and mushroom is key for life functions," I say. "It's brain food."

"Mushrooms are vile, and pineapple is the only real accompaniment to pepperoni," Zane says, glaring at me.

Dom and Logan make gagging noises. Mads and Kaden walk in holding hands. "Not a freaking pencil," Mads says. "Mrs. James, can't it be something else?"

Mrs. James grins. "I need you all to at least try to beat these heathens and their weird pizza tastes."

Kaden says, "That'll do it."

"Are these class pencils?" Zane asks.

"No, these are special ScholEx pencils." She holds up a fresh pack of deep blue pencils with Lovelace Academy's silver logo that she buys special order through the school store our entrepreneurialism class manages. The plastic still pristine. This year's class pencils are green. I know because I already have two.

"Excellent," Zane and I say together, and the whole group laughs.

"Are we still having trouble recruiting another Pathfinder scholar?" Mrs. James asks, looking around at the gathered team.

"No, Mrs. J. I've got someone," Zane says, dropping into the exact same seat he abandoned about fifteen minutes ago.

I wedge myself into my seat on the other end of the circle, with Mads and Kaden close behind me. Logan gets up and starts pulling desks out of the circle and says, "Come closer, all of you. We can still do a circle, but this is too many seats."

He doesn't just move the desks out of the way, he gets them mostly back to where they go, and we all start helping until there's a much smaller circle at the front of the classroom.

Mrs. James nods. "Thank you, Logan. I should give you a pencil for being so considerate."

"Not fair! I was already doing that when you and Dom stopped me!" I shout as she winks at him.

"Don't worry, Mrs. J. Someone has to help keep these wild nerdlings in line." He makes a face at me and shoves his backpack under the open desk beside Dom. Kaden is next to Zane, and Mads acts as another buffer as I take the seat on the other side of Dom.

"So when will our new scholar be joining us?" Mrs. James asks, looking at Zane.

"I messaged her," he says, looking at me. "She's thinking about it."

"Who is this young lady?" Mrs. James asks.

"Her name is Joey Harrison. She's Zane's debate partner," Kaden says.

"Is this Josephine Harrison, the flautist?" Mrs. James asks, and all the debate members nod. "She's talented. I saw her solo performance with the orchestra last month. Does she have time with her practices?"

"She needs more extracurriculars," Zane says. "She's thinking of double majoring at Oberlin in Ohio."

"Didn't she perform last year with the philharmonic?" Mrs. James asks.

"Children's choir at Carnegie Hall," Kaden says.

Mrs. James nods, clearly impressed. "And you're certain she qualifies for Pathfinder?"

"Technically," Zane says. "Her homeschool program and testing are super competitive but don't really translate to a good GPA. She almost had to drop debate last quarter because of it."

"That's why I don't think she's going to want to mess with this," Dom says.

"She's considering it," Zane says. "She just wants to talk to Sky first."

I exhale loudly.

"You asked for someone, I got you someone," Zane says with a superior smile on his face, like he's actually accomplished something and I don't have to do all the real work.

"We have four Achiever scholars, so we're set for that round of Quizposition even if someone can't make it, but we need another Pathfinder if we're going to participate in any of the meets," Mrs. James says.

"I'll message her later," I say.

Mrs. James smiles. "Well, that's settled. Now should we begin the competition?" She makes her way into the middle of the circle. "This is what you're thinking, right, Dom?"

Dom nods. "Yes, ask the question and then point. I'll keep score. Just try to keep it fair. If the first person doesn't get the right answer, then you go to the next one."

I open my mouth to say that we should use the flash cards from Study Buddy, but Mrs. James says, "I like this, I may need to steal it for class." She looks down at her sheet. "These are all multiple choice in sets of four, so I'm going to say second or third guesses get half points."

Dom says, "Oh, that makes sense. So no points for the last guesser."

"What if we knew the answer?" I ask, even though I should have given my idea instead.

"That defeats the purpose of your app, doesn't it?" Logan asks. "I mean, if you get it right and we don't, what does it matter?"

"Good point, Logan," Mrs. James says. "It's so important all of you realize that Quizposition is round-robin. Everyone needs to know all of this. You can't guarantee your art genius will be the next to answer when every art question comes up."

Of course, they're both right. And Mrs. James likes it. We can do this one time and then work on the flash cards next time. I take a deep breath and close my eyes. There's a small pinprick back in the corner of my head I'm trying to ignore. It could be nothing, or it could be the beginnings of a migraine. I should go take my medicine, but I don't want to miss our first real practice. Each one is necessary to track our improvement. It's two weeks until Thanksgiving, and two weeks after that will be our local meet. This is just a tension headache. I'll be fine . . . probably.

I take another deep breath and can feel Mads look at me, but Mrs. James is already reading the first question.

As the questions progress, that small pinprick expands, slowly, first to my eye and then across the right side of my head. My stomach starts to turn, and I keep stretching out my neck as question after question lands flat. Some people get it on the second or third try, but too many aren't getting any at all. Not even in their expert subjects. And as I fail question after question—especially in my own subject—I can feel their eyes burning into me, adding to the screaming in my head.

This is too much. There's no way I'm going to figure out how to get everyone trained up enough when I don't even know music myself. The pain is blooming bright. I haven't had a headache like this for months. Not since the new meds evened out. And now it's too late to go to the nurse's office to get meds for a headache that's actually happening.

"Mrs. J," Logan says, "can we stop?"

Mrs. James says, "We only have a few questions left."

"Sky's gonna hurl if I don't get her home," he says. And as he does, I can feel my eyes watering up.

I knuckle my fingers into them. "I'm fine. We should finish." This is hardly the worst pain I've ever felt. I can handle this if it means we get more study time. I just need to push through.

"Skylar, are you okay?" Mrs. James asks.

"It's just a headache," I say.

"Just a headache," Logan says, but with more mocking in his voice.

"You should have said something," Mads whispers.

"I'm fine," I say.

"You're really not," Logan says way too loudly. "We already flubbed this session; three more questions won't change that."

"Who won?" I ask.

Dom says, "Kaden with a whopping four points. I guess we all have to study more."

Mrs. James closes the workbook and nods. "You really do. Have you been reading the materials I sent you?"

Everyone nods but half-heartedly.

"There's a lot there," Kaden says, and everyone nods much faster.

"I know you all have a lot of homework and other clubs, and I'm sorry, but keep reading, we still have a few weeks until our first session. This is probably a good measure to show how much work we have yet to do. Next time let's talk through a topic. Dom, where'd we fall down?"

"Music, by a lot."

I can feel Zane's eyes on me even though now my own are closed and the ice pick has wedged itself firmly into my right parietal lobe and probably directly into my ocular nerve. It's like I can see my MRI scan looking back at me. Judging me, too, probably. "I'll figure it out," I say, but weaker than I want to sound.

The desks start moving, and I can feel Logan's hand under my arm. "Come on, sis. Let's get you home to your stash."

"It's just a regular headache, it's not a big deal," I say, opening my eyes enough to get myself out of the desk and grab my bag.

"Pretty sure what you consider a regular headache would knock out an elephant."

"Is she going to be okay?" I hear Mrs. James ask, and Mads answers her, "She gets wicked headaches."

"She collapsed in the hallway last year," Kaden says. "Had to be rushed to the hospital."

Zane says, "They've been better this year."

"This new doctor is helping . . ." Mads trails off. I'm glad she didn't finish, but I know she's just as relieved my mom found a neurologist willing to treat what's actually wrong with me and not what society makes him think is wrong with me.

Logan gets my things, and everyone makes the noises they make when you're really not okay and they don't know what to do about it. I know they'll keep talking about me when I'm gone.

JoeyJoJoIII

Hi, are you Skylar Collins? This is Joey Harrison, Zane's debate partner.

I know you just got out of your practice for this ScholEx thing, but is this a good time to talk?

Yeah.

I mean, yeah, this is Skylar and it's a fine time to talk.

Zane said you're the captain of LA's ScholEx team.

Yes, that's right.

And you wanted me to join the team.

This is for real, right?

You knew I was going to message you, right?

No. No, that's me.

I mean, that's right.

I mean, sorry. I'm just dealing with a headache. Sorry.

We can do this another time.

No, no! I'm sorry. I'm here. Just a little slow.

He said you desperately need help with music.

Is that what he said??!@!??

He also said you'd explain it all.

Ugh. He's the total worst.

You think so?????

He seems pretty cool to me.

You just don't know him well enough yet.

Maybe . . .

He's been really great in debate. He's just so talented.

That's because he's a show-off know-it-all.

He seems pretty smart to me.

He's not . . . you know . . . seeing somebody or something, right?

ZANE?!?!!!!?@#@@!

I'm guessing that's a no.

He likes . . . someone, though, right?

How would I know that . . .

You don't?

I mean, no. Why even would I?

He talks about you a lot . . .

I mean they all talk about you a lot, but he really talks about you.

I figured . . .

That I'm the actual worst human on the planet?

No, not like that.

Never mind, clearly I'm being silly.

OK, but he said you wanted a favor from me.

And well, after today's practice we may actually be desperate, I guess.

You need me?

Well, we need someone. It sounds like you know stuff. Especially about music.

Oh, I know plenty of stuff about music.

It's basically my whole life.

You performed somewhere?

Mostly with the orchestra.

That's why I'm homeschooled . . .

No, somewhere fancy.

Oh, just Carnegie. And we went to Sydney once. And I had a concert in London one time, that was super fancy.

But you're a Pathfinder?

My grades aren't the best, but my parents kinda don't care as long as I'm keeping them manageable or whatever.

I'd rather be practicing anyway.

Zane said you were smart.

He said that?????

Yeah, and that your grades are like technicalities or something.

I mean, I guess. I'm not great at writing.

When I actually went to school, I did all right. Bs mostly or whatever.

I don't like the structure so much.

But you like policy debate?

That's different!

You can practice policy debate until you get it right.

Isn't that basically what school is?

Not really.

I'm not explaining it well.

No, it's fine. Do you know what ScholEx is?

He told me a bit.

Well, at least he did that much.

Hee, yeah, I guess.

I guess it's better than school for someone like you since we only have a few things we have to practice until we remember them all.

Exactly!!! But it seems like it takes a bunch of time and I'm not sure I have it.

It doesn't have to take THAT much time.

I mean there's the events, but those are all next semester after debate has wound down.

Weekends are better . . .

And when we win it will look great on your résumé.

You think we'll win?

I have a secret weapon.

Your app?

You heard about that?

From Kaden?

Zane was talking about it. He thinks it's got a lot of potential.

UGH . . . I hate that word.

Potential?

Yeah, it means I've failed somehow.

Potential says that?

I'll have to look it all over again tonight I guess.

You're intense.

I get that a lot.

But you seem super confident.

Uhm. I guess?

I'm wondering if I join your club you'd . . . like . . . help me with something?

So this is the favor?

Yeah, this all sounds fun, and if you can help . . . it would really be worth it.

What is it you need help with?

So . . .

I kind of have a crush on Zane . . .

No way.

He's so smart. And he's so nice. And his hair flops just right and those suspenders he wears . . . and ack!

Like a million things.

65

You don't see it?

I mean, I've seen him wear suspenders.

But I don't see why you need my help.

I'm . . . not confident.

You do policy debate. I thought that was a requirement for the job.

Good breath control is a requirement.

OK, I can see how that can help.

But what do you need me to do?

Just . . . help me figure out if he likes me?

You mean like ask him if he likes you?

No! Not that exactly.

But something like that.

I guess. It's just . . . I can never tell.

And you think I can?

I think if you think about it, you can figure it out.

While I THINK about joining your club.

I'll think about it.

Cool.

CHAPTER FIVE

I'M STILL THINKING five days later when I have to work the school store during first lunch. I signed up for entrepreneurialism as an elective because I thought it would help with the non-coding bits of SkyLessLimits, but mostly it's just inventory management and spending one day a month in this closet with a classmate.

What makes today special is the classmate is Dom.

It's about fifteen minutes into his terrible dad jokes about pencils that I finally work up the courage to ask him what Joey specifically told me not to.

"So, I heard somewhere that Zane likes somebody."

I swear if Dom had a drink at that second, he'd have done a spit take. "You heard that, did you?"

"I mean, I didn't exactly hear it. But someone thought maybe there was someone he could have liked."

"This person is observant. I'll give them that." He leans back against the shelves, crossing his arms. "And so you've come to me. His best friend. For what? Advice on how to handle it?"

"What? No."

"Confirmation?"

"I mean . . . Maybe?"

"I can, in fact, confirm he likes someone," he says, nodding sagely. "I cannot, in good conscience, be the one to tell you who it is."

"No, that'd be a huge betrayal of trust," I say, putting my tablet pencil down. "I'm just curious how one would go about figuring out who it was he liked."

"Well, now, I know this is a really out there concept, but you could . . . maybe consider, I don't know . . . asking him." He's grinning so big right now.

"Why would I do that?"

"Of course, what was I thinking? Too forward." He's trying to look ashamed, but he's still grinning. "You could pass him a note, maybe?"

"What is this? Fourth grade?" But he's not wrong—it's about all I've got. *Do you like Joey? Yes or No. Circle one.*

When I don't say anything else, he says, "How about I tell you what kind of person he likes?"

"Yeah, yeah, that would help." Would it, though? I just need an answer, not a guessing game.

"He likes smart girls. Ones who get his references."

I grin. "Has he seen a movie in this millennium?"

Dom laughs. "He has, he just doesn't like them as much." He leans forward like he's confiding in me. "So, look, he likes confidence. Like, a lot of ego is not a problem for him."

I feel like I should be writing this down, but that'd be too obvious. Also, I'm trying to decide if Joey saying she's not

confident enough to ask Zane herself is more or less confident than asking a complete stranger to find out for her. It
could really go either way.

Dom says, "See, he's good if you stand up in front of everyone and make a spectacle of yourself."

Well, that Joey does. She has to, between debate and
orchestra. Didn't Mrs. James say she was a soloist?

"He's more the Katharine Hepburn type than Audrey
Hepburn, if you get what I mean." When I just kind of stare
at him, he adds, "Yeah, me either. I think it's more about
attitude than appearances. Also that he's way too into those
old movies . . . look at the way he dresses."

I nod, holding down a little laugh. It would be really weird
if he wanted a typical hot girl while he goes around dressing like he fell out of a classic movie. Waistcoats, pressed
pants and shirts, too-shiny shoes. Even his hair is just a
little too long on top to be cool. I haven't seen Joey yet, but
that doesn't mean a lot. Dom's right, Zane doesn't really care
about looks. "He went out with Issy last year, yeah?"

He laughs, covering his mouth. "You heard about that?
Do not worry about that. Like not at all. It's very over."

"Issy's nice."

"Yeah, Issy's great, but it was just a thing. But not, you
know, a *thing*." He puts a lot of emphasis on the last word,
and he's really looking at me to make sure I get it.

"Yeah, I heard she went out with Sal after."

"Exactly, exactly. You get it."

I really don't, but that's beside the point.

"Debaters. It's a whole mess. Especially debate boys. You don't even know."

Okay, that I get. All the girls Logan's dated have been debaters—a couple of the guys, too. He calls it lazy dating. They all spend way too much time together with all those meets and weekends and practices and everything, making it easier to hook up. Which is why Joey asking for my help is so weird.

"ScholEx is good for us. Gets us out of the debate crowd. Interacting with normals."

Now that I have to laugh at. "You mean like Mads and me?"

He nods. "No, you're right. You're right. You two are honorary, aren't you?"

"I don't know about that."

"You're cool, though. This is cool. It's about time. You know?"

"What do you mean?"

He shakes his head slowly, "Nothing, nothing. I'm just glad. It's hard to figure out crushes in this day and age."

"Crushes. Yeah," I say quietly. He's right. I know all too well there's no way of knowing when the other person likes you back.

"Like, you can sit and pine and pine, and meanwhile he's over there doing the same and you'd never know."

Or he's not and you're convinced he is.

"Don't get me wrong, half the fun is the pining. But sometimes . . ." His head isn't in this booth anymore. He's watching the empty hall, eyes and brain far away. "It'd just be nice, you know."

"To put it out there somewhere they could confirm it?"

"Yeah, yeah, but, like, if they don't, they don't. No harm, no foul. Do it in a way that isn't . . . I don't know . . . scary?" He shakes his head, waking himself up. "Don't mind me. Too many debaters. Right?"

I fake a laugh as the bell rings. That's probably Joey's thing. They're partners. They're going to State. If she makes a thing of it and it's not totally unrequited, she could mess that up.

Dom nods and walks backward out of the closet, letting the counter swing open. "This is good. About time we had this talk."

I roll my eyes. "Bye, Dom." I grab the counter to pull it back closed, pushing the top half of the door with my other hand so it turns back into a door and stops being a counter.

Crushes. They're the actual worst. But what if there were a way to confirm that the feelings you're having aren't just yours without messing everything up? Wouldn't that have been so much easier with Nate? If I could have confirmed he was just playing with me or whatever before I made it more than it was? And Joey could confirm Zane likes her without ruining their partnership. And Dom and whoever he was talking about could figure their stuff out.

I'm still thinking about it as I walk to lunch and get my salad. I'm definitely thinking about it as I watch Mads and Kaden talking at the lunch table.

There's something here. I can feel it.

CHAPTER SIX

THE NEXT DAY at the doctor's my fingers are itching. I'm sure I'm finally going to get the spark of inspiration I've been trying to find since yesterday and I'll have no way of doing anything about it.

The only time I have no technology with me is in the MRI room. It's a solid twenty minutes with nothing but me staring at a big white magnet. Weirdly, I find it relaxing. Which is good because over the last ten months I've had a bunch. They're fewer and further between now that my brain isn't as interesting. The doctors have assured me hundreds of times it's quite interesting; it's just that they're not finding anything new or different when they convince it to emit a radio frequency.

Before they figured any of my migraine triggers or medicine that would help, they left me in one of these tubes for about an hour while the right side of my brain tried to implode and the left just sat there and did nothing about it.

That first MRI discovered a "thing."

It sounds a lot more dramatic than it is, but half as dramatic as my mom made it out to be. She tried to be normal the whole time. Pretend the "thing" was nothing but a lump of dense cells, which . . . it totally is. But whenever she thought Logan and I weren't looking she cried like the "thing" actually was cancer. Even the doctors never admitted most of the tests were to confirm it wasn't. They just kept poking and prodding. Hospitalized me twice. Had my spinal fluid sampled. Blamed it on my weight. My genetics. My stress.

My new neurologist is pretty sure it's congenital. Or, as she described it, "Just how your cells decided to code that part of your brain." But that, combined with the rest of the stuff they found, means my migraines have a nice pattern they can keep repeating.

I like my new neurologist.

She explains things like a coder. Which, I guess, makes DNA the code base she works on.

It turns out my migraines are tied to my hormones and a bunch of ridiculously normal vitamins and minerals. Once a month I'm basically guaranteed a headache, but that's the not-as-bad kind. The kind that, if I feel it coming, I can stop with an array of medication my mom has distributed among the school nurse, Logan's car, and around the whole house.

Then there's the head splitters. The ones that come seemingly out of nowhere but actually have triggers. Things brains don't like. For some people it's chocolate or caffeine. Others it's loud noises or lights. For me it's cats and sweeteners of any kind. Well, and stress. They're really big on stress being a migraine trigger, but they don't go to Lovelace.

Aura are their own whole level of fun. They're an early warning system that are special to migraines. They're like when your code calls the wrong function and weird stuff starts happening right before the whole thing crashes. Most folks' aura is stuff like tunnel vision and light sensitivity. Mine include hand-grip problems, blurry vision, trouble focusing, and nausea. But if I'm already at the nausea, it's way too late and I'm riding that sucker out.

As far as the migraines themselves? Some are not great and others are the worst pain I can imagine. You can tell they're migraines and not, say, tension headaches, because the pain is only on one side of your head.

The "thing" in my brain, not my migraines, is why I'm in the tube today. Despite everyone staring at it, it has done a whole lot of nothing. Which is good, because there's not much anyone can do for it. For my migraines I take my vitamins and the pill to regulate my hormones. I take muscle relaxers when those don't cut it. And I avoid stress.

Fine, I do the first two, and things have been better.

The humming starts, and I can feel my body relax.

I don't know what it is about the hum, except I can feel it through my whole body. I close my eyes and let my mind wander away from here. Away from everything.

Except all the stuff I have to worry about now that my brain is under control. My future. Study Buddy. ScholEx. Joey. Zane.

Joey and I talked again, and she said she'd at least try to join some of the online chats. I said it was the only way I could really tell if he liked her, but I'm not sure I actually can. Talking to Dom didn't help. And it's not like I can ask Zane . . .

Or can I?

I keep coming back to the note idea. But if I were the one who sent it to him, he'd think it was a trick or a joke.

I can't text him . . . that'd be weird.

If only there were an app.

The magnet makes a few more revolutions, bouncing waves off my brain for my neurologist to pore over later. I wish it wouldn't actually be dangerous to have access to an app store right about now. Someone has to have something for this.

All I can think of is Tinder, which would take mental gymnastics I can't even imagine to help in this kind of situation. Even if the mere idea of it weren't extra skeevy. What I need is Tinder for teenagers. Something that confirms the other person likes you back.

I start to work out the story of the app. Person A likes Person B. A obsesses. A asks random person to find out if B likes them back. Random person checks and gets a yes or no from B. A wails because no one ever gets the real answers that way.

The problem isn't when B says no.

The problem is when B won't actually say anything.

The problem is when you can't quite tell.

The win is the yes.

So all I need is to get to a very clear yes.

What if A took a picture of their crush . . . HubBub has those new image recognition tools they just gave me access to with the priority track. The user tags the person they like to confirm it is actually who they took a picture of. It can't hurt to know B is who they say they are.

Plus, A really should check to see if B is posting nearly daily pictures with someone they've never quite mentioned to you, no matter how regularly you talk. That clears up any crush real fast.

So this is just a data table of tags with images.

It wouldn't be hard to run a compare against that.

Thrum. Thrum. Thrum.

Notifications are trivial.

Thrum. Thrum. Thrum.

Something has to come after that. So A and B match, so what?

Private bubble chats!

I nearly sit up, but I literally can't move. The voice intones somewhere overhead, "Almost done, Sky. You're doing so well."

Right. MRI. Brain scanning. I wonder if it saw the brain wave I just had. But probably not—I think they need special dyes or a PET scan or whatever and I haven't quite made it that far on the neurology testing ride yet.

So. Where was I?

Table match generates a unique chat inside but separate from the rest of the HubBub system.

So simple, so elegant.

It's a four-screen problem.

I can almost see it in front of me. A welcome/login. Picture. List. Chat.

People can have multiple crushes, can't they? I know Mads and Logan have before, even Kaden has, and they're about as picky as I am.

Probably better to let everyone have more than one.

Also, delete them.

Even I know how important a delete is in the world of crushes. That should be able to delete the chat, too. It's basically an insta-block for someone who turns out to be a slimy creep. That should reduce service requests.

HubBub's login. HubBub's camera permissions. HubBub's chat protocol.

HubBub's logout interface.

Get a theme from Mads.

Done.

Too easy.

Then it's just a matter of convincing Zane to install it and take it seriously.

But who cares? It's just a fun thing. I have tons of practice apps like this in their store that I make everyone play with. It's barely more complex than something Dad's company would come up with.

It wouldn't be obvious I made it just for Joey. The debaters could have a good time with it.

I'd be helping.

But it needs a name.

Crushed?

No. Too negative, even if it's the most likely outcome.

The humming stops and the table starts moving.

"We're all done, Skylar." The tech is at my feet, ready to help me get the cage off my face and sit up.

I don't have the will to tell them I've only just begun.

"You can change back into your clothes. Your doctor should have the results in a few minutes."

"Thanks!" I shout, practically running out of the room and back to where I left my tablet. So many ideas to get down before my messed-up brain forgets it all.

You have joined LAScholEx.

Joey, Dom, and Zane are here.

There are 5 unread messages—click <u>here</u> to unroll the history.

Dom says, "I think someone added something in Latin."

Dom says, "None of it makes any sense at all."

Joey says, "It actually is Latin. A lot of musical notation is."

Dom says, "That explains it."

Skylar says, "I thought you were in French?"

Zane says, "I'm in German."

Dom says, "I still am. But that's not actually the same as Latin."

Skylar says, "Cool, I'm in German."

Zane says, "HELLO, SKY, HOW ARE YOU?"

Skylar says, "I started freshman year. I was going to try French after I finished the requirements, but I really like Frau."

Zane says, "Fine, Zane, it is so good to see you. And I'm glad you made it, Joey."

Skylar says, "Oh, hey, Joey, I'm glad you got on! Did you have any problems getting Study Buddy working?"

Joey laughs.

Joey says, "It came up fine."

Zane says, "Phhht. Is this thing on?"

Skylar says, "Oh, good, I wasn't sure if the invite would work since you're not in our school program."

Joey says, "I am. Thanks to Zane. He got me in the debate chat."

Dom says, "Joey was just explaining the music terms while I think Zane is somewhere around here."

Zane says, "You all encourage her too much."

Logan has joined LAScholEx.

Logan says, "Zane! Joey! Dom! Nerdling!!!!"

Skylar says, "I thought you weren't going to make it."

Logan says, "Dad picked me up."

Logan says, "How was the appointment?"

Skylar says, "Fine. Did you have any problems with the music stuff?"

Joey says, "Appointment?"

Logan says, "She had her brain looked at again."

Zane says, "Everything OK?"

Skylar says, "Everything's fine. No changes. Not a big deal. UNLIKE THE MUSIC STUFF."

Logan says, "You mean because it's in gibberish?"

Joey says, "Latin."

Logan says, "Bleep."

Dom says, "That's French."

Zane laughs.

Joey laughs.

Kaden has joined LAScholEx.

Kaden says, "Mads can't make it"

Skylar says, "Yeah, she messaged me."

Dom says, "Everything OK with her?"

Kaden says, "Just art stuff"

Dom says, "Oooh."

Dom says, "Mysterious."

Joey says, "Who is Mads?"

Kaden says, "My girlfriend"

Skylar says, "Our art expert, and my best friend."

Zane says, "Sky's BFF and the person Kaden rats us all out to."

Joey says, "What?"

Kaden says, "Ignore Zane"

Kaden says, "Sky does"

Dom laughs.

Logan laughs louder.

Skylar says, "Anyway. Dom, what were you saying about the music section?"

Dom says, "THAT BLEEP IS LATIN."

Joey laughs.

Skylar says, "Yes, it is. Joey, did you figure out how to flag terms for flash cards?"

Joey says, "Do what now?"

Skylar says, "I switched the lead for music to you, so you should be able to see everyone's notes."

Skylar says, "It's the green plus."

Joey says, "OH! Is that what that is?"

Joey says, "What am I supposed to do with it?"

Zane says, "Check our work."

Skylar says, "Go in and put a plus or a minus next to everyone's notes. If it's a minus, put in the correct answer."

Joey says, "What if it's not wrong, just not entirely accurate?"

Skylar says, "Still wrong. Still a minus."

Dom says, "Oh, oops."

Skylar says, "Haven't you been doing that?"

Dom will do it tonight.

Kaden says, "What about incomplete answers"

Skylar says, "For you . . . . . ."

Skylar says, "Just use your best judgment."

Logan says, "What about me?"

Skylar says, "Learn all of this because we could be asked how our booth relates to literally anything."

Logan says, "I still don't quite get the booth."

Zane says, "It's just answering questions."

Joey says, "I suck at impromptu."

Logan says, "This isn't impromptu, it's extemp."

Joey says, "Memorization? But aren't they going to ask us questions to test our knowledge?"

Logan says, "Sorta. The trick is talking your way to an answer you know. Like when your nosy aunt asks about your future plans."

Skylar says, "Speaking of . . ."

Skylar says, "Next week is Thanksgiving, so we won't have a training session. But the first local meet is two weeks after that."

Kaden says, "Is that the aunt with the seven kids or the one who rescues dogs?"

Logan says, "Eight, they had another this summer."

Zane says, "What's the theme going to be for our booth?"

Skylar says, "The local meet is where we can see examples of past booths and get to ask questions of the teachers who worked with the teams."

Logan says, "Bleep yeah. Practice."

Zane says, "Do you think she actually muted me?"

Skylar says, "I can hear you. I will worry about the theme after we see examples at the local session."

Joey says, "That's December 5?"

Skylar says, "12. You can make it right?"

Joey says, "Pretty sure, but I'll check my schedule."

Skylar says, "I should have the answer to what you were asking me about by then."

Skylar says, "But you'll need to be there for it."

Joey says, "For real? Already?"

Skylar says, "No, but I will."

Logan says, "What's this about?"

Zane says, "Are you keeping secrets?"

Skylar says, "Nothing like that."

Joey says, "I'd have held out longer if I'd known there was bribery on the table."

Zane looks between Joey and Skylar.

Kaden says, "Told you"

Logan says, "This was all your idea."

Joey says, "Wait. How bad do you need me?"

Joey says, "I need to know if it's too late to ask Sky for baked goods."

Skylar says, "You do NOT want my baked goods."

Logan says, "No, Joey, save yourself!!!"

Zane says, "NOOOOOOOO!!!!!!"

Dom tries not to be sick.

Kaden says, "Joey. No"

Joey says, "What did I say?"

Skylar says, "You mix up sugar and salt ONE TIME and no one lets you live it down."

Kaden says, "We almost died"

Dom says, "Worst bake sale ever."

Skylar says, "You know what, this meeting is over. Go make fun of me elsewhere."

Zane says, "I still have nightmares about those cupcakes."

Logan says, "Mom doesn't let her near the kitchen anymore, we're all safe."

Skylar says, "Have a good Thanksgiving if I don't see you at school next week. We won't meet again until after. Just keep studying!"

You have left LAScholEx.

CHAPTER SEVEN

IT'S THE SECOND Thanksgiving of the day, and I am wasting time here at Aunt Sadie's house, the one with the eight kids, because it's easier for us to go there than them to go anywhere else. The first Thanksgiving was a nice brunch at Mom's mom's house. She has one sister who only brought one dog and no date. Dogs are better than cousins, but neither is better than coding.

I should be at home working on my social app.

"Pass the gravy, dear."

I look at the glop in front of me and then at Great-Aunt Ruth. "I think Logan's gravy is at the other end. You should ask someone down there to pass it."

She laughs and says, "Oh, you," watching me until I hand her the vastly inferior gravy bowl filled with actual lumps. There was a logistical failure, the kind that happens regularly on the Collins side. We ended up bringing a second serving of gravy. We also brought Mom's corn bread, which I don't even see on the table. Grampa Schmidt would never tolerate this level of chaos. Which is why he and Grandma are happy they had only two daughters and have two grandchildren.

"So I hear you're still trying to make apps like your dad,"

Uncle Richard says on the other side of me. "Or have you taken up something useful? You know Aunt Jenny has a shop on that Etsy that's doing all right. You should help her with all that tech stuff."

"I got an app approved by the Education team at HubBub," I say, knowing he won't get it.

"HubBub? Watch it, or you'll end up doing bookkeeping for your father," he says, even though he's the kind of guy who spends more time golfing than actually working. He's in sales. I assume he actually sells something. I've never heard what it was.

"Still no boyfriend?" my older cousin Iris asks from Richard's far side. Like that's important.

"Your father was a late bloomer, too." Uncle Richard laughs, even though he didn't know my father before he married Aunt Sadie.

"I hear your brother is going to the State tournament for debate," Great-Aunt Ruth says. "Such a charmer, just like his grandfather."

"Yeah, Logan's the best," I say, not correcting her that he does speech, not debate, and he has one more qualifier next weekend before his spot is assured.

I can feel my phone vibrating in my pocket, but I don't even want to know what would happen if I looked at it. No one but Ruth is eating anymore—we've all declared ourselves far too stuffed to continue. And yet we're waiting to be dismissed by Grampa Bob, carrying on these awful conversations in the meantime. But Grampa Bob is sitting at the far end of the table, his hands folded over his belly, and he looks half asleep.

Dad takes pity on all of us and says, "Isn't the game starting, Dad?" and we all take a collective breath, hoping for freedom. Or at least I am. I'll bet Logan is, too, even though he's halfway down the massive table, lodged between Uncle Bernie and our cousin Jon.

"You're right!" Grampa says, wobbling his head and then hoisting himself up. "Kickoff is in ten minutes." And with that, we're free.

Richard gives a sad little "Can't miss the game" and disappears into the bonus room. Ruth keeps munching on the mush she's made out of her dressing and yams.

I pull my phone out. With Grampa gone it's relatively safe to check my messages, but it's nothing, just an email about Black Friday sales.

"Everyone's busy doing holiday stuff, nerdling," Logan says. "Come downstairs and spend family time with the cousins."

I just look at him.

"Unless . . . you're getting a headache." He says it really intentionally, with the small lift of an eyebrow.

"Oh, well . . . that was a lot of carbs. And that doctor did say excessive carbs can be a migraine trigger." Maybe the awful weight loss guru neurologist can be useful for something.

"You and carbs." He shakes his head, feigning disappointment. "We should tell Mom before your horrible migraine gets bad. Grandma was quite worried about your health, and Aunt Sadie's still very concerned it might turn out to be brain cancer."

"But what about the game?" I ask, looking toward the living room.

"Somehow Dad will find a way to get over squinting at the seventy-inch TV in 720p Uncle Richard won't stop bragging about."

I can't help it, I actually gasp. Uncle Richard bought a TV without consulting Dad? And he got something so big with such a small resolution? Dad will thank me for a migraine.

"Is Mom talking to Aunt Jenny?" Logan says. "I wonder if she's pulled her Pinterest page up yet."

If I laugh now, there's no chance for a fake migraine, but Mom being forced to stare at mason jars and bath bombs for an hour is not the best setup to a weekend at home. Plus, a migraine wouldn't be the worst excuse to be in my room coding.

"Ow," I say half-heartedly.

"MOM!" Logan shouts immediately. "Sky doesn't look so good."

Mom's back in the dining room before he can finish his sentence. "Are you all right, sweetie?"

Dad's beside her. Clearly what I'm doing is a public service. "Do we need to get you home, sunshine?"

I smile weakly at them. Well . . . what I imagine is weakly.

"You should get the car, Dad," Logan says helpfully.

"I'll grab the leftovers from the kitchen," Mom says, meaning her corn bread no one even touched. There's cheddar and whole bits of corn in it, and she even brought special maple butter that is actually a crime to waste.

"Thanks, sis, I couldn't handle another conversation

about my hot girlfriend who is already at the Ivy League school I'll be going to next year."

"You don't have a hot girlfriend, and you're not going to an Ivy."

"Exactly. I was getting desperate."

I shake my head. "Glad to be of service."

He puts his arm around me and helps me up, as if I actually did need it. "Let's get you home, poor sick baby."

I put my head down and give a tiny moan so no one can see me roll my eyes.

The next evening there's a knock at my bedroom door.

I don't have time to answer it because this ridiculous API call is not returning the right results. I'm supposed to be able to send it a picture and a tag, and it's supposed to send back a validation, but all it's sending back is a picture of this woman they've been using to test image compression for about fifteen billion years.

"Skylar Myrtle Collins, what are you looking at?"

The picture, Lenna, is from a *Playboy* in the seventies, but while the developers might be a bunch of frat boys, it's just a shoulder and a come-hither stare.

My breath catches in my throat, and I spin around in my chair. "Crap, Logan, I thought you were Mom." The last thing I need right now is family time. If I can just figure this out, I may even get this done before Monday.

Logan is too busy leering at my screen. "She's pretty."

"I didn't know you went that femme." There's a plate of

cookies in his hand that threatens to topple over, so I grab them and spin back to my desk, closing the window with the picture. "I'm coding. Don't you knock?"

"I can appreciate a pretty girl. Also I did knock, but I heard you make the noise you make when someone isn't doing what you want them to do, so I figured you were talking to Zane."

I take a bite and realize the cookies are his espresso chocolate chip, and they're still warm. They take at least twenty-four hours to make. "When did you start these?"

"Yesterday after we got home, nerdling, which is the last time any of us saw any of you. Mom thinks you actually have a headache."

That must be why I haven't been called down to participate in some kind of family time.

He tousles my hair, then smells his hand. "Have you even left this chair?"

"I slept," I say, shoving another cookie in my mouth.

"Nerds do not live by protein bars alone. Since you're clearly not laid up, do you need a leftovers sandwich?"

"With Grandma Schmidt's turkey?" I try not to drool.

"And my gravy," he asks. "Mom stole some of Aunt Jenny's cranberry chutney."

I look up at him. "Why are you being so nice?"

"It's Thanksgiving. It's the law." He drops onto my bed, not intending to make me any more food immediately, it appears. "What was that picture? What are you working on? She's too modern to be from the Second Industrial Revolution."

I chew the cookie, considering how much I should tell him. "Are you adding porn to the rewards in Study Buddy? Will schools allow that?"

"No, doofus. It's a sample image. The dude-bros of programming have been using it since the early days of dude-bro programming as an image compression test. They kicked all us women out for fifty years so they could do stuff like this."

"Are you, er, compressing her?"

"No, I'm really not." I turn back toward the screen. "I'm trying to send them an image." My exasperation leaks into my fingers as I punch heavily at the keys. "They're supposed to send me a confirmation, not a freaking picture."

"Why are you sending anyone pictures of anything?"

"It's for a new app." I pull up the wireframe I made after my MRI and show him. The only other person who has seen it so far is Mads, and that's just because I needed a theme and a logo so it looked professional. She was too excited about the idea to ask me why I decided to make it.

Logan stands up and leans over me to get a better look. "So you take a picture of someone and then it creates a chat?"

"No, it creates a record of your picture," I say. "It only creates a chat if the other person also takes a picture of you."

"What if they haven't?"

"Then it sits here in the potential matches area."

"Sky . . ." he says, his voice very far away.

"What?" I freeze. "Did someone already do this?"

He doesn't answer immediately, and his eyes are wide, looking between me and the wireframe.

"Logan, you're freaking me out."

"Skylar, this is something," he finally says.

"It's another app. That's all." I sigh, pulling my code up next to the webpage to see where exactly I screwed up. "I'll be done by Monday if I figure out this dang call."

Logan grabs my chair and turns me around to look at him. "No, you don't get it. This is something. You're not randomly judging strangers like some dating app. You're not invading someone else's space with a private message. You're just putting your dreams out there so they can possibly become real."

"It's just a does-he-like-me note with broken code that doesn't even freaking work." I try to pull away and turn back to my work, but he has me tight.

"No, Sky, this is something. Just you wait."

"It won't be anything if I wait." I tug again. "And it really won't be anything if you don't let go."

"I should definitely feed you. You need your brain working if you're going to do something this big."

"I have cookies and protein bars."

"Brains need nutrients," he calls from the hallway. He's already halfway downstairs when he adds, "This is really something, Sky."

I shake my head, turning back around. Maybe I'm using the wrong API. I pull up another website that has similar code that actually works to see how they did it. And now I have to be extra careful with this identity verification, lest my poor brother ends up catfished and I never get another espresso chocolate chip cookie because he blames me.

From: Mark K. <socialteam-approval@hubbub.com>
To: Skylar Collins <Sky@skylesslimits.com>
Subject: Requite—Social; Spoke: Personal Interest

Skylar Collins,

SkyLessLimits's social application "Requite" has been approved for the AppHub.

Per the development agreement, we have added the necessary support channels for chat management to your admin panel. As the developer, you are responsible for handling disputes, abuse, and other issues related to your social application. See the HubBub Requirements for additional information. Such reports are available within the Flags tab of the administration environment. Regular audits will be performed on your reports, and failure to properly address issues may lead to the removal of your app and/or development credentials.

Social apps are entitled to monetization at 1,000 downloads. At that time, enhanced marketing support will also become available through the Marketing tab in your admin panel for super administrators and users in your org designated with the marketing role. If you don't know the difference between KPI (key performance indicators) and SEO (search engine optimization), you'll be able to learn more through our Sales and Marketing Hub.

Be sure to complete the monetization process in your administration profile to ensure funds are properly deposited. There will be no payment made on apps with incomplete monetization profiles or those without an active administrator.

Thank you for your contribution to the HubBub Social Network.

Mark K.

App Approvals, Social Team

HubBub, Inc.

CHAPTER EIGHT

"OKAY, SO . . . I have a new app," I say, dropping my lunch down on the wrong side of the table because Zane is in my spot. Again. It's Thursday, and this has become a thing. Much like when the debaters gather the day before big events. Only our event isn't until next week, and the tolerance is so low with the debaters that they've started invading our table for regular meeting days.

It's only been five days since I initially submitted Requite, and the email from the testing team came this morning. Probably because no one cares if social apps crap out, or maybe because of all of their code I used.

"Already?" Mads says at the same time Logan says from his new seat across from Kaden, "It's more than just an app."

I shrug at Mads and ignore my brother, who should really be halfway across the lunchroom. I don't look at Zane, who refuses to let me have my seat next to Mads back, as I say, "It's just something silly."

"It's not silly," Logan says. "You all have to download it like right now." To me he asks, "It's in the store, right? What did you call it? Request?"

"Requite, like in *Romeo and Juliet*," Mads says. "It's here."

She flips her phone around and shows everyone the cute little pink-and-green logo she created. She made me promise not to put her online name in the credits. Her legion of followers would never believe the goth queen LeBrat made this adorable abomination.

"Sky made a safe teenage dating app, and it's going to make us rich," Logan says, only partially correct. This app is never making it past this table. It's a footnote in the story guaranteeing us a Pathfinder, to get the team to Nationals.

The rest of the team has their phones out and are searching for the app—even Kaden, who will never use it. Meanwhile, I pick at my lunch. "You all have a debate tournament this weekend, right?" I sneak a peek at Zane to make sure he's downloading with everyone else.

Next to me, Dom says, "You made this, Sky?"

"It's gonna take over everything," Logan declares.

Zane is the only one who answers me. "Yeah, just a local . . . at Southdale."

I stiffen, mad at myself for even thinking about Nate as I continue, "You should use it there." I've already emailed the link to Joey with instructions. Hopefully by Saturday she'll get her answer. At the very least, she should have it before our meet next weekend. It'll be a full Quizposition, where the points will contribute to our overall total at the end of State. We have enough Achievers that we could survive without Kaden, Dom, or Zane, but Joey needs to be there or we won't have enough Pathfinders to participate.

"This is going to be huge," Dom says, and Logan agrees.

Kaden asks, "Did you really think this through, Sky?"

I look up from my tray. "What do you mean?"

"It's kind of invasive . . . taking pictures of someone," Kaden says.

"Like people don't have stealth pictures of their crushes already," Logan says.

"It's not going to change the world, K," I say. "I'm just passing a note."

"What's the harm?" Mads asks. "It's cute."

Kaden shakes their head. "Just don't come to me when this all blows up."

"You really made this?" Zane asks, still poking at his phone. And then there's a second when he looks up, eyes framed between the sharp plastic of his case and the soft curls of his hair, and I see it. What Joey was saying. About the way it flops. Kind of like my stomach just did.

I blink, probably too much, and clear my throat nervously.

"In a freaking weekend," Logan says. "Can you believe it?"

I can feel Zane smile at me from behind his phone, and I look back down at my salad. I should just look at him. Looking at him is normal—I do it all the time. "It was just some API calls." I glance at Mads instead, who is trying to convince Kaden my latest monstrosity is harmless, and I for some reason want her to convince me, too. "Mads did the graphics. It's nothing really." I clear my throat again and stand up. "I should get to class."

"Lunch just started, nerdling. Sit down and let us be the ones to say how awesome you are for once."

I drop back into my seat, realizing I don't have anywhere to go anyway. They really won't stop talking about the app, and after wolfing down his burger, Logan runs off to another table. I work at my salad, ignoring as much as I can.

". . . Bismarckian realpolitik of it all."

I look up. "What are you saying?"

Zane laughs. "I knew that would work."

Dom is also laughing.

"We were wondering what we needed to wear next week to the thing," Zane says.

"The meet?" I ask, looking around the table. They're all staring at me with assorted amused expressions. Logan's still not back; in fact, he's at a third table, gesturing wildly at his phone. "It's just the local, but we have to be onstage for Quizposition."

"So dress up," Zane says.

"No." I shake my head. "I mean, yes, for like what I think is dressing up, but not top hat and tux or whatever you think dressing up means. I mean, Zane. I mean, you're fine."

As usual, he's wearing clothes more appropriate for a high-powered business lunch than the cafeteria. He never quite goes so far as a suit jacket, but somehow that makes it seem even more formal. Simply getting dressed involves things like starch and waistcoats for him. He's got this extreme debonair thing going on that no one really needs right now.

"So, biz caj," Dom says.

"Sure. Polos and khakis. Whatever you need to be

comfortable in front of a crowd. Joey could wear a dress if she wants. Mads obviously will."

Mads says, "I resemble that remark."

"But I won't . . ."

"Sky's allergic to knees," Zane says to no one in particular.

"So Joey shouldn't feel like anything she wears is going to stand out."

Dom says, "Joey will wear an A-line skirt, pressed shirt, some sort of cardigan."

"Did you ask her?" I ask.

"No, that's what she always wears," Kaden answers for Dom. "It's her signature, you know, for performances."

"Oh, that make sense."

"Plus, she doesn't want to be outshined by Dapper Dan," Dom adds.

I think about the black pants and gray sweater that I always wear to these things. It looks fine. It'll work, but at no point will anyone ever accuse me of matching dapper anything. It's comfortable and sufficient for what we're trying to do. That's all that matters. If I were really trying something, I could go for a black turtleneck, but I'd have that thing stretched out and awful-looking by the time anyone saw me. I don't know how anyone in tech wears those things.

"Who all will be there?"

I pull myself back into the conversation. "Uhm, us, East, Riverside. Oh, and Southdale."

"Two weekends in a row?" Dom groans.

"They are the actual worst," Logan says, appearing from whatever he was doing with half the lunchroom. "But it's a great chance to destroy them twice in a row."

"Z, you cannot get into a fight with that jerkwad," Dom says.

Kaden tries to shush them, but not before Mads asks, "Which jerkwad?"

"This complete dweeb named Nate from Southdale who thinks he's the supreme debater. They faced off again this weekend, and again Zane destroyed his soul while Joey handled his girlfriend," Dom says, and this time Kaden kicks him under the table—and accidentally me in the process.

I look at Zane, and he's very much not looking at me.

I look at Kaden, who totally is, with pity.

I rub my eyes with my thumbs and try to remember my breathing techniques.

Zane says, "So . . . you do know him?"

I look at Mads, then Kaden, eyes wide. "Did he actually—"

And Kaden stops me. "Nate's partner asked Logan if you were his sister at last week's meet."

Of course Nate never even said my name in public. My stomach is back on its nonsense, and the headache I was pretty sure I was imagining becomes all too real. Logan and Mads are trying to shush everyone, and Zane is apologizing, and all I can say is "And now you all know?"

Logan finally says, "She said some things . . . about you knowing the jerkwad, so Zane had to crush them again."

Zane says, "'Things'? She was totally out of line. And we didn't crush them all over again for that. We crushed them because they couldn't handle us."

I lift up my tray and drop it back on the table to a loud clatter, and everyone looks at me.

"Sky," Mads says softly.

"It was nothing." The adrenaline is buzzing in my ears, but that's not the only reason everything is a little blurry. "It was a long time ago, and it was nothing. This has nothing to do with me."

"It wasn't nothing," she says.

"I can't right now. I need to go get meds." I pick up my tray again and rush to the tray-return area next to the kitchen. The nurse's office is just out the door. If I make it, I can get my meds before the next bell.

That's all that matters after the world's most humiliating lunch ever.

You joined LAScholEx.

Dom, Joey, Kaden, Logan, and Zane are here.

There are 173 unread messages—click here to unroll the history.

Skylar says, "WHAT ARE YOU DOING IN MY CHANNEL?"

Dom and Logan are grabbing lunch at the McD's next door. Join us when you're done.

Dom says, "Joey and Zane, not you, Sky. You stay home."

Logan laughs.

Skylar says, "You are at a DEBATE TOURNAMENT not a SCHOLEX EVENT. Why is the debate team in MY CHANNEL?"

Logan says, "It's not the whole debate team, just the good parts."

Joey says, "We JUST got done destroying our first pairing. Judge is giving notes."

Skylar says, "What the bleep are you doing coordinating lunch FOR A DEBATE TOURNAMENT in my channel?!?"

Logan says, "Uhhh, so we can study, potty mouth?"

Kaden says, "If you scroll up, you'll see I did try to warn them"

Skylar says, "I'm not scrolling through 173 lines of nonsense."

Logan says, "I am taking care of things for you, so it's fine."

Skylar says, "For me . . . how?"

Zane says, "Logan is calling us a street team."

Joey says, "I wouldn't be surprised if the folks working at McD's haven't already downloaded."

Skylar says, "Downloaded what?"

Dom says, "Don't they let you know when someone installs your app?"

Skylar says, "They need partners to use Study Buddy."

Kaden says, "Not Study Buddy"

Kaden says, "I told them you'd be bleeped"

Skylar says, "572 Requite downloads?! @!#@!!!!@!@!"

Logan says, "Is that all?"

Dom says, "Bleep, that's twice the number of people who are here today."

Zane says, "We HAVE been telling them to tell all their friends."

Logan says, "Well, keep in mind that includes most of the school downloads from this week."

Skylar says, "There are almost 2K images already."

Kaden says, "Figures"

Zane laughs.

Dom says, "Debaters."

Logan says, "Arguing leads to bleep."

Dom says, "LOGAN."

Logan says, "L-U-S-"

Logan says, "T"

Logan says, "How is that even a bad word??!?"

Joey says, "It is one of the seven deadly sins."

Skylar says, "How have they made 700 chats already?"

Dom says, "You can see the chats that are created?"

Skylar says, "I can see the total chat channels my API calls have generated."

Skylar says, "If there were only a few people on it, I could probably infer, but this is ridiculous."

Dom says, "Good, perv."

Skylar says, "Perv?"

Dom says, "What do you think people are doing once they have chat rooms created?"

Skylar says, "I didn't think that far."

Kaden says, "Obviously"

Logan says, "Don't be such a negative nelly, K."

Zane says, "What did you THINK would happen when you made it?"

Zane says, "Where are you guys sitting?"

Logan says, "BY THE SLIDE"

Dom says, "By the slide!!!!!"

Logan says, "Hey, Sky . . ."

Skylar says, "Yes?"

Logan says, "Can I borrow your tablet later?"

Skylar says, "Where's yours?"

Logan says, "Do you want me to do well at the ScholEx meet next week?"

Skylar says, "Is this a trick question?"

Logan says, "Then loan me your tablet later."

Skylar says, "Let's talk when you get home."

Dom says, "You should do it, Sky. What could Logan possibly do wrong?"

Logan says, "You're not helping, dude."

Dom says, "I'm totally helping. You watch."

Mads has joined LAScholEx.

Skylar says, "You're not helping."

Mads says, "What's wrong with you people!! @*#@!@!#@!!# $33531@"

Kaden says, "Now you've all done it"

Skylar says, "And you thought you needed to be afraid of me."

Logan says, "I'm sure we can double the installs by next week's meet."

Logan says, "We've awakened the BEAST!!!"

Kaden says, "You have no idea . . ."

Mads says, "If I get another bleeping notification, I'm bleeping coming the bleep down there and placing your phone exactly where you think I will!!@!@#!!!"

Dom says, "You can always turn them off."

Logan says, "Dude, no, run while you can."

Kaden says, "They'll all be quiet now . . ."

Mads says, "Simply because you all wake up at the bleep crack of dawn to argue with other nerds doesn't mean the rest of us didn't bleeping stay up till 3 a.m. working on commissions!!@!#$@!!"

Zane says, "We're moving to the debate channel."

Mads says, "See that you do!!!"

Mads has left LAScholEx.

Requite on HubBub | @RequiteApp
Saturday, December 5, 8:48 p.m.

He loves me?

She loves me not?

Stop guessing and find out with @RequiteApp.

 ★35 💭3

Requite on HubBub | @RequiteApp
Saturday, December 5, 9:14 p.m.

Don't you wish there were better ways to communicate with your secret crush than climbing walls and sending messages through priests?

Now there is!

With @RequiteApp the path to true love runs real smooth.

 ★25 💭1

CHAPTER NINE

THERE ARE TOO many people in this cafeteria. And it's not my cafeteria. This is Nate's cafeteria—Southdale, enemy territory. I don't know where to sit or how to be here. I pull open my app and message everyone a quick Where are you? but nothing comes back.

Logan's parking.

I'm in here alone.

I weave my way through the folks gathered near the front to a table kind of in the back with a useful landmark: a big post with purple-and-blue banners all around it. I tell the chat room where I am and take a seat in the middle of the table to make it clear that I'm claiming the whole thing.

After a couple of minutes spent staring at my phone, hoping for any sort of response from anyone, I hear behind me. "Ugh, it's her . . ."

"The stalker?"

"She thinks going to Lovelace is enough to make up for her other shortcomings. You think she's back here by us looking for him?"

I look over my shoulder to see the girl from Nate's HubBub feed. So, yes, they're talking about me. Which means either

Nate has mentioned me out loud or, more likely, she also found out I exist from the comments I used to leave him in HubBub.

"Did you hear she's the one who made that ridiculous app everyone was talking about last week? I bet she thought it'd help her get him back. But, I mean, look at her."

I'm about to stand up. To tell her that the "ridiculous" app has nothing to do with her and her awful boyfriend, who, by the way, was the one who led me on. At no point was I stalking anyone. But before I can figure out how to start, I hear someone shout, "Sky!"

"Oh! It's him," her friend says. "You should go talk to him."

"He's just so yummy. If Nate and I weren't still together . . ." the girl in Nate's pictures says, debater lust in her voice. "Do you think he's coming over here?"

Something between anger and embarrassment blooms deep in my stomach and runs like a live wire through me. He is absolutely coming this way, but instead of talking to either of them, Zane drops into the seat in front of me. "What's wrong?"

I shake my head, and he looks around, asking, "Where is everyone?"

I clear my throat and blink a few times, but there's still something trapped inside me—shame, maybe. "Logan's parking. Or he stole my tablet again and is posting more awful poems from my admin account. Who knows."

"He's probably stopped to talk more people into downloading your app."

"He wouldn't."

"That's all he did last week. That's all any of us did," Zane says. "He bribed us with hot apple pies to help."

I try to clear my throat again. I can't hear them behind me anymore, so I don't know what awful thing they're saying about me . . . or Zane. They probably think I'm throwing myself at *him*, of all people. They definitely think he could do better.

"Are you okay?"

"What?" I say, looking up at him for the first time. "No one's here yet."

"Are you getting a headache?" he asks, frowning.

"No, I'm fine. The app's fine. I'm about three downloads from monetizing, which is something I've never had to deal with before. Logan really needs to stop."

"This is way past just Logan now. I heard two kids talking about it when I was out to dinner with my family last night," he says, a strange glint in his eye.

"You didn't."

"Totally did." He adds, "How is it working for you?"

"What?"

"The app," he says. "Have you made any matches yet?"

I frown at him. "Why would I?"

"You didn't . . . you know . . . do this to get someone's attention?"

"You think I did this for Nate?" I ask.

"No!" he says a little louder than he clearly meant to, based on the way he looks around. "I mean, I figured you did this for someone."

"I didn't make it for me."

"Or for Mads," he says, kind of prompting me to explain.

"No, Kaden would kill me and eat me."

"Logan, then?"

I laugh. "Logan has never once in my life needed my help with getting a date."

"I think you overestimate your brother."

"How about you?" I ask, trying to sound casual. "Have you matched yet?"

He shakes his head, looking over toward the doors to the cafeteria, probably trying to find anyone else to talk to except me.

"What about Joey?" I ask, trying to be even more casual.

His head snaps back at me. "What?"

"You and Joey. I thought maybe . . ."

"Thought what?"

"I don't know?" I suddenly can't be casual, and I definitely can't handle this eye contact right now, so it's my turn to scan the door. "Arguing, lust, whatever."

"You're really not using the app for yourself?"

I shake my head, but only a tiny bit. It's never once occurred to me that I could actually use the app. That I should. That there'd be someone I could use it on. I don't think the final version is even on my phone.

"Why not?"

"I just never . . ." I trail off. Why would I use it? That's not what it's for. "Why does it matter?"

"I don't know. I just thought . . ."

"Why? What have you heard?" Could he actually believe random girls from Southdale? Would he think I'm some kind of stalker?

"I haven't heard anything."

"It's not like I made it for myself or anything. Let's be real. Who would even match with me?"

Why does this matter to him? I made this app to get him with Joey, not for him to give me the third degree.

"Is that what you think?"

"There's no reason for you to be concerned about what I want out of Requite when you have a cute debate partner sitting right next to you." I say the obvious because clearly he's not going to get us there.

"Joey doesn't even like me."

"You sure about that?" He cannot be this oblivious. They spend all this time together, how can he not know she likes him?

"Will that help? For me to prove no one else likes me like that?"

"No, what would help is you leaving me alone." I mean, of course I want him to confirm she likes him, but if I just say that, it would be a waste of my Thanksgiving weekend. He should go take her picture and leave me out of it.

"Maybe I should. Maybe then you'll get it."

I think he's actually upset. Even though he's clearly the one who isn't getting it.

Maybe he's scared she won't be there. Maybe he just really wants a fight. But for good measure I add a firm "Maybe."

And then I see a way out of this conversation and stand up, "Mads! Kaden! Over here!"

When I turn back, Zane is gone, probably looking for Joey. I don't know why, but for the first time since sixth grade, I almost wish I hadn't started yet another fight with him.

CHAPTER TEN

"INTERPRETING THE AGE of Enlightenment in your school colors of green and gold is a lot to carry off, but at least it was a choice," Mads says as we look at the display that got Old North High to State three years ago. We Achievers finished our Quizposition round before lunch, and Mads has probably about fifteen minutes before she and the other Pathfinders need to check in for their round. I haven't seen Zane since our quiz ended. Not that I've been looking for him. We've been so busy going over the booths in minute detail.

It's only about two thirty, but trying to find the solution to what makes a good booth great is starting to wear on all of us. I say, "At least they have more than one color. The last one was so very blue I thought I was having aura."

"They all have some color, though, don't they?" Kaden says in a thoughtful voice. "That's the risk of the Second Industrial Revolution—grayscale. Everyone assumes because of photography the world was black, white, and shades of gray while in reality it was just as colorful as now."

Mads nods. "We could colorize images."

"That's not enough, though," I say. "We need a theme."

"Where is everybody else?" Joey asks, coming up on the three of us.

Kaden says, "Logan is doing Logan things with Dom in tow. Zane said he was going to go grab some snacks for all of us." They look at their phone. "But that was almost two hours ago. How was your practice this morning?"

It's a good thing Pathfinder is this afternoon, because evidently she forgot she had a commitment this morning. All that work, all this planning, and she almost ruined it.

"Fine," Joey says, but her big eyes are a little wild behind her tiny wire-frame glasses. "Today has gone better than I expected."

She's even cuter in person than I imagined, in her giant cardigan and pencil skirt matched against a tiny pixie cut that perfectly suits her size. *Adorable* would probably be a better way to phrase it. Down to the tiny bow clipped in her strawberry-blond hair.

"I didn't miss my Quizposition, right?" she asks me. "You said three?"

I look at my watch and nod. "You have a little bit of time. I might bio break before we head in."

"I'll go with you," Joey says as Kaden says, "I'll save you a seat."

Mads and I both give Joey a strange look, but I agree, so we start making our way through the crowds storming the handful of booths in the gymnasium.

It's not until we're in a quiet part of the hallway that she says, "It happened!"

"What?"

"We matched! There's a chat and everything, just like you said!" She's jumping up and down and has a death grip on my arm.

Prying her hands off my sweater before she stretches the arm out, I ask, "Really?" I mean, yeah, I said to Zane he should match with her. But . . . he really did it fast.

"Yeah, we met up on my way in! He was playing with his phone and all of a sudden I had a notification!" She holds her phone up to me, showing me my app and a single match with Zane's ridiculous smirk next to it. "I had almost given up, since he hadn't done anything last weekend, but I guess maybe he was too busy with all the stuff Logan was asking us to do . . ." She keeps going on, probably ready to give me a complete rundown of the debate tournament.

"Why is he still using that picture?" I ask, and try to keep us moving so she's not late for check-in.

"I think it's cute."

"It's from ninth grade," I say, remembering the field trip to the historical society, where he was trying to mimic the statue out front while Dom shouted instructions at him like a professional photographer.

"Still cute," she says defensively, and clicks her phone off.

"So how's the conversation going?" I ask.

"What?"

"The conversation? In the chat? How's it going?"

"I haven't actually talked to him! It's been five minutes." She's nearly squeaking. Her eyes even bigger than before.

"But you like him. He likes you. So . . ."

Her face goes gray, and she looks about to faint like a forlorn waif in one of those black-and-white pictures of a workhouse we were just discussing colorizing. Maybe we could make her grayscale instead.

"Talk to him," I say, pushing open the door to an available stall. "What's the worst that could happen?"

"I don't know," she says from the other side of the door. "I say the wrong thing and he's mortally offended and we have to duel at dawn?"

I have to laugh at the image. "Zane wouldn't duel. At best he'd write a strongly worded letter."

"What if he doesn't like me?" she asks pleadingly. As if I have some form of reassurance.

"Then you find someone better," I say as I exit the stall and head straight for the sink.

"What if there is no one better?"

"Then you become the best flute player in the whole world and make him regret all his life choices." I grin at her reflection, and she laughs.

She finally agrees to at least try. She's strangely reluctant, considering the whole time we're signing her in for Quizposition she spends gushing about his hair and clothes and awesome personality. After dropping her at the stage, I find my seat next to Kaden halfway down the auditorium a few seats into the row. Dom is already there, on their other side, and even though there's a seat next to me, Zane makes us stand up so he can sit next to Dom. Which is fine—I didn't want to sit next to him, anyway.

He's not smiling like I would have expected him to be, and clearly Dom's concerned, but no one can ask anything because they lower the room lights and raise the stage lights on the competitors.

It's different being on this side of it. I expected to be less nervous, but I'm even more. At least when I was up there I had some control over the outcome. Now it's all up to my best friend, my brother, and a stranger who thinks I'm her hero.

The announcer explains the rules again. Each team will have one person buzz in to answer the questions. If the answer is wrong, they get a negative point; if it's right, they get a positive. Points are both for the individual and the team overall. The answerer is determined by round-robin. Basically the order they sit down in is the order they answer things, but since all topics are random, there's no guarantee that they'll get something they know.

I'm sure Logan is going to screw this up for me.

"What's with you?" Kaden whispers in my ear.

"What?" I whisper back.

"Are you and Z fighting?" they ask.

"No, I'm trying to watch the quiz."

Questions are flying. I'm suddenly less worried about them getting a question wrong than them not buzzing in at all. It takes something each is confident in for them to start buzzing in on other questions. Except Logan, who buzzes in the fastest and then asks, "Can you repeat that?" Which is an automatic negative point ... which he now realizes, I hope.

Kaden and Dom are conferring next to me, and I shush them both.

I can hear Zane say, "She's in a mood," but I don't rise to the bait.

The whole Pathfinder round goes a lot slower than the Achiever round. No one buzzes in before the question is asked, more people get answers wrong. It's why they're last today and first in the State meets. This is their chance to practice and learn from us, but outsiders don't want to see mistakes. They come for the excitement of the Achiever rounds.

Okay, mostly they come to support their children and significant others.

When all is said and done, our Pathfinders aren't first, but they're in the top three. And that's more than I expected.

"If Logan can listen, we'll actually do all right." Kaden says what I was thinking.

"I don't suck," Zane says loudly.

"They all just need to study, and we'll be fine," I say, almost relieved.

"You could thank me," Zane says.

"For?" I ask.

"Finding you Pathfinders," he says.

"I did thank you," I say.

"No ... you didn't."

Dom stands up so he's between the two of us and turns to Zane. "Whoa, whoa, there, champ. This is no way to treat Sky."

Zane sighs and turns, leaving our seats from the other direction.

"He should be happy," I say.

"What'd you say to him?" Dom asks.

"Nothing," I say. And then, "Well. We had a little argument this morning."

"I knew it," Kaden says.

"Requite," I say.

"He asked about that?" Dom says, looking after his friend, who has been slowed on his pouting march out of the room by huddles of people congratulating their friends.

"For some reason he was mad I didn't even have it installed. Like I have to use the thing just because I made it. Ridiculous."

"Yeah," Dom says. "Ridiculous." But he's not laughing, he just shakes his head.

"You did awesome!" Kaden says suddenly, and Mads appears in the row in front of us.

"I screwed up that question about the Rockefellers," she says.

"Carnegie is the steel and libraries. Rockefellers are Standard Oil," they say. "I can explain it all later."

"Oooh," Logan says, "someone's in trouble."

"Yeah," I say. "You."

"What did I do?" Logan asks, affronted.

"You need to listen to the question and only buzz in when you know the actual answer," I say.

"I know that *now!*" he replies.

"Where's Zane?" Joey asks.

"Pouting," Dom says, and Joey's face falls.

"We were supposed to talk," she says, looking at me pleadingly.

"You can do it online when he's not a big grumpy pants," I say with a half-hearted laugh.

"Cruel, Sky," Dom says.

"Oh, he'll get over it." I grab my backpack.

"It's done now, right?" Logan says.

"Yeah, we need to get home. Mom wants us there by five."

He looks at Dom and shrugs. "Tomorrow?"

Dom smiles at him. "You know it." He does a little dance step and backs down the aisle, away from us. "I'm going to go check on my boy."

"Later, Dom," I say.

We all say our goodbyes. Mads and Kaden are off to yet another date, leaving me to talk to Joey as she waits for her mom. I don't know if we would have done anything together, but it would have been nice to be invited.

Instead I encourage Joey to message Zane in the app, but she's still scared. Not that I blame her. Who gets grumpy when they confirm that their crush likes them? But I guess that's Joey's problem now.

ADMIN: This is the transcript of Chat 12X329W231
between Requite users JoeyJoJoIII and NotThatZane
on Saturday at 6:54 p.m.

JoeyJoJoIII submitted for review at 8:48 p.m. with the
following notes:

I CANNOT DO THIS!!! WHY DID YOU THINK THIS WOULD WORK?!

Please evaluate for possible improvements.

So . . . uh . . . JoJo?

Yeah.

Hi.

Hi, Zane.

I have to admit I didn't expect you to be here.

Me?

Why?

Oh, no reason.

Did you not mean to tag me?

Maybe Sky can fix it, or whatever. Should I report this to her?

NO!

I mean, no, I did tag you.

I just didn't think you'd tag me.

Oh.

Well, I did.

Tag you.

On purpose.

Yeah, so here we are.

Yeah.

So maybe we should talk later?

Oh yeah, good idea.

Bye.

Administrator Options:

___ *Ban one or more user*

___ *Flag the chat for HubBub Standards Team*

___ *Request controls of Chat 12X329W231 from one or more user*

CHAPTER ELEVEN

I DID WHAT I promised I would.

They matched.

He likes her.

Question answered.

Yet it's Monday night, and here I am . . . helping more.

I'm here, I send Joey from one window while her chat with Zane is visible in another. The only difference between this and any of my normal windows is that there's a faint chat ID at the top and everything has a light gray sheen over it. She gave me read permissions on the chat. This useful tool was created so the admin can watch someone replicate an error. And Joey got a really big error.

Message him and ask him if you can try this again. I tell myself this is customer service, though I'm not sure which I'm worse at, customer service or flirting.

OK, she sends me, and then in the other window I see: Hey, Z, is now a good time to talk?

It's a couple minutes before I see: Hey, JoJo, what's up?

Nothing, she says before I can stop her.

I send her, Tell him sorry for how things went last time, you were just nervous.

Sorry about last time, she sends. Then on another line: I was really nervous.

I get it, Zane sends. It's hard talking to someone you have a crush on.

I send her, Say, I guess we were both pretty awkward.

You and me both, huh? she sends.

Hah, Zane sends back. Right.

We're losing him. Which is just so weird. He normally has about a million comebacks to everything. He must actually be nervous. More nervous than I've ever seen him. Tell him you want to take this slowly.

If it's all right with you, can we just chat for a while? she asks instead.

I shake my head at the screen. I know she understands English. I've heard her use it. But it's like we're talking two entirely different languages.

Sure, Zane answers. What do you want to talk about?

And now we're stuck in awkward small talk, which I'm terrible at on the best of days.

What should I say? she asks me in our window, and honestly I don't know what to tell her.

I don't know, ask what he's doing for winter break? I send back.

His mom's family's coming into town, she says, and I already know that, but I didn't expect her to.

Fine, ask him about the weather, I send, ready to give up on this whole ridiculous fiasco.

I can't do this!!! she sends back.

Are you still there? Zane asks.

Help me! HELP ME HELP ME HELP ME!!!! she sends where he can't see.

I sigh loud enough to wake the dead and click the menu button that asks her to give me full control. She's definitely replicated the error. Now I have to see if I can isolate the issue.

Her permission comes back almost instantly, and the gray background turns white like any other chat I can type into.

So I start figuring out what exactly has gone wrong with this chat. On her behalf I send, You said before that you were surprised I was here.

I didn't say surprised, he answers.

You didn't expect me. Isn't that the same thing? I send back.

Not exactly.

Then what kind of thing is it? When he doesn't answer, I add: Isn't the whole point of this app to match so we can do something about it?

I honestly don't know what the point of this app is, he responds, and I want to scream at the screen that this here is the whole point of the app. These two in a chat, talking to each other so I can get on with my life. But no, I have to intervene.

Instead I send, But we did match.

Yes. And now we're here, he sends.

Yes.

Ask him about the State tournament, Joey sends me in the other window, and I had forgotten she was there.

We haven't qualified for State yet, Regionals are next, I answer her.

She sends, No, for debate.

So I hold her off with a quick I'll get to that.

Shouldn't we do something about the fact that we matched? I send.

We are, he sends. We're chatting.

It takes every ounce of self-control not to throw my keyboard across the room. If I hadn't spent so much time on the identity verification, I'd swear I was talking to an entirely different Zane. There's not a single smart comment. It's almost like he's not even smiling. I can't imagine Zane talking and him not smiling at his own cleverness. But here it is, right in front of me.

I have to ask. Are you nervous?

What?

You're just so quiet. It's weird.

I'm always like this, he sends.

He is, Joey confirms in our window as he asks in the other, Aren't I?

I guess you are, I send. But he's not. I don't know this Zane or how to talk to him. I definitely don't know how to flirt with him.

You're the one being weird, he sends. Intense.

This is important, I send.

And then as an afterthought I add, To me.

Isn't it to you? I ask. Diagnostically. Of course.

I mean . . . he sends, but that's it. He doesn't finish it. And I don't help him.

State is coming up, he finally puts in.

And? I send.

Joey sends to me, I don't want to make State awkward. Please don't make State awkward.

Maybe this whole matching thing was . . . too soon. Maybe we should hold off on doing anything about THIS until after THAT? he sends, and I want to ask why he matched on Saturday if he doesn't want to talk now. I want to ask him why he doesn't want a date for tomorrow. Why they're not in some corner making out like Mads and Kaden were as soon as they confirmed their feelings for each other. I want to scream at him to be Zane again.

But mostly I want to yell at him for trying to hide this thing he has with Joey.

But this is what she wants, too. So instead of any of that, I send, That's fine, at the same exact moment that Joey sends in the same exact window, If that's what you want.

Isn't it what you want? he sends.

But neither Joey nor I answer him immediately because I blocked her ability to do it again, and I'm too busy sending to my window with her, STOP IT! You're the one who didn't want it to be awkward.

I'm sorry. I just couldn't help myself, she sends.

I get it, I send her, even though I don't, not entirely. I don't know why she wants Zane when he's always like this with her. I don't get why he matched when he doesn't seem to actually want to do anything about it. I do get why she's anxious to figure this out without a clear definition of what *this* even is. But mostly, I really don't want to be in the middle of it. And now I need to talk both of them down.

Isn't it? Zane has asked again in their chat, so I flip back to it and stare at those words.

I don't want debate to be awkward, I send, giving him Joey's feelings.

Good, he sends. I don't want this to have made things awkward with you.

Good, I send back.

Are you OK with all of this? he asks.

With what?

With this not being a THING.

Yes.

Are you? I add.

Absolutely. But after State maybe we can just, I don't know, maybe we should try to get to know each other better? he sends.

It's not nothing. But it's not what you say when your crush admits they like you, too. None of this makes any sense. This is not the Zane I know. It's not remotely how I'd want him to be if it were me. But this isn't me.

Yeah, cool. If that's what you want, I send, while Joey is filling our chat with little heart emojis.

Look, I have to get going, he sends.

Bye, I send, and when he doesn't say anything else, I take in a massive breath as if I'm coming back up for air from being under water too long.

Was that OK? I send to Joey's window, where she's still heavy on the heart emojis.

I'm going to go do homework now, I send her.

Thank you, Sky!! Now I can practice talking to him like a person before I have to actually flirt, she sends. You're a lifesaver.

We'll see, I think, my fingers hovering above the keyboard—but I don't actually type it. I can't. She doesn't seem to know there's something more wrong here than her inability to flirt, and I don't know how to tell her. I fixed the glitch, but it's temporary. A patch at best. There's a real problem with Zane, and if he were mine, I'd fix it. But he's hers now, and she's going to need to do her own bug fixing.

Or maybe it's a feature.

Maybe confirmation is actually all she wanted. Maybe she only wants the idea of Zane. Or maybe this is just how it always goes.

I don't know why I wanted Zane to be better.

I don't know why I'm so mad.

This doesn't have anything to do with me.

You have joined LAScholEx.

Dom, Joey, Kaden, Mads, Logan, and Zane are here.

There are 14 unread messages—click here to unroll the history.

Skylar says, "We have to have a theme for the booth by the time we log off or we're dead."

Kaden says, "We were just talking about it"

Mads says, "K was explaining while waiting for you."

Dom says, "And Logan was pointing out that it's the first day of winter break and we should all just chill for five minutes."

Zane says, "And I was saying that those are brave words for someone who is literally across the hall from you right now."

Skylar says, "Actually, he's in the basement."

Logan says, "Yeah, see? She has to cross two whole floors and both parents to get to me. Basically immune."

Skylar says, "But I can always burn his Christmas present."

Logan says, "You wouldn't."

Skylar says, "If we have a theme for the booth by the time we log off, you get your present."

Joey says, "What's in it for us?"

Skylar just LOOKS at Joey.

Joey laughs.

Zane says, "Satisfaction of a job well done?"

Mads says, "We are allowed to live."

Kaden says, "We don't have a panicked Sky bubbling up at us for two whole weeks"

Skylar says, "Kaden gets me."

Kaden says, "Which is why I'm saying we should focus on the plight of the laborers . . ."

Dom doesn't see how that showcases anything other than social history.

Skylar says, "Dom makes a good point."

Zane says, "Teacher's pet."

Dom says, "Jealous?"

Joey says, "What about the art of the laborers?"

Mads says, "That might just work . . ."

Skylar says, "I was thinking something more along the lines of the influence of the railroads."

Joey says, "Right, Mads? Like ragtime and the rise of sheet music."

Mads says, "Arts and Crafts. Barbizon. Realism vs Impressionism."

Mads says, "This could work quite nicely."

Dom says, "Oh, bleep! Electricity and wrought iron."

Skylar says, "Or, I guess, we can do something else."

Zane says, "And Mark Twain and investigative journalism."

Kaden says, "This sounds very bourgeoisie focused . . ."

Mads stares.

Kaden says, "What?"

Mads says, "We're going to have a nice talk about Arts and Crafts after this."

Logan says, "Ooooooooooh. Someone's in TROUBLE!!!"

Zane says, "You really stepped in it this time, K."

Kaden says, "Like you know anything about Arts and Crafts"

Zane says, "I know it's a movement."

Skylar says, "Arts, music, literature, science, history (after Kaden gets a lecture). I guess that's all the bases covered."

Mads says, "PHOTOGRAPHY!!@!@#@!!!!"

Joey says, "PHONOGRAPHS!!!"

Zane says, "Kaden, we can work together. There might be something in the Standard Oil reading. And isn't The Jungle from that period?"

Dom says, "Yeah!"

Dom says, "Social influence through creativity."

Mads says. "THAT'S IT!"

Mads says, "Social Change and Creativity"

Skylar says, "Lacks a certain panache."

Mads says, "But you get what I mean."

Logan says, "I'll work on the title."

Skylar says, "What an excellent contribution."

Logan says, "YOU'RE WELCOME."

Zane says, "Sounds like we got it."

Dom says, "That was pretty easy. Thanks, Joey!"

Zane says, "Yeah, thanks, JoJo."

Skylar says, "Yeah . . . right . . . thanks, Joey and Mads, for finding a connection."

Logan says, "So I can go finish my game?"

Skylar says, "I can hear you playing through the vents. Don't pretend."

Logan says, "I paused!"

Logan says, "Peace out."

Kaden says, "Zane"

Kaden says, "I'll bubble you after I read The Jungle."

Logan has left LAScholEx.

Zane says, "Cool."

Zane says, "Thanks, Sky."

Dom says, "Yeah, thank you, Sky. This is gonna be bleep."

Skylar says, "I didn't actually do anything."

Zane says, "Why are you swearing at her?"

Dom says, "I just said bleep."

Dom says, "BA."

Dom says, "That doesn't make sense. I give up."

Dom has left LAScholEx.

Zane says, "Sorry about him."

Mads says, "Joey, bubble me and we can coordinate our movements."

Skylar says, "You don't need me?"

Mads says, "Don't I always?"

Mads says, "Kaden."

Mads has left LAScholEx.

Kaden says, "I guess I have to go get lectured now"

Skylar says, "I'll be there by three tomorrow. OK?"

Kaden says, "Can't miss cookie day"

Kaden has left LAScholEx.

Joey says, "Cookie day?"

Zane says, "Those two make a massive amount of cookies over break while Sky is allowed in the room for who knows what reason. They keep her from baking, you know, for all our safety. Sometimes they all share if there are leftovers by the end of break."

Joey says, "Mmmmm, stale cookies."

Skylar says, "Actually, I'm in charge of packaging and distribution. They're in charge of measuring and mixing. And baking."

Skylar says, "We freeze half the dough in batches so we always have fresh cookies."

Joey says, "Oooh, so you have a dough pile?"

Skylar says, "If that's your poison."

Joey says, "Yes please!"

Skylar says, "I'll mark you down for unbaked."

Zane says, "Of course she gets special treatment."

Zane says, "I'm lucky if there's a peanut butter kiss left."

Skylar says, "Blossom. They're peanut butter blossoms."

Zane says, "WHO CARES IF I CAN'T EAT ONE, SKYLAR MYRTLE COLLINS."

Skylar says, "Now you get none."

Zane says, "We'll see about that."

Sky rolls her eyes.

You have left LAScholEx.

CHAPTER TWELVE

WHEN I ARRIVE at Mads's the next day, the baking is already in full swing and there's a sonorous voice growl-singing about hair dye and burning leaves while Kaden and Mads shuffle-dance in the middle of the kitchen. I take a second to just wrap my head around the whole scene. Of the two of them without me. It's no different than the three of us together, but in a way it is. And for the first time since I suggested cookie day all those years ago, I feel a little left out.

Mads finally notices me and shouts, "Sky!!!" I can hear all her extra punctuation even if I can't see it. "Come dance with us!"

"I need help getting all the containers out of my car." I stumble up the last of the stairs, dropping the overly full bags onto her floor.

"Get that up here before Rufus eats it."

"Where is my best boy?"

Just then a giant bouncing pile of muscles and jowls launches himself into the kitchen and right at me. He wiggles and dances around me and into me, almost knocking me back down the stairs. And whatever feeling I had of being unwanted is wiped away by an onslaught of dog kisses.

"Rufus," Mads shouts. "Stop it, leave Skylar alone!"

Kaden has already moved my shopping bags out of the way so Rufus can't decide to play keep-away with the paper.

Rufus and I have been friends almost as long as Mads and I have. This massive bulldog has snored his way through all our sleepovers since we were in elementary school. He settles down long enough to start backing into me.

"Scratches first," Mads declares as Rufus's official voice, "then wash your hands, because we've already started."

"I'll go get the rest of the stuff out of the car," Kaden says.

"It's unlocked," I shout after them as they jog down the stairs. I doubt Kaden gets this much love from Rufus. Though Kaden probably sees this pile of grumbles more than I do now.

Satisfied with the butt scratches, Rufus turns and shoves his face into my hands and starts snoring, standing up, staring at me. I'm glad at least someone still loves me best.

"What have I missed?" I ask, managing not to sound disappointed.

"We just started the shortbread since we need tons of it."

"Six batches," I say, having calculated the official amount.

"Are we trying to drown someone in cookies? Because I can think of far worse ways to go."

"I'm trying to save you time. The shortbread goes in the pressed cookies and the lemon bars, plus the crumble from the offcuts goes in the date fingers."

She sighs and turns back toward the counter. "Fine, I'll make more," she says as she pulls the bowl out of her stand mixer, gracelessly dumping the first batch of shortbread onto a waiting sheet pan that already has some sort of fine white powder on it. "But I make no promises I won't drown anyone in them."

Rufus seems to be done with me, so I stand myself back up and head to the sink to wash the dog off. "What can I do?"

"Just stand there and look pretty," she says, making air kisses at me. I roll my eyes, and she says, "Fine, measure out the flour."

Kaden reappears with the correct bags from Mom's trunk. "This is everything I could find."

"That's all there is," I say, drying my hands off on a nearby towel. "I bought in bulk."

"How efficient," they say, leaving the bags on the far end of the counter. "No, let me measure, you get the containers ready for the freezing."

"We're making another three batches, my love," Mads says.

"This explains the butter," Kaden says.

I sent them the official ingredients list two days ago, and if they bought to spec, our three families will have enough plates of cookies for thirteen total Christmases, a dozen or so plates' worth to give as gifts, and sufficient snacking for the rest of break.

We start working our way down the list, me giving instructions while they both measure and time things and stop me from making helpful suggestions that would taste better because chemistry doesn't care what would taste better.

"This is why you need me," Mads says.

"What?" I say.

"Our creativity is different," she says. Kaden has gone downstairs to put a load of dough in the extra fridge down there. Mostly to keep it safe from our snacking. Even three batches of peanut butter cookies aren't enough when we start snacking.

"I'm not creative," I say, and she laughs—like full-on bends over and laughs.

"You're kidding me, right?"

I shake my head, counting out the cookies we've already made in the last batch and calculating what remains.

"You're, like, super creative, but only when there are all these rules."

I look up at her and frown. "That's not creativity."

"It is." When she sees Kaden coming up from the basement, she says, "Kaden is creative socially."

"What did I do?"

"You're gonna save the world, babe."

"I can only do that if we get enough people to realize how much the old white dudes have rigged the system."

She laughs, winking at me. "See?"

"Okay," I say slowly.

She runs her fingers through her bangs. "I'm creative visually. And, you know, murderously."

"You haven't actually killed anyone."

"That doesn't mean I haven't been creative about it in my

head." She looks at Kaden and then at me and takes a deep breath before adding, "That's why you should let me handle the booth."

"The booth is really important," I point out, trying to keep my voice even despite the sudden buzzing in my ears. "Plus, it has to fit the rules and the judges' expectations." I think I need to sit down.

"It's entirely visual," she says carefully. "I love you enough to help you win." She puts the tray she just pulled out of the oven down on the protective circles of cork that keep the counter safe. "You know that, right?"

"We have to win," I say flatly, even though my face feels hot.

"No, that I love you . . . platonically."

I look at Kaden to see if they'll side with me, but they make a face back telling me I'm on my own.

"Well, I do, and loving you means doing what you need, not what you want," Mads says.

"What is that even supposed to mean?"

"You kind of get a bit . . . intense, Sky," Kaden says.

"I mean, I guess," I say, suddenly needing to be doing something. So I move the too-hot peanut butter blossoms off the rack and into a container before they're ready, thus deforming the Kisses on top with my rough handling.

"So I'm going to help you," Mads says, too cheerful, like she's delighting just a little in my pain. "Because the result is more important than the journey."

"I need to be the leader," I say, rubbing at the flaming-hot chocolate napalm on my fingers.

"Delegating is being a leader, genius," Mads says, popping the next tray in the oven.

"She's right," Kaden says.

"That's what you always say."

Kaden shrugs. "She's hot."

"Traitor."

"So you're delegating this important task to me, Captain?" Mads asks, knowing it's time for the gingerbread people.

I don't say anything.

She just watches me, her eyebrows raised.

I look at Kaden, and they cross their arms, very clearly not interested in taking any side.

"You can make a proposal to the team," I finally concede. It's the best I can do.

She laughs and rolls her eyes. "What's next on the list?"

"Just get the nutmeg," I say.

"See, you can still be bossy even when you're not doing all the work yourself."

NotThatZane

How's your break going?

Sky?

Hello?

What if I said this is a ScholEx question?

What if my house was on fire?

What if I needed a kidney?

What if I said I needed you?

What if we hadn't known each other for years?

What if I were a stranger?

Nothing?

CHAPTER THIRTEEN

"CHIPS!" LOGAN SCREAMS from the kitchen. "And guac," he adds, following his words through the door and straight into me. "Oh. Is that what you're wearing?"

It's the other end of winter break. We've survived three Christmases with various family members (and each other) and only have to make the long slog through New Year's before we're back at school and can start really working on the booth again.

I look down at my sweatshirt, which reads *!False (it's funny because it's true)*, and the stretchy yoga pants I slept in last night. I have so much to do that the only time I left my room was for forced family time. Part of it was studying for ScholEx and coming up with a backup idea for the booth if Mads's doesn't work. The rest has been coding. I spent a good chunk of break working through a few dozen tickets in Requite that didn't require a code fix. My help files have grown exponentially. Yesterday I had to make it even clearer you could delete a chat and that would basically block someone.

Turns out not every crush should be requited. Which I

could have told everyone before they started using this ridiculous app.

I thought of asking Mads to help, but she's got her own family stuff to deal with over the holidays. And Kaden. And the booth. Stuff that isn't my stuff. Plus, then I'd have to admit to myself I wanted to be working on Study Buddy more than hanging out with my best friend over break.

Not that she called.

"Yes, this is what I'm currently wearing? Why?" I ask, scratching at my scalp under my ponytail before taking it down and redoing it.

"I figured you'd want to look nicer, but you do you," Logan says, turning back around and entering the kitchen.

I follow him. "What do you mean?" But I'm pulled up short by a massive spread of food. "What's going on?"

"It's New Year's Eve, nerdling."

"So?"

"So . . . folks will be here in like half an hour," Logan says.

My phone pings in my pocket before I can even process what he's saying. "Why is Mads asking me to ask you what they can bring?"

"Tell her sugar," Logan says loudly over the fridge door. He's holding a huge tray with one hand and moving things around with the other.

I type the answer back to Mads, assuming she'll bring extra frozen dough or something, and ask Logan, "Why don't you put that in the downstairs fridge?"

"That one's full already."

I stare at him.

He finally gets the tray inside and stands up. "You're really wearing that?"

"What is happening?"

"I thought it was obvious." He grins. "We're having a party."

I shake my head. "What?"

"I told you like three days ago?"

"You didn't." I try to think back. This break has been a whirlwind of tickets, studying, and coding. I remember him stopping by my room on Saturday with some sort of turkey-pasta-bake thing and reminding me it was New Year's soon, which, duh. But I don't remember a party.

"I did. You agreed."

"I agreed it was a holiday today."

"Well, you can hide in your room if you want, but I don't think Mads will stand for it."

"Who all did you invite?"

"Just a few people." He laughs at me. "Fine, wear that, see if I care. Or, you could go up and put on that new black sweater Mom gave you and those jeans I got you."

"The jeans have holes in them."

"It's called fashion, nerdling, try it." He looks me over. "And, I'm saying this entirely out of love: at least comb your hair. I get you're going for a tortured-genius thing, but this is a party." He looks around. "And a kitchen."

I open my mouth, but my phone pings again with an

apology from Joey saying she's not going to make it because of a concert or something, and I realize this is way more than just a couple of people coming over. I flee upstairs for a shower and clothes that are intentionally holey and not just the victims of my nervous habit of chewing at the collar of my sweatshirt when I'm focused.

The doorbell rings as I'm sliding my phone into my jeans pocket. These are ridiculously comfortable despite their fashion. I should thank Logan, but then his head would get even bigger. Mom is shouting that my friend is here as I open my bedroom door, so I run down expecting Mads, but it's not her. It's not even Kaden.

"What are you doing here?" I ask Zane, who is standing in my hallway. Wearing jeans of all things. Jeans and a pressed white shirt, so I know for sure it's him. But still, jeans. And his hair is extra floppy.

"I was invited?" he replies, seemingly unsure.

"Not by me. I didn't even know this was a party."

"Didn't know or didn't remember?" he asks.

I make a small grunting noise and turn on my heels. "Follow me, we're probably downstairs." But I make it to the kitchen door and he's standing halfway down the hallway looking at my great-grandmother's spoon collection. While she was alive, she collected tiny sugar spoons from all over. When I was little, I used to polish them with my mom for fun.

"Are these them?" he asks.

"Are they what?"

"Your grandmother's spoons."

"My great-grandmother's, but yeah." I cross back to look at the spoons with him. "How did you know about them?"

"You told me, remember?" He's looking down at me, and I forgot he'd gotten tall. We always seem to be sitting around each other.

"I don't," I say shortly, and clear my throat.

"In sixth grade. We were working on those family reports and you said the only cool thing about your family was that your grandmother had spoons from everywhere."

"Great-grandmother," I correct. I don't remember this. I don't remember being nice to him.

"And Abby Perkins suggested you start using those tiny spoons to eat, and you threw your book at her and got detention."

Now that I remember. My first and only detention. She moved away in eighth grade, and my life got so much better. Why does he remember this? Does he have a list of my most embarrassing moments?

"I should have known you'd be first!" Logan shouts from the kitchen doorway, quickly joining us at the spoons. "You like GiGi's spoons? They used to be a lot shinier." Logan nudges me with his elbow.

I move away from them both, putting as much distance as I can between me and Zane's casual starched shirt. "We're in the basement, right?"

Logan says, "Yeah, can you put some more pop in the fridge? I just pulled some out to put on ice, but knowing this group it won't be enough."

Then the door swings open behind Logan and Zane, and Mads appears in her goth queen best, screaming at the top of her lungs, "I have the sugar!" In one hand is a two-liter of Mountain Dew, in the other a massive stack of Pixy Stix. There's more in a bag hanging from her wrist.

This is going to be a very long night.

First we watch Logan's favorite movie of all time, *Furious 7*. Then we have to endure the inevitable lecture that follows about how the introduction of Shaw shifts the tone of future films and contextualizes the events of the third movie, which actually should be the sixth movie. Really, he likes it because everybody's fighting all the time and it has the best explosions, but he'll never just say that. He's clearly trying to impress someone tonight.

Then we are forced into a rousing game of charades that actually kind of works as a study session because all of Logan's clues were topics from ScholEx, even though half the people here are debaters. Throughout the course of the evening we have managed to drink way too many glasses of Mountain Dew with Pixy Stix in them. Well, they did. I've been good. Mostly.

Dom showed up right after Mads and Kaden. Sal and a bunch of folks who graduated last year stopped by halfway through the movie and left after charades, taking the other debaters who had trickled in over the course of the festivities with them to the next party. When Mom's old clock strikes eleven, everyone still in the basement is both a ScholEx teammate and has a tongue of a different color. Mads's tongue is a purply black from a steady mix of blue and red. Kaden's is bright red. Dom's is blue. Logan's is a more brownish black because he couldn't choose just one color. Zane's is a calmer purple from only eating the purple variety. Mine is probably a teal from the green and blue I've been going back and forth between, because they're the only ones that make sense with the flavors of Mountain Dew.

"It's an hour till midnight," Logan says. "What should we do next?"

"Not Pictionary," I say. I hate that game; I cry every single time.

"Truth or dare!" Dom says, and Logan agrees immediately.

Kaden says, "You sure?"

Mads says, "I'm in."

Zane looks at me and says, "Me too."

I sigh. Even if I don't want to, this is clearly happening anyway.

"Yes!" Logan says, jumping up.

"Ground rules," Mads says. "All dares must occur in this room."

I start laughing and she glares at me, but I can't stop laughing.

"There's a story here," Zane says.

Logan says, "They cannot involve people not participating in the game."

I was already sitting on the floor, but now I'm practically rolling.

Dom says, "There's definitely a story here."

Kaden, also laughing but less hysterically, says, "One time Sky dared Mads to scare Logan, so Mads hid under his bed and . . . well."

Mads says, "No going under Logan's bed."

Logan says, "No crawling out toward me like you're some sort of Japanese movie ghost while screaming like a banshee."

Mads says, "No explaining what all those socks were under your bed!"

"Deal!" Logan practically screams, and now the rest of them are laughing as hard as I am.

When we've calmed down a bit, Zane adds, "You can turn a dare into a truth but no backing out of a truth."

We all nod.

"Everyone must consent to a dare," Logan adds, and Kaden and Mads both nod vehemently.

"No being a jerk," Dom says.

Logan puts one of the empty Mountain Dew bottles in the middle of the circle we've all formed and says, "I'll go first," as he sets it spinning. The next half hour or so is a series of headstands and impossible pool shots on Dad's table. Quiet little truths like how many people they've matched with on Requite, to which Logan's answered two and made the whole room quiet, and Kaden matched none and kissed Mads, and everyone oohed or gagged on their cuteness according to their maturity level.

And then Logan lands on me, and there's no way I'm

telling him the truth, he knows too much, so he dares me. "Install Requite on your phone."

"What?" I ask, expecting far worse.

"You heard me!" Logan says.

"You really don't have your own app installed?" Dom seems astonished.

I pull out my phone. "I side-loaded the alpha for testing, but no one but me is on it."

"What does that mean?" Dom asks Logan softly.

"She has a version she can code, but not the actual app folks can match to," Mads explains.

"There." I hold my phone out to show them all Mads's new logo. Once it hit fifteen hundred downloads, she decided that her quick Thanksgiving graphics were not going to cut it anymore and sent me a whole new skin, which almost immediately jumped the downloads to three thousand.

"It's hard to hype for a brand when the CEO doesn't even believe in it," Logan says.

"Now she just has to tag someone," Zane says.

"Keep dreaming," Dom says.

Kaden adds, "She's a slow burn, but she'll get there."

I make a face at them all, then spin the bottle and end up daring Dom to snort a Pixy Stix, which turns out to have been a terrible idea, and we waste a good ten minutes just trying to clear his sinuses out even though he barely got any up there. Fortunately Mads is already planning on spending the night and has her neti pot with her.

At almost 11:50 we're back at the game and Zane having

confessed his match to Joey with a cryptic "Yes and no," and then spinning the bottle only to have it land on me. Fearing his dare more than I had Logan's truth, I ask for a question I have to answer.

"Why do you hate me?"

The entire room goes, "Oooooooooh," and looks at me.

"Wha . . . I don't . . . Why do you think that?"

"You literally screamed 'I hate you' across the lunchroom a few weeks ago," says Dom, who I never expected to chime in.

"You once drew a picture of yourself pushing him out a window," Mads says.

"That was seventh grade!" At least I have an excuse for that.

But I do hate him.

No, I did.

I want to.

I should.

"Do you even have a reason?" he asks, not breaking eye contact, which should be reason enough to hate him and his floppy hair and starched shirt, and the little tug at his mouth that's almost a permanent smirk that should be there because it's always there, but it isn't right now, and there's way too many people looking at both of us and I can't think of all the extremely valid reasons. I know they exist. That they used to have something to do with stolen grades and the eighth-grade variety show. And while they seemed utterly valid a mere month ago, I know they're not nearly enough anymore.

Then I think of how he left things with Joey. "You infuriate me," I say weakly.

"That's for sure," Dom says, breaking some of the tension, but only for people who aren't me and Zane.

"I don't hate you," I finally say, meeting his gaze and trying to convey the truth of it.

"Anymore," he says, but it could be a question.

"We're teammates," I say too brightly.

"Teammates," he says flatly.

Dom hits him in the shoulder. "That's all you're getting tonight, dude. Live with it."

"Sky, your turn."

But my phone starts vibrating. "It's almost midnight."

And Logan screams, "Oh no! Places, people!" And he leads us all to one of the side tables that has an old plaid blanket on it. I thought he was protecting some of Mom's tchotchkes, but underneath are actually some bottles of sparkling cider and fluted glasses. There are hats and streamers and noisemakers. "Grab one and fill your glass," he says, struggling to open one of the bottles while Dom works on the other.

"One minute," I warn, looking at my phone.

"Hurry!" Logan says, and Mads is giggling as she chooses hats for everyone, and Dom is putting some Pixy Stix in the glass before Logan pours the cider in, making it bubble everywhere, and Zane is next to me.

"Sorry," he whispers practically in my ear.

I ignore him. "Thirty seconds."

Kaden shoves a plastic flute in my hand, and Mads put a glittery top hat on my head.

The countdown and the sugar and everything is getting my adrenaline up as I say, "Ten!"

And the rest start counting with me very loudly and laughing at nothing.

And then we all scream, "Happy New Year!"

And then Mads and Kaden start kissing. And Logan kisses Dom's cheek, and then everyone's doing it. And we're all laughing. So I kiss Mads on the cheek and Kaden on the ear because they twist away. And all of a sudden it's Zane in front of me. I should just kiss his cheek like the others. Prove I don't hate him.

But I can't.

Because his hair is flopping in that way again. Or it's just flopping normally.

But it doesn't feel normal.

The smile that is only a ghost on his lips also doesn't feel normal.

And I can't stop looking at his lips.

So I stare up at him and he stares down at me. Maybe he's just waiting for that kiss on the cheek. Or maybe he's not waiting for anything.

But his hand comes up and just barely touches my elbow, which makes my stomach flip over in the most devastating way, and every nerve ending from my arm to my toes lights up. And time slows down so nothing else happens for a second or an hour but the two of us looking at each other.

Until he bends closer, like he's going to say something. He's so close I can tell his breath smells sweet. Something deep and urgent inside me wonders if he tastes sweet.

And that's it. It's too much. Instead of waiting for what he's going to say, I turn away from him and immediately kiss Dom on the cheek, and then Logan has us all put our arms around one another and we're singing "Auld Lang Syne" even though that's something I'm pretty sure you're supposed to sing *before* the year flips over and it's immediately clear none of us knows the words.

And through all of it Zane is staring at me. Which I guess I should have expected. He probably still thinks I hate him. That's probably why he looks just a little sad. And I wish I did hate him, because that's what I'm supposed to be feeling right now. Because he's Joey's. Or he will be Joey's. I need to stay focused on Study Buddy, and ScholEx, and all the things I have yet to accomplish.

At the very least I should be having fun with my friends right now. But no matter how hard I try, I cannot focus on whatever it is Logan is saying we should all do that will be totally awesome.

New Year's Goals

TODAY

Figure out the bug in Study Buddy.

Make sure team is using the app.

Refocus!!!

THIS WEEK

Get the booth figured out.

THIS MONTH

Win @ Regionals!!!

NEXT MONTH

State tournament—win it!!!!!!

Begin getting teachers at school on Study Buddy.

(invite + attend!)

IN 6 MONTHS

Win Nationals!   Young Programmers' Camp @HubBub HQ

Write-up of SB in national paper!

IN 9 MONTHS

Apply to Stanford early decision!

Figure out next app after Study Buddy breaks out

Tech mag piece about ME!!

NO MORE MRIs

IN 1 YEAR

Accepted @ Stanford

Monetized enough apps to cover housing if not tuition!

YEAR AFTER NEXT

On track to drop out?

Internship @ HubBub (? if desperate)

IN 5 YEARS

CEO of own company

Self-funded (may sell, but only if new company has better name)

CHAPTER FOURTEEN

"WE NEED TO make a newspaper," Joey says as she approaches the table I'm occupying in the school's library the following Thursday. In the days since New Year's, I've recentered and reprioritized. Less Requite and more Study Buddy. Mrs. James had a meeting or something after class, so we couldn't use her room, which is why I told everyone to meet in the library. She made it a point to remind me good booths need the whole team's excitement to drive us to victory.

"What do you mean *a newspaper*?" I ask, and for some reason I can't look directly at her as she puts her flute case on the chair next to mine.

"Shh, Joey, no giving away our ideas until the big unveiling." Mads appears from around one of the bookshelves with Kaden close behind. Both are hauling bags I know are Mads's. "Put that one there." She nods toward the far end of the table.

"We ran into Mrs. James in the hall," Zane says as he and Dom come into the room. I'm too busy watching what Mads is pulling out of the bags to look at them, and after a second Zane takes the chair Joey is removing her flute from for him and Dom is sitting across from him.

When I focus on my tablet rather than him, Zane says, "She says to tell you she wants us to have a rough display next week when we meet. And can we make this fast? This weekend is State for debaters and we need to run cards." And now the mystery of Joey's presence makes sense.

Joey says, "I've got my laptop in my bag so we can go straight there."

Everyone wants me to ask them what they're talking about, but I'm not going to. Not today.

"Never fear, Logan's here!" Logan says, and he gets a faux chiding from the librarian, who we know loves him best of all of us. "Sorry, Ms. Kelly." He hands her one of the chocolates he's holding. "You know you're my favorite."

She warns us all not to eat in here as she puts the chocolate on her desk and Logan puts the rest on the table. "Sustenance. For my intrepid debaters." He looks over his shoulder at Ms. Kelly and says, "For later, when you're far from the precious books."

Dom grabs a whole handful and shoves them in his backpack. "These are my favorites."

Logan winks. "I know," he says, and takes the empty seat next to Dom.

"If you're done?" Mads says, clearly rhetorically. "Joey and I have the perfect booth."

Wait. Joey? She asked *Joey* to help her with the booth?

She spent all that time convincing me to let her do it so she could work with Joey?

Hurt swirls in me and I want to argue, but I promised to give her this chance, and the least I can do is let her finish. Plus, if they fail, I have a backup proposal ready. But as Mads puts down a large piece of paper that has the model of a booth measured out precisely as what looks like a very formal living room, I realize the few hours I put into mine aren't nearly a match for what she's got here.

"What is this?" I ask.

Mads says, "It's a tableau." She unrolls wallpaper with a very busy print. "We'll cover some board in this replica William Morris wallpaper and make a window with, like, a view of a factory or whatever."

Dom says, "For us science nerds, what's a tableau?"

Mads says, "You know, like a slice of life. So we show what it was actually like back then?"

Kaden says, "If you were a factory shill who sold your soul to the machine for the faux respectability of the middle class." They make a face at Mads, who is scowling at them, and add, "Because it's got a clear aesthetic and has good wallpaper."

Entirely ignoring Kaden's socialism, Joey adds, "And we can fake a phonograph by putting a speaker inside it." She points toward a tuba-looking thing in Mads's picture. "That's both music and science." She looks at Zane for approval, and he gives it to her in one of his smiles.

"And I can get some old books," he offers.

Joey adds, "And some serials."

Mads says, "And Sky and I can make a newspaper. No, two! A Hearst and a Pulitzer." She looks far away and then says, "Kaden, do you want to put together some sort of article about robber barons or something?"

"I have the paper for a tabloid," Kaden says.

Logan says, "And as we sit at the booth we're like living history interpreters in a museum?"

"Docents!" Mads says, at the same time Joey says, "Exactly!"

"Do we all have to dress like Zane?" Dom asks, making a face at his best friend.

"What will we do about the table?" I ask, trying to sound like I'm excited and not entirely steamrolled by my best friend and the girl we desperately need on the team to win State. There's no way I can bring up my railroad station idea after Mads and Joey have invested this much effort. Mads is clearly excited, and the last thing I need is a real full-blown fight.

Mads is still explaining each of the details in her sketch at about a mile a minute. "We're going to put a table skirt on it, but I was going to ask my dad to make me little wedges to put over the legs so they look like Stickley."

"That's brilliant," Logan says.

"Like you know what Stickley is," I say. Because he's the only one here it's safe to pick a fight with and suddenly I need at least that.

"Gustav Stickley was a furniture designer who established United Crafts in 1901." Logan recites from the information in the Mrs. James packet, then sticks his tongue out at me. "I have been studying, thank you very much."

"Well, how are you going to contribute?" I ask.

"I could make the Stickley sticks." He sticks his tongue out once more for good measure and then says to Mads, "I'm pretty good around Dad's shop now." He shrugs. "I made a shelf."

"That'd be great!" Mads says, and gives him a high five—and now I really want to fight with him.

"You don't actually need me for the newspaper, do you?" I ask.

"I mean, no, but you could help Zane find serials," she says, and Dom oohs and elbows Zane.

"Right," I say, really hoping it doesn't sound snotty, but the look she gives me tells me I'm not doing a good enough job.

Joey says, "Great, so I'm working on the phonograph. Zane and Sky will do the reading materials. Oh." She giggles, actually giggles. "And Kaden, too, I guess. And then Mads and Logan can do the set dressing."

This is supposed to be me delegating, not them taking control.

"Me too," Dom says. "I can help fake the wrought iron and stuff." He grins at Logan. "That is, if I can come over later and get in on some of that woodworking action."

Logan says, "Right on, but next week?"

Dom says, "Oh yeah, after State, of course."

Mads says, "So we're all in agreement? We're doing the tableau?"

There's generally positive noises around the table, and she looks at me. "Sky?"

I hadn't really thought about it before, but with only three Pathfinders, I need Mads every bit as much as I need Logan and Joey. And while the booth theme is important, she's even more important. And I hate that I have to worry about losing Mads of all people. She's supposed to be the one person I know for sure will be there. Ride or die. But now I'm not sure, and I say, "Yeah, fine."

"You sure?" she asks.

"The team's excitement about the booth is the best path to victory," I say, and try to smile. This is better than her quitting in a huff and taking Kaden. I know things are weird, and I don't think I'd actually lose my best friend over this, but she's clearly invested a lot more time and effort into it than I expected, and I can't just tell her no, even if I kind of want to.

"Excellent," she says. "Everyone should bring their things next week so we can do a run-through before Saturday."

Joey says, "We just have to get through this weekend and then everything changes, right?"

"Looks like it," Zane says.

"So, I guess, you guys can go do your practice stuff," I say, trying to maintain even some control over the meeting.

Mads starts gathering everything back up. "And I can just leave."

"I'll meet you there," Kaden says to the debaters, helping

Mads pack up, and the two of them coordinate things for the project and this weekend—and very clearly leave me out.

Logan says, "All right, cool, let's do this."

Zane says, "At least it's not just me."

"What's that?" Joey asks brightly.

"Nothing. Should we go to the coffee shop?" Zane asks Joey, and she says yes enthusiastically.

Logan asks them, "You want a ride?" And they both agree, because the coffee shop is close but not that close. He looks at me. "Can you get home? We're going to be late."

"I'll take her," Dom offers.

"Don't you have to study?" I ask.

He shrugs. "Impromptu doesn't study. Impromptu lives in the moment."

"Will you clean up the passenger side? The nerdling is precious and cannot sit on your to-go containers," Logan says.

"I'll shove them all on the floor just for her," Dom replies with a laugh. This seems to be a well-worn path of teasing, and I wonder when Logan's ever even seen Dom's car.

"See that you do," he replies with mock solemnity. Then to Zane and Joey he says, "Let's go crush these losers." Joey falls immediately into step behind him. Zane lingers a second longer, so I ask Dom about what he's going to do with the wrought iron, and Zane sighs and leaves.

When it's just Dom and me, he says, "I thought you were going to lock that up."

"What?" I ask.

He nods at me. "He's not going to wait forever."

"What are you even talking about?" I ask, genuinely confused.

"If you don't stop playing with him, he's really going to give her a chance."

"I don't know what you're talking about."

"You're kidding me," Dom says. "Logan said he needed to help you two get out of your own way, but I told him you were already on it. At least I thought you were until this nonsense with Joey started."

"What do you mean? They like each other."

"I mean, there's liking someone and then there's *liking* someone," Dom says.

"No," I say. "Wait . . . so that party was some kind of setup? To what? Break them up? Don't you like her?"

"No, it's not like that," Dom says.

"They matched on Requite. They'll figure everything out after this weekend. Once State is over," I say, but I'm not sure if I'm trying to convince him or me.

"Look," Dom says, "you should talk to Zane."

"Talk to him about what?" I ask. "I thought we settled this on New Year's." I start shoving all my books and stuff back into my bag. Books that would have explained everything about how a rail station could reflect various levels of society and technology. Useless now that I'm letting Mads and Joey have the booth theme.

Dom says, "It's pretty clear there's something going on here."

I push my tablet in the bag so hard I'm worried I broke it. And then what would I do? "No, Dom, there's nothing going on here but studying for ScholEx."

I don't like Zane. He doesn't like me. And my brother needs to stop focusing on all the wrong things. Requite doesn't need more users, and I don't need to make up with Zane. I throw my bag over my shoulder and start for the door.

"Wait, Sky, I'm giving you a ride," Dom says.

"Don't worry, I'll figure out my own way home," I say, practically running from the library.

Mads 🕷 ♛

> Did you know?

> I need to know if you were in on it.

> I need to know if you helped Logan with that whole Zane thing.

What Zane thing?

> That truth or dare garbage. Did you know about it?

It was a game. What was there to know???

> I think it was some kind of setup.

> Knowing Logan, the whole thing was probably to embarrass me.

Wait . . . . . . I'm confused . . . . .

> He and Joey matched on Requite.

How do you know that?!!!?

> She told me.

What does that have ANYTHING! to do with you??????!!!?@

> Why do you think I made the app????

Practice with the social APIs?

. . . .

That's a good reason.

I should use that.

But you made it for Joey to hook up with Zane??????

Not hook up with.

Just figure out if he likes her.

And he does???

They matched.

And Logan thinks . . . what, that Zane likes you instead?

No, I think Dom does.

Or he doesn't like Joey.

I can't really tell.

He does . . . .

I'm just so tired of everyone telling me what to do. First you take over the booth and then Logan tries to trick me into . . . whatever with Zane, and I'm just done with it!!!!

I swear on my undying soul, I had nothing to do with whatever ridiculous plan Logan and Dom may have had.

Seriously?

Sincerely.

Now . . .

I KNEW you were mad about the booth stuff!???????##@?

I'm not mad.

Why did you lie????

I'm really not mad.

You've decided to put your whole life and future and dreams and whatever into ScholEx and now you're mad that I'm trying to help????!@@!??

You're helping by being there.

You're ridiculous!!!

You don't have to do everything by yourself, you know?

I mean, I guess.

How is this ANY! different from doing skins and logos for your apps?

It's half the points.

It's putting an aesthetic on YOUR! vision, Sky!!!@!#!@

......

Plus, you have MORE! than enough to do right now.

I can see the tickets coming in from Requite, REMEMBER!!?!

I definitely don't want to think about that.

Right now I just want to be mad at Logan.

You know I'm always here for that!!!!!!!!!@!!!!

He apologized for the whole Minecraft debacle three years ago.

And he can keep apologizing until we're dead and buried in the ground, but still I must destroy him.

Don't destroy him.

Can I draw pictures of him in awful scenarios?????????

OK, you can do that.

Can I profit off it?

Oh definitely.

Excellent!!!

Feeling better?

No.

As I see it there are two choices:

Fight with me or fight with everyone else.

You can't do both at once.

Well . . . . . I'm DEFINITELY fighting with everyone else.

This is serious.

I just have to hold on until we win and then everything will be fine.

This is the first of three competitions you have us slated to win in order for you to be happy.

If we win Regionals, I'll be OK with you completely taking over my booth.

Fair.

I take it you're not coming out for spaghetti with the debate team tomorrow.

You would have to drag me kicking and screaming.

CHAPTER FIFTEEN

I AM TRAPPED in this car. Tricked. Held against my will.

My parents told me we were going out for supper. Dress up, they said.

I had assumed we were going over to one of their friends' houses. Yet this car is pulling into the parking lot of the university's alumni building. The very building that hosts the State debate tournament. A tournament happening right now.

This is cruel and unusual punishment. I tried a headache and Mom just handed me my medicine, but she knows if I take it when I don't actually have a headache, it'll give me an even worse headache than the one I'm claiming to have. I only half considered just taking it. Except then she'd say I was fine and drag me along anyway. And then I'd have a headache and I wouldn't be able to think or deal with what was about to happen.

"I have to go to the bathroom," I say the second the car stops.

"You went before we left," Mom says. "Finals starts in ten minutes. We have to go get our seats."

"How do you know he even made the finals?" I ask,

trudging through the lobby beside her, my dad on the other side waving and nodding at people I'm pretty sure he doesn't even know.

"He sent me a message using this little thing called the internet," Mom says. "Perhaps you've heard of it?"

"Hey, sunshine, look, it's Maddy," Dad says louder than he knows what's good for him. No one has called Mads "Maddy" in almost four years. Not since the eighth-grade sleepover when we discovered Hannibal Lecter and she discovered her dark soul. She took to the weird serial killer like I took to the first JavaScript I stole off Stack Exchange to get my little kitty puzzle working. Formative experiences do that to you.

"It's Mads, Dad," I say, and extract myself from the arm link my mother has kept me in. She's fine letting me go knowing that so long as Mads is here, there isn't any likelihood I'll make a run for it.

"Kaden! How did you do?" I ask, running up to them both.

"Lost by decision, but it was really close and there's always next year," Kaden says, happier than I expected for having lost in an early round.

"You all better get seats," Mom says, walking past.

"We're sitting with the team, Mrs. C," Kaden says.

Mom smiles at them. She always liked Kaden the best. "I'm sure you did great today."

"There's always next year," my dad says.

Mom and Dad go find seats, while I turn back to my friends.

"With the team?" I ask, but to Mads, not Kaden.

"Logan made it through to finals, and so did Zane and Joey," Mads says flatly.

"I . . ." I really don't know why I haven't started kicking and screaming yet. I should be at home fixing a bug or something.

"Later—they're starting," Kaden says, and grabs Mads, who grabs me, and we all run toward the front of the large auditorium.

I hate it, but it's amazing. The Lincoln-Douglas debate finals make me think about the morality of recycling plastic way more than I expected to. It's sad Kaden didn't make it into the final, but these two debaters are super talented. It may not be as popular as policy debate, but it should be. First of all, I can understand what they're saying. And second, they're actually trying to convince me of their side instead of yelling facts at each other. It's perfectly Kaden, but no one else in our school gets it, so they don't have a chance to practice at nearly the same level all the policy folks do.

Then it's Logan's turn. He does an impressive job with his extemp, a seven-minute speech about Brexit, of all things. I didn't even know he knew where the UK was, but he pulls it off. We just won't know how he did until everything's over.

We got here at four, and it's almost seven and there's only one event left: policy debate.

I'd like to say I didn't care, but Zane is standing on the stage with his hands in his pockets looking like he's waiting to chair some executive board meeting or star in a play, and my throat feels tight. Even though all he's going to do is argue the merits of criminal justice reform against a kid in Dockers and, oh no.

"That's not . . ." I whisper in Mads's ear.

She makes a sound loud enough to be heard throughout the room and not only do Zane and Joey look straight at us, so does Nate. Easy to do, since we're basically in the front row. Joey is waving frantically, and Zane glares at Nate and then looks back at me. Nate has quickly looked over to his partner, the girl I recognize all too well from his HubBub feed and the Southdale cafeteria, so I guess she must be looking at me, too.

I start to reconsider programming and Stanford and the whole social media track and wonder why I've been so quick to dismiss MIT. They make great things at MIT. They might even know how to make an invisibility field. I need that way more than an app that fills my ticket pile with teenagers who don't know how to flirt. Like I even know how to flirt. Clearly not. Or my life wouldn't be like this. I wouldn't be here. Those people wouldn't care if I were, that's for sure.

"Breathe," Mads says in my ear, and I shake my head. "Breathe or else."

I suck in some air but only to make her happy. No one's looking at me anymore. Okay, his pretty debate partner might be, but I refuse to look at her.

All I see is the boy with floppy hair who's one jacket short of a three-piece suit, and I decide that I'll consider not hating him anymore if he makes Nate and his partner cry in front of me. Somewhere in the back of my brain I remember how close he was on New Year's Eve and wonder just for a second if his breath still smells sweet.

Breathe. That's all I have to do.

"Why are they talking?" I ask under my breath.

"They're flashing," Kaden whispers back.

"Oooh." Mads sits up in her chair.

"Down, girl, they're just emailing their files so the other team can follow along." Kaden puts their hand on Mads's arm and leaves it there.

"Follow along?" Mads asks. She's never been to a policy debate before.

The judge taps the mic on the table, and every eye in the room is on them. They go over the rules for the audience and read the resolution, which is what the teams will be debating about. Joey and Zane are arguing in favor of prison reform, and Nate and his partner are arguing against it.

Mads whispers, "Figures," and I cover my smile with my hand even though no one can see me anymore now that the house lights have gone down.

What follows is an hour of sustained breath control. Joey starts it all off, reading their arguments like she's playing the flute. High and light and so fast I wish I had the arguments in front of me, and yet I'm glad I don't. I can follow her words better than I can most policy debaters, which is a testament to her talent.

She lays out a very viable case about the economy, the Thirteenth Amendment, and how the whole thing undermines the electoral college, which seems sideways except when I stop and think about it, it starts to makes sense. There are a couple more arguments in there I don't entirely follow, but when Nate starts asking questions, it's clear he followed just fine.

Then Nate is reading his arguments. He's a lot more of a mumbler, although I might be biased. His voice is a low rumble, but instead of watching him I keep looking at my friends. Zane is swiping back and forth between taking notes and circling things on his tablet, and I wonder if he's using the same app I use for my planners because the update does a good split screen and he could do both at the same time.

No, I'm not telling him about it. He doesn't need my help. Neither of them do. Joey is asking Nate clarifying questions about their argument, and I only half care. Nate keeps implying that there's no reason to change what's working, which I know that Zane is going to demolish. I'm sure Nate's a fine debater, but Zane has that tiny little tug at the corner of his lips like he knows how he's going to win. I should know—he's used it with me plenty of times.

And I'm right—speed-reading and obscure clarifications go back and forth, arguing about whether something is on topic or not, whether their arguments matter to society, and whether the status quo is something worth saving.

Then the round is over and the judge is making notes and the competitors are supposed to shake hands. The girl from HubBub who, turns out, is named Maia, is trying to shake Zane's hand, and he's just looking at Nate, who looks pissed.

They trade quiet words and act all sportsmanlike while the audience applauds, but I want to throw something at the stage.

"That was so cool," Mads screams into my ear over the applause.

Zane and Joey are coming offstage and we're all still clapping, but I stop when I realize that the only spots in the team row are between me and the aisle.

As the crowd quiets and the judge says to hold on a few minutes while the awards ceremony starts, I find myself next to Zane in a room full of people who want to tell him how perfect he is.

Despite all the calls for attention, he leans over to my ear and says, "We need to talk."

I look at him and then at Joey laughing on the other side of him and shake my head. She's so happy.

He leans back in. "Sky, please."

Joey's tugging at his arm since their coach is trying to get his attention, and I gesture. "You're being summoned." Because they won for policy debate, of course. Logan came in second for extemp. Kaden was fifth overall for Lincoln-Douglas debate, which is a fine place to be junior year. At least Kaden's now actually invested in us getting to Nationals for ScholEx. Socialism is one thing, but Sarah Lawrence is an entirely different creature, and they'll need some first-place wins for an early decision application.

"What did Zane want?" Mads asks into my ear as the audience applauds all the winners.

"Nothing," I whisper back. Or it will be nothing soon. As soon as he and Joey figure out their relationship.

Now that State's over.

CHAPTER SIXTEEN

"I NEED TO borrow your tablet again," Logan says, not even bothering to knock this time. It's barely a full day after debate's State tournament and he's already pestering me. He's such a pain in off-season.

"Why?" I ask, looking up from my tablet. I'm working on some of the music cards Joey had put together. "So you can post more bad poems with the admin account?"

"They're not bad!" He looks genuinely offended. "The *Romeo and Juliet* one has almost three hundred ups."

"Because you made it look like I endorsed it."

"Because you're not doing any kind of marketing at all."

"Because it's an awful app and doesn't deserve attention." I wave my tablet at him. "Study Buddy is the important one. And I'm using my tablet right now."

"Just five minutes."

"Where's your school tablet?"

"If I knew, would I need yours?"

I sigh, holding my tablet out to him. "Five minutes." He never keeps his nearby. I'm the only one who really uses mine. It's a total waste of school resources. They'd be better off buying me the new version and handing him a notebook.

"I'll be done in three."

He starts flipping around, presumably to the school's blackboard app to get some homework assignment or something. "You have a lot of tickets in here for Requite."

"Stay out of my admin!" I grab at the tablet, but he turns away, putting his whole back between us.

"Almost . . ." He trails off, clicking around.

"If I see another one of your campy poems, I'm deleting it," I say, trying to reach past him but not actually bothering to get off my bed.

"Trust me, I'm way beyond poems at this point." He holds the tablet back at me. "See, not even close to three minutes."

"What did you do?" I start flipping through my apps, trying to figure out what he actually could have done. He didn't have time to cancel my account. He really didn't have time to delete anything.

The official Requite Hub is clear of all bubbles and messages.

If he did anything, he deleted all evidence of it.

"If you can figure out what I did, nerdling, I'll admit it." He smiles at me, taunting. "But I doubt you even know it was possible."

"If you ruined anything, I'll kill you."

"If you were actually as good at computers as you think you are, I wouldn't be able to ruin anything." He rests against the edge of my dresser. Probably not sure where to put himself while I'm on the bed, where he usually perches. "So, you and this Nate guy . . ."

I look up from my tablet, still not able to see what he did. "I do not want to talk about that right now."

"Did he break your heart, because I can kill him if he broke your heart."

"Logan."

"His knees, then. I can break his knees?"

"It's not his fault."

He just stares at me, arms crossed in front of him.

"Okay, it's entirely his fault and he's a jerk. But my feelings are my problem, not his."

"That's enough to go egg his house. I'm sure I can get help."

"It's below freezing out, you're not egging his house."

"I just want you to know I'm here for you." His jaw is set, and he actually does look like he's capable of egging Nate's house. Fortunately there's no way he even knows where he lives. I don't even know where he lives.

"I know you're here for me, Logan," I say, and mean it. It's nice knowing my big brother would defend my honor, even if it's also in service to a debate rivalry.

"And that dude is not worth ruining good stuff for."

"Yeah, I figured that out."

"I can still break his knees."

"I'll let you know, okay?"

"I guess that's all I can ask." He pushes himself away from the wall. "Zane and Joey were pretty awesome yesterday, though, right?"

"Yeah," I say with a sigh. I look back down at my tablet and all the tickets I have no idea what to do with. More and more of the chunk is Requite. "They were great." Hopefully they're happy. Hopefully soon it will be Study Buddy making Requite look like a blip. A bad dream. A memory of something that shouldn't have been.

"Another big weekend this week, too." He's hovering over the edge of my bed. "You're going to be nicer to Zane, right?"

"I mean . . ." I look up at him, and he's got a strange look on his face, not quite smiling but not quite angry. "I need him." I don't finish the sentence with what I'm thinking. I need Joey. We can live without Zane—there are more than enough Achievers.

"Well, that's a start." He bounces my bed with both hands. It doesn't send the whole thing wild like it used to when I was younger. I keep it down pretty good at this point. Plus, he's not nearly as strong as he thinks he is.

"Tell me what you did."

"Figure it out, nerdling."

"If you ruin things, it's your knees you'll have to watch out for."

He's already outside and halfway down the hall. "I only make things awesome, Sky."

NotThatZane

Tell me the last thing you watched on TV, song you listened to, and book you read.

What?

Don't think, just answer.

A documentary on the Triangle Shirtwaist Factory fire

Truth Hurts

Anne of Green Gables

ScholEx has taken over your brain.

What?

The factory fire is pretty intense.

It's a pivotal moment in labor history.

And the history of social services.

It's a tragedy.

It was.

They died to save a few bucks.

Make a few bucks.

Stuff like that makes K's rants about capitalism make more sense.

Capitalism BAD on Life GOOD?

Something like that.

But Kaden never quite has an answer on how to convert us away from a scarcity economy.

It's like they're not even trying.

Hah. Right?

So the Lizzo makes sense . . .

But Anne? Is that one of the alternate readings?

Oh yeah, I guess it is.

Huh.

That's not why you read it?

No.

You like books about redheads?

What?

OHHHH!

Oh no.

Why did you read it then?

Why does Lizzo make sense?

The flute thing?

That's what I thought.

Did I say something wrong?

No . . .

I did.

But this was going so much better!

I know.

I'm sorry. Can we try this again?

But it's the day after State.

Yeah I know, but . . . later.

Are you busy?

Something like that.

Got it.

I'll try this again later.

Tomorrow?

Yeah.

Good idea.

Try then.

All right.

I'm sorry.

For what?

I just figured I owed that to you.

And I wanted to say it.

While I could.

You OK?

Later.

You got it, JoJo.

CASE: 191218-1723-REQUITE-1-232534382-JOEYJOJOIII

Status: [In Progress]
Chat Name: JoeyJoJoIII-NotThatZane-12X329W231
Notes:

Current Admin Access:
@JoeyJoJoIII [Full Access]
@NotThatZane [No Access]

Would you like to close this ticket?

Confirm the following fields are updated to close:

Chat Status: Resolved
Admin access: No Access
Case Reason: User Error
Next Steps by Admin: None
Why are you closing this case: There's literally nothing I can do to
make this better.

*Once you confirm these values, you'll no longer have
access to this chat.*

*To regain access, one or more users needs to submit a new
ticket.*

Are you sure you're ready to close this case?

CHAPTER SEVENTEEN

IT'S BEEN FIVE days since the tournament. Four days since Logan told me to be nice to Zane. Three and a half since I was nice to him when I mistakenly answered Joey's chat as if it were mine. I don't know why I thought he was actually talking to me. Or why I even answered this time. I'm sure it's fine. I covered well enough. I'm sure he and Joey are happily chatting along now. They don't need me.

Clearly whatever he wanted to say to the real me at the tournament wasn't that important. I haven't heard from him since.

Zane probably only needed to talk to *me* about gathering reading materials for the booth.

Something else that doesn't need me. I should be at home fixing the one thing that does seem to need me—my code. But here I am, trying to lead my team to victory this weekend or whatever. But maybe they don't even need me to do that. Maybe I could sit home and work on Study Buddy. Zane, Dom, and Kaden can handle the Achiever round. Mads clearly has the booth handled.

But I'm not at home, I'm here. Because it's Thursday

practice. And tomorrow is setup. And Saturday we have to win. Because my future's still at stake.

"Skylar, you made it," Mrs. James says. "I was worried you were looking a little green in class."

"I'm fine," I say, but less to Mrs. James than the half-built booth in front of us. We're in the drama room instead of her classroom because it has the space for the booth and the spring musical tryouts aren't until next week. Plus, it's right near the auditorium, so it has access to the basics: tables, chairs, rails. There's also a fake hot rod from last year's school production of *Grease*, but we won't need that.

"Grab me the window frame," Mads says, "and some of the Velcro."

I am loaded down with a bag of supplies, including Velcro strips they definitely didn't have in the Second Industrial Revolution, though Stickley would have probably done some amazing things with it. It's not really a window frame, it's a picture frame, but a good-sized one.

I hold my provisions out to her, and she tells me what specifically to get her and what to do with it, which gives me something to do as everyone else arrives. Joey's first, thankfully, and she's happy to fill every ounce of space with talking.

Unlike her online persona, she's also kind of intense. Which is a relief, because the last thing we need is this group to scare her off. She's got her fake phonograph in a little cabinet with something that looks less like a tuba and more like a trumpet. She's explaining how it's closer to Edison's original design when Zane and Dom arrive.

Even after that she doesn't stop talking—if anything she talks more, pulling them into figuring out the pairing for the Bluetooth speaker she brought with her. Zane looks like he's about to tell her to have me do it when she goes off about what a terrible time she had finding one that fit exactly in the little compartment but was also loud enough to be heard.

He's not wrong; I could fix it, but then what?

No, I am helping Mads tack down the fake wallpaper so it lies seamlessly, which is a lot harder than I expected.

"No, no, no, no!" she screams at me for the hundredth time. "Don't let it droop."

"Here, let me help," Zane says. "I'm taller."

"Fine," I say, backing away. "I'll pair the speaker."

"Fine," he says, "see you in like three seconds."

I roll my eyes and go over to Dom and Joey. "Dom, they could probably use you, too," I say.

"I'm not using paste," he says.

"It's not wet. It's got a sticker backing. Mads is overreacting," I say.

"Fine," he huffs, but picks up the pace when Logan appears with an armload of wood. He's so proud of those ridiculous legs. Like they're something far more complex than the two pieces of wood nailed together they actually are.

"Can I . . ." I ask Joey, and she hands me her phone.

"Did you see that?" Joey asks while I pull up her settings. First problem, she didn't even have Bluetooth turned on.

"See what?" I ask, putting her phone in pairing mode.

"Zane came right up to talk to me," she says.

"Push the power button on the speaker," I say.

"What?"

"The power button."

"That just turns it off," she says. "Plus, he wants to talk more tonight. What do you think that means?"

"Nothing," I say, but she looks sad and won't let go of the speaker. "It means you should talk to him tonight."

"Maybe I should ask him to go to the coffee shop again. That was fun," she says.

"You should." I grab the other end of the speaker and twist it around. There's only three buttons on it—power and volume up and down. "Where are the instructions?"

"Oh, I threw those away," she says, finally letting go of the speaker. "Do you think they need help over there?"

I sigh and hand her phone back. "I'm sure they do."

She skips off to help line things up perfectly and be yelled at by Mads.

I turn the speaker over and find the model number. I'm pulling it up in Google when I hear behind me, "It's been more than three seconds."

"Mads will solve that being-tall problem you have if her wallpaper is less than straight." I refuse to look at him, instead trying to find where to change the manufacturer's website to English.

"Not easy, is it?" He pulls the speaker out of my hand.

"She went over there to help you," I say, finally turning around. "Least you could do is be there to be helped."

"I came to see what's taking so long."

"Your girlfriend threw the instructions away," I say off-handedly, staring at my phone.

There's a silence, and I look up at him. The smile's gone again. I did that. It's weird how now that I don't hate him it's so much easier to make him hate me. I can't watch, so I glance down at my phone, finally finding the instructions.

"Sky" is all he manages to say.

"I found it. Give me that." I pull the speaker out of his hands and head to one of the nearby chairs. I need two hands for this and to stop dealing with that conversation.

When I look up as the speaker announces that the pairing has been a success, I see he's still standing there. But not looking at me. He's kind of looking toward the booth and the wallpapering that now involves Mrs. James, Joey, Kaden, Dom, and Logan. Even with Mrs. J here, Mads is still screaming at them all that they're dropping it.

"I'm going to get more stuff out of the car," I say, too quietly for anyone to hear me over Mads, especially Zane, and disappear out the side door through the backstage, like the cowardly captain I am.

Joey ♪

I should message him, right?

You haven't chatted yet?

Things have been busy with the booth stuff?

Do you have your small talk ready?

What if he doesn't message me?

What should I do?

Should I ask him something?

Something about ScholEx?

No. Nothing about ScholEx or debate.

Ask him about him.

What is there to ask about?

Ask him about music.

I've tried that.

He's not really into music.

Then books.

I guess.

I could ask about TV.

He doesn't really watch TV.

Movies?

Maybe anime? It's my absolute favorite.

Huh.

Maybe just let him ask the questions.

You sure?

Yeah, he's good at it. I promise.

What should we do if he isn't?

Just trust me.

You have joined LAScholEx.

Dom, Joey, Kaden, Mads, and Zane are here.

There are 8 unread messages—click here to unroll the history.

Mads says, "These bleeping panels don't fit together."

Joey says, "What happened to them? They were perfect when we left yesterday!!!"

Logan has joined LAScholEx.

Logan says, "I finally found a parking spot outside the gym. They could have found a school with a bigger lot for Regionals. I'll be there in a sec to bleep them in for you."

Mads says, "This is our first chance to be judged on this booth and it needs to be PERFECT!@#!@!"

Skylar says, "I need to meet with Mrs. James to confirm the roster and get us all signed in for tomorrow."

Skylar says, "We have three hours tonight to get the booth set up and then another hour before the Regional Expo opens to judging tomorrow. Are you going to be able to handle this?"

Dom says, "No need to get nasty with the panels."

Mads says, "Sky! I have this!!! LOGAN!!! GET HERE NOW!!!!@!@#!#!"

Dom says, "We're in the snack aisle, what do you need?"

Zane says, "No sugar, this is a brain food day."

Skylar says, "Why aren't you here?"

Joey says, "I am in the wings of an orchestra concert."

Skylar says, "Not you. I know where you are."

Kaden says, "Mads sent them to get supplies"

Kaden says, "Velcro not snacks"

Skylar says, "We should all be in there working on this together, not online."

Kaden says, "Mads also has deputized me as her official online coordinator"

Kaden says, "And as her coordinator she would like you to know that she has this"

Logan says, "And I have the screwdriver!!!"

Kaden says, "We're in the third row toward the back"

Zane says, "We have the Velcro, and the blue tape. We can't get spray paint because fascism, but we have some craft paint."

Zane says, "Ask Mads if that's good enough."

Kaden says, "She says to get a primary blue and an orange closer to ochre than actual orange"

Kaden says, "And sponge paintbrushes"

Zane says, "I'll go back for brushes."

Dom says, "I have nuts!"

Kaden says, "But do you have Phillips head"

Logan says, "And I have the WRONG screwdriver . . . Whomp whomp."

Skylar says, "Turns out there's a whole orientation for the captains. I'm trapped in the auditorium!!!@!"

Dom says, "Don't worry, I'll fix it for you."

Zane says, "They don't have sponge paintbrushes."

Zane says, "They do have SPONGES and I'm in the arts and crafts area."

Kaden says, "One sec Mads is still yelling at Logan about the screwdriver"

Skylar says, "Look, I paired the speaker to her phone during practice yesterday. Put the murder podcast on, that should calm her down."

Kaden says, "There's a ton of people around . . ."

Skylar says, "Just do it, K. You know it's the only thing that works."

Kaden says, "True"

Zane says, "I'm buying the sponges. If they're wrong . . . well, there's a Michael's two doors down and I'll use any excuse not to get yelled at by Mads."

Logan says, "I'm sorry for letting you all down. I'll do better in the future."

Skylar says, "Why does SHE get an apology out of you?"

Logan says, "Stop being a brat."

Skylar scoffs.

Dom says, "I have a multi-head screwdriver!!!"

Dom feels manlier already.

Logan says, "Bet you look manlier, too."

Zane says, "It's true, he's like five inches taller and built like a football player."

Logan says, "We definitely have the best booth so far."

Logan says, "Most of them are posters and pictures."

Dom scoffs. Amateurs.

Dom says, "I'm getting pop."

Kaden says, "Get me a Coke"

Dom says, "Poseur."

Logan says, "Get me an iced tea."

Dom says, "Anything for you."

Zane says, "Sky, you want a water?"

Skylar says, "I'm fighting something, Dew me please."

Dom says, "It's about bleeping time."

Logan says, "Skylar!"

Logan says, "This is a SCHOOL channel."

Kaden says, "You OK"

Skylar rolls her eyes.

Skylar says, "You're all children."

Skylar says, "Zane knows what I meant."

Dom says, "He'll be cried out by the time we get there. No worries."

Zane says, "I'll get you both."

Zane says, "Like a grown-up who has no idea what these children are talking about."

Dom says, "Who knows what ochre looks like?"

Logan says, "Google it."

Logan says, "Dear lord."

Kaden says, "Please don't come back with the wrong color"

Logan says, "Don't come back at all."

Logan says, "She tried to chew my arm off when she saw the screwdriver."

Logan says, "I'm pretty sure she's going to kill us all in our sleep."

Dom says, "This may be her villain origin story."

Skylar says, "Is the podcast still running?"

Logan says, "It's not working."

Kaden says, "It's a live show . . ."

Logan says, "They keep talking about pockets!"

Skylar says, "You're doomed."

Skylar says, "Should have let me stay in charge."

Zane says, "Uhhhhhhhhhh, we're going to Michael's."

Dom says, "In Canada."

Logan says, "Take me with you."

Dom says, "It's too late for you."

Dom says, "I'll remember you fondly."

Zane says, "No one fear. I have googled ochre."

Dom says, "He's also carrying a bag of chocolate-covered pretzels."

Dom says, "He's breaking the sugar rule."

Skylar says, "There's always an exception for chocolate-covered pretzels."

Dom says, "IS THAT SO?"

Kaden says, "Please get an 11 x 14 canvas and a pack of oil paints"

Kaden says, "Cheap is fine for this she says"

Zane says, "Will do."

Skylar says, "Mrs. James says she's going to take us all out for pizza after the ceremony tomorrow. Win or lose."

Dom says, "SCORE!"

Zane says, "I'll bring my pencils."

Skylar says, "SO WILL I!!!"

Logan says, "I'll bring money to buy pizza that actually tastes good."

Dom says, "I will be sitting with Logan."

Kaden says, "If we don't focus, I am afraid for us all . . ."

Skylar says, "OK, time to focus."

Zane says, "We'll be there in 15."

Mads says, "I can hear you!!@#!$@!!@!!@!@@!!!!!"

Skylar says, "I'm almost done!"

Mads says, "Come help!!!! NOW!!!!@! Or else!"

Mads says, "I know where you all sleep!!@!#@!!"

Zane says, "Yes, ma'am."

Dom says, "Hail dark queen, mistress of the universe and all its evils."

Logan says, "It's too late for us, save yourselves."

Joey says, "You guys are funny."

You have left LAScholEx.

CHAPTER EIGHTEEN

"YOU'LL BE OKAY?" Mads asks, all her nerves from last night gone. Given to me. The booth came together, and it was still standing when we got into the Expo this morning to put on the final touches. We're all on edge, but it actually looks good and has stayed pretty stable through the rush of people.

The early shifts have been fine, and everyone has done at least one interpretation of the booth for a judge, guaranteeing them points in the final. Our Achievers even scored pretty well in the Quizposition earlier, so Regionals nerves are finally wearing off.

"Pathfinders' Quizposition is in twenty minutes," I say. "Go sign in. If you miss your window, I'll never speak to you again." Even I have to admit that the booth is actually a really stand-out concept. Mine would have been great, but it was too close to the other booths around ours. Mads and Joey's booth is more of an experience than an explanation, and like mine it covers a lot more than just one or two elements, but theirs is immersive. The judges so far have been really impressed, but it means nothing if she doesn't sign in.

"Lies!" she hisses, but steps away from the booth. "If you

burn down my booth while I'm gone, I really am murdering you in your sleep." She winks at me, while some teachers huddled nearby eye her. They've been discussing the blurry tree drawing Mads made last night with Zane's ochre paint, canvas, and sponges while lying on the floor and not hurting us all. Evidently it's an excellent example of tonalism. But I'm hoping they don't want me to interpret it for them. I'll lose points. I can handle the literature stuff, but Mads went deep on this last-minute picture. I want to take it down, but this place is full of people. We need to have top scores across the board if we want even a chance of making it to State.

This morning was spent explaining what a tableau is and why we think we're representing our topic. Kaden worked up an excellent default speech for all of us on the rise of the bourgeoisie and the leisure class's manipulation of labor for more creature comforts.

Mads, when not scandalizing people, explains how art became home and how, rather than taste being a thing for rich people, everyone could have a little color in their lives with well-made pieces.

I overheard Zane talking about affordable paper and the rise of print journalism and personal libraries. I only caught the end, but it was really good. I was coming to the booth as he was leaving. Somehow our shifts have never overlapped.

I steal pieces off everyone, but mostly let others do the speaking. Dom almost seems to make things up as they come along. Most of it's right, but no matter what he says it sounds right. I have to admit, Logan's the best at it.

Whatever someone's interested in he makes them even more interested. But right now my teammates are all gone and it's just me in the booth, trying not to lose us any points.

"A tableau, you say," Nate says, appearing by the aisle. There's no pretty debate partner in sight. There's no one I know. No one he knows. Because that's the only time he speaks to me. When there's no one to confirm or deny my existence. Something that didn't happen at the local event.

He picks up the broadsheet and starts skimming the page. "You went all out."

I close my eyes, and when I open them, he's still there.

He's not going away.

My throat is tight, so I croak out, "We're going to win."

"That's cute you think so." He looks at me and stares in the way that once convinced my brain I was the only person in the world he could see. But now I know it's a lie.

He steps closer, grabbing one of Zane's serials. "You haven't seen our booth."

I have. It's not bad. But it looks like a science fair exhibit. It's a narrow dive on the transatlantic shipping industry. Their table is a large model of the pre-*Titanic* Cunard steamships.

"These are good," he says, putting down the serial Zane actually made without my help.

"Do you need something?" I ask, trying to find anyone at all to come to the booth so I can explain how the legs we Velcroed to the table represent Stickley's desire for the art world to return to products created by hand in an ever more machine-produced world and the bourgeoisie's eagerness to pay top dollar for it while managing the very factories the artists were railing against.

"Maia thinks you made the app to get me back."

Debate partner thinks too much.

"But that's not true," he says.

"Wouldn't I have needed to have you in order to get you back?" I finally look at him, and he brightens considerably. Attention. That's all he wants. I wish he'd go somewhere else to get it.

"You're not going to ask how I know?"

"No."

"We didn't match," he says with a grin.

I hate him. Like for real. Not like I thought I hated Zane. I can't believe I wasted so much time on Nate. I hate his polo shirts and his khakis. I hate the warm smiles and sweet words he had when no one else was around. I hate the way he'd make me feel like I needed to earn him. I never liked him. He was playing with me.

I can't believe I thought this jerk was going to give me that same sense of togetherness that Kaden and Mads found without me.

"You're right, Nate." I say his name like it's sharp and I could cut myself on it. "We're not a match. Also, you have a girlfriend. A fact you seem to forget quite a lot."

"Who? Maia?"

I just look at him.

"We're not together."

"Does she know that?"

He shrugs.

"Well, go deal with that and leave me out of it. As you said, I'm not interested."

"Come on, Sky."

"Can we help you?" Joey asks, overly bright. Zane is beside her, channeling some of Mads's violence. "Oh, it's you!"

He turns and sees the two of them, and clearly they don't have the kind of attention he likes because he seems even smaller. Maybe it's because, like me, he's several inches shorter than Zane, or at least Zane's hair. But probably it's because Zane and Joey smashed him at State.

"He was just leaving," I say to her. "Just like you should be."

"But we just got back from lunch," Joey says, oblivious.

"Mads is already in line for Pathfinder, and you should be signing in," I say to her, while Nate keeps eyeing Zane awkwardly.

"No, really," Zane says. "Is there something *we* can help you with?" He puts the emphasis on *we*, and Nate pales.

"No, I was just . . ." Nate looks at me like I'm going to protect him. He sidesteps so he's not between them and the table anymore. He's closer to me, but Zane moves forward to fill the gap, making Nate step back farther. Joey's just standing there smiling, and I'm trying to keep my stomach in check.

"Goodbye, Nate," I say firmly.

"Yeah, uh, bye," he says, and scuttles away, past the curtain dividing our booth from the next.

"Why was he here?" Zane asks me.

212

"Checking out the competition?" I reply, knowing full well it isn't the answer.

"You should be a better winner," Joey says, nudging Zane in the rib cage. Her smile is like the sun. And I can't help it—I look for his reaction as something tightens in my chest.

That he's still mad at Nate shouldn't make me happy. But it does. Even though Joey and Zane being together means success. I know he's not doing it because of me or my anger with Nate, but for a second I pretend he is.

Even though I shouldn't do that, either. I need to be rooting for them to look at each other adoringly.

"Where's Dom?" Zane asks me, ignoring Joey's teasing.

I shrug. "Not here."

"Obviously." He breaks eye contact to scan the thin crowd. "He was supposed to be here."

"He's helping Logan," Joey says. "You know, with that important project he's working on."

"Not that important," he says.

Joey pulls a sheet out of her pocket. "I'm going to go check in."

I nod. "You should. The lady is super slow."

"Would you come with me, Sky? Your shift is over." She looks up at Zane. "Will you be okay by yourself?"

He nods, his phone is in his hand. "I won't be alone. Dom's coming."

"Oh goody." I grab my bag from under my chair.

"Sky," Zane says.

"Don't even think about it," I say.

"What?" he asks.

"You're going to tell me what to do. And whatever it is, it's something I already know. So, again I say, don't even think about it."

"Sky," he repeats, a bit more pleading.

"You're not the only one who can make jerkwads cry." I grin at him.

He smiles back, and if I thought Joey was the sun before, I was entirely wrong. This smile is so warm. It's not the smile I usually get. Not the confident smile. This one I can feel deep inside. This one could be addictive. Maybe this is the smile Joey gets, what she saw that I didn't. But what if I had? What if I'd seen this first?

"Wish me luck?" Joey asks him.

"You used Study Buddy, you don't need it," Zane says, making my stomach turn over again. He drops into the seat I had just occupied and crosses his arms, phone tucked up under his arm until it's hidden by the pinstripes of his shirt, eyes scanning the crowd again.

Joey links her arm through mine and tugs. "Wait in line with me." And I've never heard a better idea. I need to get away from here.

At least Nate won't be back while Zane's around. And if I'm not here, I won't have to be part of whatever his debate partner, Maia, would do if she showed up. But mostly, I won't be leaving Zane alone with my traitor brain, which has found a whole new way to mess with my life.

My apps always work. It was these two who matched. I just need to remember that.

"Let's go," I parrot back, and we walk off together so I can watch my brother, my best friend, and the girl who just got to have lunch with Zane answer random bits of trivia to prove that the only app that matters works, too.

You have joined LAScholEx.

Zane and Dom are here.

There is 1 unread message—click here to unroll the history.

Kaden has joined LAScholEx.

Mads has joined LAScholEx.

Skylar says, "The results ceremony is about to start. We should all be sitting together as a team. Why is it just me, Kaden, and Mrs. J?"

Zane says, "Where are you?"

Logan has joined LAScholEx.

Mads says, "Joey and I are in the back on the left. We ran to the bathroom."

Dom says, "You're late! We're at the front!"

Skylar says, "Who's we?"

Mads says, "Shhhh! They're announcing Pathfinder top scorers."

Joey has joined LAScholEx.

Logan says, "THAT'S ME!"

Skylar says, "How did that happen?"

216

Dom shrugs.

Logan says, "MY SISTER IS A GENIUS WHO MAKES GENIUS APPS."

Kaden says, "Tenth is respectable . . ."

Mads dances.

Mads says, "And I take fifth! THANK YOU!!!@!@!!!@!#@"

Dom says, "Congratulations, Joey!"

Zane says, "Second is excellent!"

Joey says, "Oh, wow! I didn't think I did that well."

Skylar says, "You dominated the music questions. Cornering one of the lesser known areas is a common technique recommended in the forums online."

Skylar says, "The rest was Study Buddy, right?"

Mads shakes her fist at the kid from Seymour.

Mads says, "I could have had it all."

Skylar says, "Dom with tenth for Achievers!"

Logan says, "Awww! We're twinsies!"

Zane says, "Gratz, dude."

Kaden says, "I'll take eighth, thank you very much."

Mads says, "Now it's just down to Sky and Z."

Joey says, "It has to be Skylar."

Logan says, "Booth points are in this too, right?"

Skylar says, "Unfortunately."

Dom says, "Boo, Southdale scum!"

Joey says, "Third's not bad!"

Logan says, "THAT'S MY SISTER!"

Zane says, "Way to go Sky!"

Skylar says, "I got second???!@!?#!#!@?"

Dom says, "Wait for it."

Kaden says, "Second is great, Sky."

Mads says, "I can kill first and then you'll be first."

Dom says, "NO YOU CAN'T!!!!"

Joey says, "CONGRATULATIONS ZANE!!!"

Skylar says, "Well, at least we definitely won."

Zane says, "It was the booth stuff."

Skylar says, "You won fair and square."

Zane says, "And all the studying I did with your app."

Dom says, "And Sky missed that question on the newspapers."

Skylar says, "Shh, it's the overall scores."

Mads says, "You did great, Sky."

Logan says, "BOO SOUTHDALE!"

Joey says, "You really hate them."

Zane says, "We really do."

Dom erupts!

Logan says, "!!!!!!!!!!!!!!!!!!!"

Mads says, "GO US!()#*@!$*@!&(#@!@!!"

Zane says, "WE DID IT!"

Skylar says, "THANK BLEEP!"

Logan says, "SKYLAR MYRTLE!"

Skylar says, "Study Buddy works!! We really won!"

Joey says, "You didn't think we would?"

Skylar says, "I mean, I was pretty sure we did with this many people placing."

Logan says, "Sky, did you see this?"

Logan has shared a link to TechMonster.com, click here to view.

Skylar says, "No, what is it?"

Logan says, "It's a blog post about you!"

Skylar says, "ALREADY?!"

Skylar says, "We literally just placed, how do they know about Study Buddy?"

Dom says, "Oh, they love Requite!"

Skylar says, "Oh, whatever, they're just a small blog."

Mads says, "It's press! None of our other apps have gotten press before!"

Skylar says, "No one reads them. It's not a big deal."

Zane says, "Isn't the whole point of us doing this to get your apps press?"

Joey says, "This is so great, Sky!"

Skylar says, "The whole point is to get STUDY BUDDY PRESS!!!!"

Mads says, "This is a good thing, Sky."

Skylar says, "It's a non-thing. The win is the good thing."

Skylar says, "When we win State it'll be Study Buddy all over everything."

Kaden says, "Mrs. J says to meet by her van . . ."

Joey says, "Which van?"

Mads says, "I got you. Follow me."

Logan says, "PIZZA TIME!"

Kaden says, "Good pizza time, please"

Zane says, "Oh, trust me, it WILL be."

You have left LAScholEx.

CHAPTER NINETEEN

"WHY ARE WE eating spaghetti?" Mads asks. "I thought this was supposed to be pizza."

Logan passes her the big platter of spaghetti with red sauce. "Fortunately for all of us the wait at the pizza place was three hours."

Zane, across from Logan, waves his pencil at him. "Do not make me use this."

Logan says, "Dude, whatever I can do to keep you from using that I will."

Mrs. James, sitting at the head of the table, smiles. "You'll get your pizza, on the way home from State."

The whole table shouts, and the unfortunate elderly couple seated just outside the nearly private room they found for us looks over their shoulders again.

"Three cheers for our high scorer!" Logan says, upsetting the elderly couple even further, but it looks like they have their check, so they'll be clear of our nonsense soon enough.

The entire table lifts a cheer for Zane, and he just basks in it, big grin plastered on his face and his pencil still waving about like some sort of magic wand.

"Don't forget our captain and her press coverage," he says when they're done, and they cheer me, too, even if I don't want or deserve it. In the end, most of our points were not from Quizposition but the booth, and I can't credit Study Buddy for the booth.

"What about Mads's perfectly aligned wallpaper?" I ask, trying to be gracious, because I can't sound like a sore loser. Not today.

"And Joey's phonograph with . . . I think they said 'a music curation that suited the scene set by the upper middle class respectability,'" Mads says with a wink for me as she lifts her glass of Coke in the air, and instead of shouting, everyone clinks glasses.

Then they all start eating and talking and laughing and shouting while I push the pasta around my plate. Mads leans in. "You okay?"

I just smile at her.

"So that's a no," she says.

Kaden leans into Mads. "Is she okay?"

"I hate you two," I whisper back, and they laugh. They're both so close I can feel it, and I smile despite myself.

Kaden says, "Get a poker face."

I spin linguini onto my fork and shove it into my face and say, mouth full, "Happy?"

They nod and go back to their own plate while Mads whispers, "You want to talk about this?"

I shake my head, chewing my way through the clams I

insisted on ordering. I just can't do the red sauce. I'm at the opposite end of the table from Mrs. James, who appears to be a very big fan of the sauce and the garlic bread. When she sees me looking at her, she gives me a smile and a thumbs-up. Dom, sitting next to her, is talking nonstop, but he's too far away, across too many conversations to tell what it's about.

Logan, in the middle, is laughing at whatever it is Dom's saying. Everyone's in such a good mood. And I should be, too. We're going to State.

I keep working my way through the plate when I hear, "Isn't that right, Sky?"

I look up, blinking, not entirely sure where it came from. "Is what right?" I ask, trying to find the speaker, and it's Joey.

"That guy we beat at State tried to match with you on Requite, Sky," Joey says, laughing, but no one else is laughing. "He thought she made it for him."

How did she know that? She must have heard more than I realized. "You know that's not why I made it," I say, almost pleading with her to confirm it, though I don't know why it matters. She'd never say why I really made it any more than I would.

"Oh, I know." She's still laughing. "I just thought it was hilarious."

"Why?" Zane asks.

"What?" she asks. "Oh, you know, Sky trying to match with that jerkwad."

"No," Zane says. "Why did he think she made it for him?"

Mads says, "Isn't he dating his debate partner?"

Joey says, "He said he wasn't."

Mads just makes a face at me. "Sky's not the type to steal someone's boyfriend," she says.

"Sky'd give her boyfriend away before taking one for herself," Dom says, and that does get a laugh out of most of the table.

And then Logan says, "Doesn't matter why she made it—it's gonna make us famous."

"It's just one blog post," I say, but everyone's talking and laughing too loud to hear me all of a sudden.

Zane, at least, doesn't seem to think any of this is funny. He keeps spinning the same forkful of spaghetti.

No one should be thinking about Requite—today is Study Buddy day.

Plus, Nate misunderstanding is one thing; he thinks everything is about him. Zane actually knows me. He knows I wouldn't do something so ridiculous over a jerk like that.

Well . . . not anymore, anyway.

I pinch the bridge of my nose and try to breathe. The last thing I need right now is a migraine.

"You aren't using it, though, are you?" Zane says when the conversation has lulled again.

"Everyone uses Requite," Logan says.

"Except Sky," Zane says.

"Oh." Logan looks down at me. "But you installed it."

I shrug. "Sure. At the party." I try to get a forkful of linguini in my mouth before he can ask a question.

"But you haven't matched with anyone," Zane says, not letting it go.

I shake my head, chewing slowly.

"Moguls haven't got time for that nonsense," Mads says, her knee nudging mine, and I look at her. She wipes her eyes with her hand, and I do the same and realize that the eyeliner she made me wear is all over my fingers.

I swallow fast and try not to rub at my face. "Exactly. I'll . . . uh, be right back." I'm out of my seat before anyone can say anything else, and fortunately the bathroom is just down the hall. It's not a lot, but my eyes are definitely red. I must look like I'm actually upset. I'm happy about all of this. We won Regionals and we're going to State. I fix the eyeliner and blow my nose. I'm just tired. I'm fine. This is all what I wanted. It doesn't matter what people think about me. It really doesn't matter what people think about Requite. I take a few minutes, just letting the conversation go on, but when I open the door, Zane's standing there.

I clear my throat and try to just walk past.

"Sky, wait," he says.

"Bathroom's free," I say.

"I don't care if you don't match with . . . anybody. But don't hold out for that jerk." He hasn't looked up from the floor. All I see is hair and his long form leaning against the wall. The suspenders he was wearing are hanging at his sides, and his sharp white shirt is unbuttoned a little farther than earlier, but his black dress pants still have the crispest line in them, and his shoes shine even in the dim light of the hallway. It's a moment right out of one of his movies, but his ingenue is in the other room, and it's all being wasted on me.

And yet, it's working, because I want it to be for me. I want this to be about more than his petty rivalry. I want my stomach to stop doing its weird fluttering nonsense.

"Do you really think I would?" I'm standing in the middle of the hallway basically ogling him. What is wrong with my brain? Do I need to mention this to my neurologist?

No, I need to turn and walk back to the table. Before anyone gets any ideas, especially me.

"Just"—he looks at me through the fringe of his hair, and something really deep inside melts—"don't. Please?"

"Look, I hate him as much as you do." Which isn't true. I definitely have more reason to hate him, but this isn't a contest.

His smile comes back, just a little, just in the corner. "Doubt it."

"Don't challenge me. You know I'll win."

"You didn't today." He pushes off the wall, and we're a lot closer than I realized.

"I was too busy making sure everything went perfectly."

"Sure, if that's what you need to tell yourself to sleep at night." He leans a little more. To the same distance as New Year's. And like New Year's, time loses all meaning. His voice a little quieter. "If you didn't make it for him, why did you make that app?"

Because I needed Joey. Because I was overconfident. Because I didn't know then what I know now. "It was a favor for a friend."

He looks at me, like really looks at me, full eye contact. "Which one? You don't have that many friends."

I know he can't possibly like me, because he wouldn't be this good at talking if he did. Dom doesn't know anything. And why am I thinking about Zane liking me all of a sudden? Of course he likes Joey. They're probably together. They had lunch. If there was a second he was thinking about me, that second is over. He's moved on to someone else.

"Fine. Don't answer."

"I thought it was the right thing to do," I blurt out.

"What?" he asks, head tilting to the side, sending his hair cascading and my concentration with it.

When I finally get myself to stop wondering if his curls are as soft as they look, I say, "The app. When I made it. I thought it was the right thing." When nothing more rational comes, I repeat myself. "At the time. When I made it."

"You said that. But why?"

"I just . . ." Why did I make it? Hubris? Greed? Why am I saying anything? Why does it matter? He doesn't care. "I thought I was helping."

"You don't think it's actually helping?"

"I didn't say that."

"Yeah. You did." The other side of his mouth quirks. "I know you, Skylar Collins. Don't think I don't."

"I . . ."

He just stands there, smiling. So close I can almost feel it. And some traitorous part of me wonders what would happen if he were even closer. So little space between us . . .

I turn on my heels and walk away. Because that's what I do. Because there's nothing I could say or do that would change that he matched with Joey on Requite. Because I could never do that to Joey. Because Study Buddy and everything that comes after matters more than my ridiculous hormones. Because even if I stayed right there, I would still be me and he would still be Zane.

He's calling my name. But I keep walking.

Away from him.

Not closer.

Away from the thought that I could move closer.

Back to the room.

Back to the table.

Back to my chair.

Back to the people who will see us.

Back to being the person he thinks hates him.

Back to my plan.

Because I'm not giving up my future.

I'm not becoming someone who steals other people's boyfriends.

Not for some floppy hair and shiny shoes.

From: Josie Fitzgerald <jfitzgerald@scholex.org>
To: Skylar Collins <skylar.collins@lovelaceacademy.edu>
Subject: ScholEx State Qualifiers

Greetings, Captains!

The final tallies are in, and below is the ranking for the twenty teams that qualified for the ScholEx State competition being held February 12–13 in Springfield! We had fifteen rousing Regional events, and the competition for the five wild card spots was really close!

1. Springfield High School: win
2. Polk County Prep: wild card
3. Newcastle High School: win
4. Lovelace Academy: win
5. Fairview–Bristol High School: win
6. Burlington High School: win
7. Southdale High School: wild card
8. Centerville–Southern: win
9. Holy Family: wild card
10. Winchester High School: win
11. North Central High: win
12. Jefferson High School: wild card
13. Saint Mary's: win
14. Pleasant Valley High School: wild card
15. East Clay County Regional High School: win
16. Pine Grove Area High School: win
17. West Lake High: win
18. Fox Lake Academy: win
19. Clayton–Lebanon High School: win
20. Central Christian: win

Details on the State tournaments and lodging options are being sent to your adviser. Please work with them to ensure that your full team remains active and eligible for competition. Teams without at least three Pathfinder and three Achiever scholars will not be eligible to compete.

And congratulations, scholars!

Josie Fitzgerald
State Coordinator
ScholEx International

From: Sophie G. <socialteam-features@hubbub.com>
To: Skylar Collins <Sky@skylesslimits.com>
Subject: ACTION REQUIRED: Requite—Social; Spokes: Relationships, Lifestyle

Skylar Collins,

Congratulations! Requite has been identified as a feature application by the social team!

We are extremely impressed with Requite and the response from the HubBub community to your application. We look forward to including it among our feature applications for the February 11–17 highlight period.

We ask that you submit an update of all your pending changes no later than Monday, February 8, to take advantage of the additional attention that a feature page will bring.

Because you are in the Junior Developer Priority Queue, our internal support crew has created a list of possible improvements to your app that may be helpful. You'll also find the suggestions as tickets in your Admin panel. Even if you don't manage to address them all before next Monday, you'll have them for future development cycles.

We realize that many of these items may be beyond your current skill level, but recommend that you do your best to include as many improvements as possible. Remember that your app has to be stable and only needs to run on the latest version of HubBub's platform, but backward compatibility is always encouraged.

We look forward to seeing your updated app.

Thank you for your contribution to the HubBub Social Network.

Sophie G.
Features Marketing, Social Team
HubBub, Inc.

You have joined LAScholEx.

Dom, Joey, Kaden, Logan, Mads, and Zane are here.

There are 21 unread messages—click here to unroll the history.

Logan says, "It's this Saturday and I hope you all can make it!"

Skylar says, "Make what?"

Logan says, "SKY!!! There you are!"

Logan says, "We're having a movie night at our house. Be dressed and stuff."

Skylar says, "On Saturday?"

Logan says, "Why? Do you have something better to do?"

Skylar says, "I mean . . ."

Logan says, "Skylar, you need a night off."

Dom says, "We're all coming."

Dom says, "Right?"

Mads says, "Sounds fabulous."

Kaden says, "These films are NOT car related. Correct?"

Skylar says, "This is an excellent question."

Joey laughs.

Logan says, "No car-related movies. I promise."

Mads says, "That doesn't mean anything...the one with the spies isn't car related."

Logan says, "This is a very special movie night, not a GOOD movie night."

Logan says, "The one with the spies."

Logan scoffs.

Skylar says, "Fine, I'm in."

Logan says, "You were coming anyway."

Zane says, "I guess I can make that."

Dom says, "You already knew you were going to be there."

Zane says, "Let me pretend to have a life, dude."

Joey says, "That sounds awesome. Plus, we've never all done anything together."

Logan says, "Does my NYE party mean nothing to you?"

Joey says, "I didn't make that, remember? I was performing for the New Year's Pops concert."

Logan says, "Oh yeah."

Skylar says, "OK, so I bet you're wondering why I brought you all here."

Dom says, "You've been spending too much time with Logan."

Zane says, "Right?"

Joey says, "I can just imagine her stroking a big white cat."

Logan says, "Too bad cats are Sky's mortal enemy. We could be so dramatic."

Joey says, "Sky hates cats?"

Skylar says, "I BROUGHT YOU ALL HERE"

Skylar says, "Because as you saw in those final results I sent, our point totals aren't enough to win State . . . yet."

Zane says, "Do you have a plan?"

Logan says, "Who do you think she is?"

Dom says, "Oh, he knows who she is."

Skylar says, "Shut up, Dom."

Zane says, "Shut up, Dom."

Joey says, "What's the plan?"

Skylar says, "So I figure we should increase the quiz rates on Study Buddy. I need to tweak some of the settings first . . ."

Mads says, "Will you have time for that? Your plate is pretty full already."

Skylar says, "I have to make time."

Mads says, "!!!!@!#@!#@!"

Skylar says, "If it's a choice, I'm picking Study Buddy."

Logan says, "What's going on?"

Skylar says, "Oh, it's just some nonsense."

Zane says, "What nonsense?"

Mads says, "HubBub has chosen to put Requite on one of their feature pages."

Skylar says, "That's a corporate secret."

Mads says, "We're not incorporated yet!!!@$!"

Skylar says, "And we won't be with that attitude."

Logan says, "FEATURE PAGE"

Skylar says, "It's not that big of a deal. There's like fifteen feature pages and a hundred apps on each feature page at any given time."

Zane says, "Sky!"

Zane says, "That's huge!"

Zane says, "Congratulations!"

Logan says, "AND MY SISTER IS ONE OF THEM!!"

Dom says, "Congrats!"

Joey says, "OH WOW! Congratulations!!!!!!!!!"

Kaden says, "Except . . ."

Skylar says, "Except they've suggested a few dozen changes. They're easy for the most part. I could get them done and in by their Monday deadline. But only if that's ALL I DO."

Mads says, "So we're going to have to pick up the slack."

Zane says, "Done and done."

Skylar says, "No, this is more important."

Zane says, "What do you need?"

Skylar says, "I need to get Study Buddy able to target questions."

Joey says, "Like DIY quizzes? My mom would love that."

Mads says, "Yeah . . . . . but instead we're going to have meatspace study sessions."

Dom says, "You mean in person?"

Kaden says, "She means face-to-face"

Skylar says, "No, I'll fix Study Buddy first and then see what I can get done in Requite."

Mads says, "SKYLAR!"

Logan says, "Skylar Myrtle."

Zane says, "We can handle this, Sky."

Kaden says, "Or . . . we could do old-school study sessions like Mads said . . ."

Skylar says, "I just need to tweak the point structure so you can assign intensive topical flash cards to individuals while maintaining a sufficient overview of the rest of the cards."

Mads says, "OR leaders will schedule in-person review sessions for the folks who missed questions in the Quizposition."

Joey says, "Not fair, Zane just has to do music and art!"

Zane says, "And lead the lit session."

Logan says, "Who all missed lit questions?"

Kaden says, "Skylar"

Zane says, "Sky."

Mads says, "Sky, you, and Dom."

Skylar says, "Thank you, Mads. And yes, I screwed up one lit question. Sue me."

Skylar says, "You don't think I can do this?"

Logan says, "You mean reprogram two different apps, study for ScholEx, and attend a party?"

Mads says, "You can, but you shouldn't."

Dom says, "You just have to study lit and music."

Dom says, "Right?"

Skylar says, "Yes."

Zane says, "She should do a coaching session with Logan too."

Skylar says, "He's not a leader."

Logan says, "What she said."

Zane says, "Sky, the only point differential between us was the booth."

Skylar says, "Much like Requite, that's not that big of a deal."

Mads says, "Logan, check Sky's temperature, she's clearly unwell."

Skylar says, "I did fine in the booth. And I can make up points in Quizposition."

Skylar says, "And I can fix Study Buddy."

Logan says, "We're doing study sessions, sis."

Logan says, "We'll still tell everyone it was Study Buddy."

Skylar says, "But it wouldn't be."

Zane says, "Sky, this isn't worth fighting about."

Skylar says, "Requite isn't that important. So what if it's on a feature page????"

Mads throws up her hands.

Mads says, "Logan, can you talk some sense into her?"

Logan says, "SKYLAR MYRTLE, YOU TAKE THAT BACK."

Joey laughs.

Zane says, "Sky, give yourself a chance."

Mads says, "If you throw this away, I'm never helping you again."

Kaden says, "Even I think this is too good a chance to pass up, Sky"

Skylar says, "Et tu, Brute?"

Kaden shrugs.

Kaden says, "Not my fault you broke the system"

Skylar rolls her eyes.

Logan says, "You're doing the Requite stuff. You're attending lit and music, and I'm going to help you with marketing stuff."

Dom says, "Booth marketing."

Logan says, "Yeah, that."

Skylar says, "Just me?"

Skylar says, "Anybody else need Logan?"

Logan says, "I am willing to coach anyone who needs my magical skills."

Joey says, "I thought it was weird that we had so many debaters on the team, but I guess it makes sense with the booth, doesn't it?"

Skylar says, "That and I don't have many friends."

Zane says, "Sky."

Skylar sighs.

Skylar says, "So we're doing this?"

Mads grins.

Mads says, "I'm glad you're finally listening."

Skylar says, "If I fix this app, I don't have to think about it ever again."

Logan laughs.

Zane laughs.

Mads says, "In your dreams."

Skylar says, "So, if you're all going to take point on studying, we need to figure out where and when."

Skylar says, "That means, leaders, give me time and place and I'll pop that on the Hub."

Zane says, "She gave in too quickly."

Zane says, "I feel I have somehow missed something."

Kaden says, "We definitely missed something"

Logan says, "What did we miss?"

Skylar says, "A perfect score at Regionals."

Joey says, "What? I'm missing it."

Mads says, "You missed Sky practicing her impressive delegation skills."

Skylar says, "Everyone just send me your session times. Logan . . ."

Logan says, "Oh, trust me, I know where to find you."

Skylar rolls her eyes.

Skylar says, "If there's nothing else."

Logan says, "No."

Logan says, "Go make us famous."

Mads says, "I'll have the button graphics without the words they were asking for within the hour."

Skylar says, "Whatever."

You have left LAScholEx.

CHAPTER TWENTY

WITHIN MOMENTS OF logging off the chat there's a knock at my door. I could stop them all from harassing me, but I cannot stop the monster in my own house.

"Go away!"

My door opens.

"I said, go away."

"Even if you fix Study Buddy, we're not going to use it," Logan says. "In fact, if you don't do the Requite fixes, we're not studying at all." He drops onto the edge of my bed closest to my desk and smiles at me in satisfaction.

"What?" I take off my headphones. "That's not fair."

"Everyone agreed. You're doing this, Sky, don't resist."

"Why? It's just a throwaway app. I've made hundreds of them."

Logan sighs. "You still don't see it."

"This one can't be more important than Study Buddy." I don't really know why I'm fighting. I should just make the changes to Study Buddy. But I need them to study. They're all being so stubborn about Requite, they probably wouldn't even use my updates anyway. Or worse, not even show up a week from Friday. So either way I wouldn't be able to prove my system actually works.

None of this is going right.

I slam my fists against the edge of my desk so hard even my monitor on its wall mount wobbles in a way that makes my heart leap into my throat.

Logan stands up, hands out. "Whoa, nerdling."

"This is ridiculous."

He puts his hand on my shoulder. "You may have made it as a throwaway, but that doesn't mean it's actually worth throwing away."

"Why this one, Logan? Why not something better? Why not the kitties?"

He laughs. "The kitties are not better. This one is amazing."

"I don't want it." I wipe at my eyes.

"You do," he says, crouching down so our faces are on the same level. "I love you, nerdling."

"Are you dying? You have to tell me if you're dying," I say, making a face at him.

"I'm not dying. I'm just . . . proud of you. And want you to stop torturing yourself. You have all the time in the world to get Study Buddy right, but you only have a week for Requite."

"Why? Why can't it just go away?"

"Look, sis, if the producers of *Fast and Furious* thought like that, we'd never have Hobbs and Shaw."

I can't help it. I laugh.

"I mean, think about it. In the summer of 2000, when they first began filming *The Fast and the Furious*, they didn't set out to make the perfect spy movie. But when they had the chance to in 2018, they took it. Even if it meant making their star and executive producer angry. They did the right thing then, and that's what I need you to do right now."

"It's not just that."

"Haven't you used the app? It's amazing."

I shake my head. "Why would I?"

"You're intent on ignoring all the chances you have, aren't you?"

"What's that supposed to mean?"

"Maybe Mom's right and you need to stop and smell the roses before they shrivel up and die."

"Are you saying I'm wasting my time on this?" I half spin back toward my computer.

"No way, you have to finish all those fixes. Work harder. I need you to be a billionaire and keep me in the style to which I'd very much like to grow accustomed."

"You plan on leeching off me for my whole life? Maybe I should stop trying."

He laughs. "I am very much intending to earn my keep. But . . ." He doesn't finish.

"But?" I ask.

"But not everything in life is going to go according to your plans."

"I know. But can't some of them?"

"Quarter mile at a time," he says, giving me a "go slugger" chuck to my chin.

"Life doesn't work like that."

"It can. When you trust family."

I roll my eyes. "You mean you?"

"I mean the team." He straightens up, clearly thinking his pep talk is over. "You don't see it?"

"There's nothing to see. They all have something they want."

He gives a low laugh. "Ain't that the truth." Then he says, "But you keep starting things you don't even realize the value of." He looks at the door as if he can see them in the hallway. "Whatever happens, you made something when you brought us all together."

"You're getting sappy in your old age," I say with an awkward laugh.

"So are we square?" He hits me on the knee, telling me I'm not the only awkward one in the room.

"Fine," I say.

"When do you want to practice demonstrations?" he asks, hitting me again, harder.

"OW! Not now, I'm almost done with their ridiculous timer."

"Timer?"

"It was among the list of suggestions that were passed along before feature launch. They had their social team look at the app, and I knew right away how to do this one, so I got started on it."

"And you're already working on their list?"

"Yeah." I turn around and pull up the mock-up that's just a screenshot with some text on top of it. "The timer is actually a cool idea. Instead of having the unmatched chats just be empty it shows how long you've been waiting for a response."

"That sounds . . ."

"Pitiful?"

He laughs. "No, I wouldn't say pitiful. Cruel?"

I look up at him where he hovers over my shoulder. "Right?" I click back to my code window, which is just a dark screen full of multicolored text. He always calls it gobbledygook because it makes no sense to him. It also seems to scare him a little, because he backs up.

"Hope. It's the worst," he says.

I turn to him. "I thought it was a good thing."

He shakes his head. "It's as much a monster as anything else Pandora let loose. It's just so cruel it stayed behind to look like a good thing."

"You have problems with hope?"

"Not me. Not anymore." He reaches out and ruffles my hair, messing up my already-messy ponytail bad enough I actually have to fix it. "You fixed that bug already."

I glare at him, my holder in my mouth as I pull my hair back into order.

"Go put more boys out of their misery. Or . . . you know . . . just one." He winks at me.

"I don't know what you mean," I say, already turning back to my coding.

"Oh, I think you do."

"You're bothering me."

"You're obtuse."

"You're a jerkface."

"You're mean."

"MOM!" I shout, but I can hear my door shut. So I put on my headphones to drown out the world, my brother, his weird implications, and, most of all, hope, with some K-pop played just a little too loud.

Because this is the only way you'll study, and I'm pretty sure you'll do it whether I want you to or not, these are the official study sessions:

Lit = 6 p.m. Wednesday, Central Library, Zane

History = 3 p.m. Saturday BEFORE THE PARTY, Coffee Joe's, Kaden

Art = 4 p.m. Monday, Coffee Joe's, Mads

Science = 4 p.m. NEXT Wednesday, school library, Dom

Music = 5 p.m. NEXT Thursday AFTER WE LOAD THE BOOTH IN THE TRAILER MRS. J IS RENTING, Joey's house, Joey

It's up to the leader to make sure everyone's there.

(But if you're not, hate yourself a little bit for failing us all.)

CHAPTER TWENTY-ONE

ON WEDNESDAY EVENING, I'm at the library by four thirty for the lit study session I totally do not need. This isn't the school library. Six would be too late for the school library, and Logan had some sort of reason not to be able to do it right after school. The public library's amazing Wi-Fi and even more impressive lack of siblings makes it a great place to kill a few more tickets on Requite.

I don't even notice Zane when he arrives. Unlike Logan, he doesn't pull my headphones off or otherwise interrupt me. When I finally get the button exactly where I need it in the menu, I look up and he's just sitting there staring at me, causing my breath to catch.

I check my computer time and it's 6:45. I pull off my headphones, hoping I'm not doing something ridiculous, like blushing. "You should have stopped me."

"You were busy," he says.

"Where are Dom and Logan?" I ask, closing my laptop after saving everything at least twice and making sure it backs up.

"They messaged about half an hour ago saying they were stuck."

"Stuck how?" I shove my laptop in my bag.

"I don't know. They didn't say."

"Do you want to cancel?" I ask him. "We can reschedule or something."

He leans forward on the table and whispers conspiratorially, "I'm too afraid of our captain for that. Plus, is there another time that works for you?"

I sigh. "Clearly even this doesn't."

"Let's just do this and then you can go home and work on being famous."

"I've been on a feature page before," I say.

"Yeah, but this is different," he says.

This time it's based on a lie.

I shouldn't be alone with him.

No, that's ridiculous. It's Zane and me. We're not even fighting anymore.

"Hey, you two." A white woman with short brown hair comes up to the table. "As cute as you are, you know we close at seven on Wednesdays, right?"

"What?" I look down at my watch, like I hadn't just checked the time. "Why did Logan suggest this?"

Zane says, "Thanks, ma'am. We'll find somewhere else to study."

She rubs her hand through her hair, and there are tattoos visible for the briefest moment under her sleeve. "Ms., please! I have a reputation."

"Sorry, Ms. Jen," he says, smiling at her, and I don't feel

so bad for how awkward he makes me if he can get a full-on librarian smile in like five seconds.

"Better, Zane. Zane's friend." She heads to another table, where an older man is sound asleep.

"You know her?"

"I know all the librarians." He rubs his fingernails on his vest, and I roll my eyes. He nods across the room. "The one in the pink cardigan behind the desk over there is the reference librarian who found the source I needed for the congressional neg that won me State."

"You come here for debate?" I ask.

"She's got the good reference books, what can I say?"

"You're the worst."

"You know it." He sits up in his chair and grabs his leather messenger bag. "So, Coffee Joe's?"

"We should cancel."

"So," he says, again, more intently, "Coffee Joe's?"

I nod and stand up, and suddenly I'm back in the chair and he's reaching out for me. "What happened?"

"I was sitting for too long." I wave him off. "It's fine."

"How long have you been here?" he asks, looking down at me.

"Since after school."

"Have you had anything to drink at all?" He's right next to me as I stand back up with more success, but my bag is wrested from my hands and he looks like he's ready to catch me if I fall again.

I shake my head.

"Forget coffee." Without actually touching me he herds me toward an old blue Subaru wagon.

"What's this?" I ask.

"My mom's car." He opens the passenger door for me. "Get in."

"Where are we going—Joe's is just two doors down."

"You need food." He still has my bag, and he's heading over to the driver's side.

"They have those sandwiches, I'll be fine. Or should we reschedule?"

"And how are you getting home?" His brows go up, waiting for my answer. "Logan's MIA."

"Fine," I say, dropping into the seat.

He puts our bags in the back and starts the car. He pulls out of the lot and turns north, away from the school and my house and even his house.

"If you'd done this in September, I'd probably be screaming bloody murder by now," I say.

"I'd never have been brave enough to do this in September." He's looking at me but only out of the corner of his eye, and we're at a stoplight. I have to credit him for his quality driving focus.

"How far are we going?" I ask.

"Just up here." He's signaling a turn onto a street that my family has driven by about a hundred times but never actually gone down. He follows a curve and winds up around the back of the mall. It's a little set of shops that we've never had any reason to stop at. "Thai?"

My mouth starts watering. "How's their panang?"

"The actual best in the west." He's smiling, but at the parking spot in front of us.

"We're here to study," I say.

"And eat. And drink water. That's it," he says.

"Do they have Wi-Fi?"

He actually looks at me at this.

"Fine, I'll bring my tablet."

He shakes his head.

"What?" I reach in the back and pull my tablet from my bag.

"You," he says, but there's about a thousand things in the way he says it that makes it feel like a whole conversation. I can't tell if it's exhaustion, pride, frustration, or acceptance.

He makes me get out and locks my door by hand before getting out on his side and using the key to lock it. "Can't have your IP getting out, right?"

"Whatever," I say. "Wait, I don't have any money."

"You can owe me." He's herding me again, his arms going to either side of me without actually touching, and if I want to keep it that way, I have to go all the way inside.

"You don't have to . . ."

"I want to," he says, plainly to me, then says, "Two," to the older Thai woman sitting behind the host stand. She leads us to a booth kind of in the back and asks what we want to drink.

"Waters," he says when we're sitting. "And a milk coffee for me."

He looks at me and I say, "Just the water, thank you."

"It's really good," he says.

"And it's really late," I say, not going into all the risks involved in having any caffeine, but especially intense coffee late at night after not drinking a lot during the day.

"Your loss." He pulls out a small paper notebook and puts it on the table. I think he had it tucked in his pocket like a phone. "Studying, right?"

"Very analog," I say.

"You should see my watch."

"What watch?" I look at his wrist and there's nothing there.

He digs in his vest and pulls out an old-school pocket watch, holding it between two fingers. I grab it without even asking for permission.

He laughs. "You like it?"

I've been obsessed with pocket watches since I was small. I want more than anything for some tech company to come out with a digital pocket watch just so I can wear it on a chain. But I don't tell him any of that, I just stare at the inlaid silver cover and the delicate hands.

"Very analog," he says.

"Pocket watches transcend analog." I look up at him. "There'd be no internet without pocket watches."

"How do you figure?" he asks, but my answer is interrupted by our drinks arriving.

I haven't even looked at the menu, but I'm ready to order.

"Panang with chicken, American-person medium hot." He laughs at me and so does the waitress, so I explain, "What? I'm a wimp."

"At least you're trying medium," she says.

Zane orders massaman curry with beef and extra potatoes for himself and then fresh spring rolls for an appetizer.

"You don't have to do that," I say after she leaves.

"You only say that because you haven't had them yet. Now explain about pocket watches and the internet."

"It's a long story, but railroad chronometers were the first universal standard time because otherwise there'd be crashes. Standard time led to a need for faster communication, which led to Morse, which led to telephones, which led to internet." I look up, and the smile still on my face matches the one on Zane's.

"I'm getting that back, right?" he asks.

"Oh, right." I click it closed, and it's such a satisfying sound that I have to do it again. But I stop myself from doing it a third time and hand it back to him.

"If I'd known you loved these so much, I would have pulled it out on you earlier."

"I mean, I still love my watch," I say.

"I would never dream of separating you from the internet." He slides the watch back into his vest pocket.

"So . . . studying?"

"You didn't mess up that bad," he says. He moves his pad out of the way so the waitstaff can put down the spring rolls. There's two of them and they're massive.

"I'm pretty sure I got Pulitzer and Hearst's New York papers confused." I mirror him as he pulls half a spring roll onto the small plate that came with the appetizer, and he drizzles both the clear sauce and the thick peanut sauce on the roll. "I also . . . kind of . . . maybe didn't actually read the Standard Oil reading beforehand."

"What?!" He gasps. "Skylar Collins didn't do the reading?"

"I meant to." I take a bite so I can leave the rest of my defense implied, and he's right about the spring rolls. These are not to be missed. I could just eat them the rest of my life and be happy.

"You've had something else going on?" he asks before taking his own bite.

"Ha-ha-ha," I say sarcastically between bites.

"So do you want to do the reading or do you want me to explain it to you?"

"I read it this weekend." I have to take a break between halves. I don't want it to end. "I think I've got it."

"So what you're staying is that if I teach you that it's Pulitzer's *World* and Hearst's *Journal*, then you don't need to study?"

I nod.

"And what if I say that Rosebud is the sled?"

I glare at him, and he laughs.

"So why are we here?" he asks, but it doesn't sound like he wants to.

"You kidnapped me," I say.

"Kidnapped?" He laughs harder, choking a bit. A waste of perfectly delicious spring roll. I should hate him again.

Instead I laugh and grab the rest of my roll. "I'm the captain; I can't skip this stuff."

"Oh yeah, I get that."

"Do you go to debate even when all your work's done?" I ask, taking more of the peanut sauce than the roll needs but not nearly as much as I want.

"Debate stuff is never done," he says. He's cleaning up the plates, stacking them nicely so it's easier for the staff to get them. "That's how you get to State."

"Exactly." I'm finishing the last bite when our curries show up.

"Exactly," he says, grinning at me over the steaming bowls.

He was not wrong about the panang. I savor every morsel, and he keeps smiling that smile I crave almost as much as the lime and peanuts in this dish. We talk about ScholEx and the alternate readings, all of which he's read.

We talk about *Anne of Green Gables*, which is the only one in the series that I read. And "The Lady of Shalott," and all the weird little layers the author put in that I never would have found on my own but he just saw.

We talk about debate and how he actually loves the research more than the shouting at each other.

He asks me about coding. Study Buddy. My future.

I was right.

He's really good at asking questions.

Because he also answers as many as he asks.

He tells me he's looking at Berkeley. I ask him why not Dartmouth, and he's impressed I know about their debate program. But, no, his life doesn't begin and end with debate. There's also history, art, and literature. He really likes movies, mostly the older ones that had to be creative with their effects. There's a whole conversation about the guy who did the special effects in the old *Clash of the Titans* movie using stop-motion animation.

But he doesn't want to make movies. He doesn't want to study literature. I get the feeling that he doesn't quite know what he wants to do, but in a way that is very focused on finding it out.

There's a small piece of my brain that runs away with the idea of us both meeting up in San Francisco, eating sourdough or whatever. Talking for hours before going back to our very different parts of the Bay.

This is not the Zane I thought I hated.

"You have big plans," he says when I've explained how I'm going to have enough venture capitalist contacts by the end of sophomore year at Stanford to drop out and start my business. "What if they don't happen that way?"

"They need to," I say.

"What if there's another way to get to the same place and you're missing it because you're so busy shoring this one up?"

"You sound like Logan."

He grins. "I thought his philosophy was that you make choices and don't look back."

I laugh. "He wishes. But, no, he likes the bits about family and living life a quarter mile at a time."

"Winning's winning," Zane intones in a very bad Vin Diesel imitation.

We both laugh.

"But seriously," he says, "you're so focused on it being Study Buddy. What if we don't win State? Will the world really end?"

I open my mouth and close it.

Yes, it will. The world I built in the wake of the headaches. The one that grew from the crushing weight of Nate. The plan that got me through my best friend having less time for me and more time for Kaden.

"You look like it will," he says, leaning forward.

"I put a lot of effort into it."

"And you think it would be a waste if it didn't work out exactly the way you wanted."

"Not a waste . . ." I say, but he's probably right. So much time spent on a bad path. I don't have a lot of time to make the waves I need to get where I want to go. "You won State, why can't we?"

"Oh, we can." His cocky smile is back. "But that's not what I'm saying."

"You don't think I can do it."

He laughs.

"No one thinks I can do it."

"Skylar." He shakes his head. "I know you're going to do it. I just wish . . ."

I don't know what to say, where he's going. I wait for him to finish, and finally he does.

"I wish there was more room in your plan." All his smiles are gone. "That's all."

"There's plenty of room in my plan," I say. "After I get my funding."

"There's a lot more here than Study Buddy. I mean, look at Requite."

I sit back. I didn't realize I'd gotten so close to him. That we were both leaning across the table, across our empty plates, closing the space between us. But now I do, and I need more space between us. "What about Requite?"

"It's amazing, Sky."

"Why? Because it worked for you?"

"What?" he asks, sitting back and frowning.

"Nothing. I don't want to talk about that app."

"Why does it seem like you hate it?"

I can't answer him.

I don't know why.

Except it's a distraction.

The posts that people have made about it.

The feature page taking me from ScholEx studying.

The ever-growing pile of tickets and requests.

The matches that have been made.

"All I'm saying is that it's . . . special." He fills the blanks I'm leaving in the conversation.

"We should get going," I say, stepping around it. Instead

of explaining what I didn't know when I created it. Instead of telling him how complicated it's made everything for me. For us.

About how my perfect plans have gone horribly off track, all because of that one app.

"Sky . . ."

I flag down the waitress and get our check, and Zane pulls out enough cash to cover it, but I'm already up and heading out to stand by the car.

"Skylar, wait," he calls after me, but I just need to go. I have coding to do. Even if it's on the app I hate.

"Skylar," he says again, coming up behind me after having fully settled our bill. "Are you mad at something?"

"No," I say. "I'm busy."

"You have a lot of coding to do before Monday?"

I nod, looking away.

"I get it," he says, but it sounds like he doesn't. "I'll take you home."

He lets me in his car by getting in his side and manually unlocking mine. I slide in next to him, waiting for the heater to start doing anything useful, but it doesn't manage to by the time we pull into my driveway.

"Sky," he says, and I look at him as I unbuckle. "This was . . . nice."

"Yeah," I say. "Thank you for supper. And for clearing the papers up."

"That's not . . ." he says, but I'm out of the car and

smacking the back hatch so he'll release it and I can grab my bag.

He does, but while it's open, our eyes meet in the rear-view mirror and I feel like I just screwed something up, but I don't know what. He's with Joey. I studied lit. This is all I get. No more. It's better that I draw the line than that he has to. I've already been through that once.

Plus, it's not like I don't already know the line is there.

"Good night, Zane," I call across the car, and slam the hatch closed.

Why do I always feel so much less sure about what I'm doing when I talk to him?

Why does it always feel like I'm running away?

Why can't I just go back to hating him?

Life was so much easier then.

Mads 🕷 ♛

What do I hear about you two going on a date?!›??!?

What?

You and Zane.

You went for dinner.

You had a nice time.

Please explain so I can understand.

Because I can't understand.

I just got back.

How did you hear about this already?

So you WERE planning on telling me???@!#@!#!@

Kaden needed something from Zane.

Zane said he'd just dropped you off . . .

Explain.

Logan and Dom ditched us.

So you went on a date??????@!@#???#?#

It WASN'T a date.

It was a study session.

What precisely did you study?

265

Each other?

We didn't actually study much.

I KNEW IT!!!@!

We just had supper because I kinda missed eating and the library was closing and it made sense at the time.

Where did you eat?

He took me to this Thai place that had the most amazing spring rolls and the panang curry was magical and why have we never been there before?

He took you for curry.

It was SO GOOD. It's right behind the mall in this tiny little area I thought was like accountants or whatever.

He took YOU for curry.

Yes, why?

Sky, he knows you.

Everyone likes curry.

No, Sky, you like curry.

I like lots of things.

You like weird pizza and curry.

And spring rolls.

THAT PEANUT SAUCE, THO.

You're so in love.

With spring rolls? Yes.

How did I miss this?

What did you talk about?

When did you start talking?

Nothing. School. ScholEx. Stuff.

Did you, in fact, study?????

Some.

That's what this was . . . a study date?

It was a study SESSION.

Mmmmmmmmhmmmmmmmmmmmm . . . . .

I will take NONE of your lip.

Did you know he has a pocket watch?

Are you still there?

It's so obvious now . . . what was I even thinking?

How you managed to pretend to hate him for nearly six years is beyond me.

He's a jerk.

A pompous jerk who likes everything you do.

He uses a pen and paper.

No one's entirely perfect.

Ain't that the truth.

What were Logan and Dom doing at this time?

Good question.

You didn't text him?????

I forgot.

He ditched a ScholEx study session, left you alone with your worst enemy, and you haven't yelled at him yet?????>??>

I was busy.

Staring at Zane's . . . pocket watch.

I only looked at it a little.

Did you really study "a little bit"?

We talked about the Standard Oil thing.

And about Anne of Green Gables a little.

I'll bet you did.

What's that supposed to mean.

Nothing, carrots.

Did you know that Anne's favorite flower, Queen's Anne's Lace, is actually a member of the carrot family?

Did he tell you that?

Yeah, he knew a ton of cool facts like that.

You're lucky I love you.

Or I'd have to break you.

Look. It was JUST a study session with food.

He likes Joey.

And?

And, I'm not going to get in the middle of that.

What makes you think she's not the one in the middle??

That's ridiculous.

You're ridiculous.

YOU'RE RIDICULOUS.

If I actually were a serial killer, I'd start with Nate.

What does he have anything to do with anything?

He messed you up.

You deserve better.

Why does everyone keep saying that?

Who else said that???????

No one.

SERIOUSLY!?@@#@!!?!

I don't know what to do with you.

Everyone keeps saying that, too.

He likes Joey.

We'll see about that.

StubBub Ticket

NAME: Skylar Myrtle Collins

EVENT: Vintage Movie Night

ORGANIZER: Logan Collins (@LoganCollinsSays)

TICKET/SEAT: General Admission

DATE: Saturday, 5:30 p.m.–12:00 a.m.

LOCATION: Logan and Skylar's

CHAPTER TWENTY-TWO

THE BEST PART of Logan's unnecessarily over-the-top movie night invitation is that I knew when it was happening so I could be showered, dressed, and in the basement before anyone arrived. I even managed to claim my spot on the couch and a full bag of popcorn. I have my tablet and pencil and am taking notes with my headphones on. I can be present and still get stuff done at the same time.

It's the perfect plan.

Until I feel someone sit down next to me. I glance over and of course it's Zane. I try to ignore him, but he waves his hand vaguely near my face. It's so polite I hate it.

I pull one earphone off and say, "What?"

"Hello, Skylar, it is nice to see you," he says, stilted with mock politeness. Then continues in a higher octave, "Hello, Zane, I'm glad you could make it."

"I'm working." I point my pencil at him.

"You've earned a night off," he says, grabbing at the pencil.

I pull it out of the way before taking my headphones completely off. "This is school."

"This is not," he says, then gestures around the room. "Your friends are here." And I can see that Mads and Kaden

have claimed the love seat to my left and Dom is helping Logan carry trays of the snackage he demanded from
them all downstairs. Someone brought a meat-and-cheese
plate with almonds and fruit on it like we're grown-ups or
something.

Joey leans over Zane from her spot on the other end of
the couch and says, "Don't let him bother you, Sky."

"Wouldn't dream of it," I say, finishing my notes for the
paper I'm supposed to have for English on Monday that,
theoretically, I've had two weeks to work on, but with the
Requite fixes and ScholEx, it has been sadly ignored. If only
I'd actually read the books I was doing this report on.

The couch suddenly seems very full and I scooch over,
but there's nowhere to go that separates me from Zane in
his jeans and starched blue pinstriped shirt and those suspenders. This is the second time ever I've seen him in jeans.
The third time his shirt's been partially unbuttoned. The
first time our legs have touched like this. How is he always
this warm?

Logan stands in front of the screen. "I bet you're wondering why I gathered you all here." He's got a pile of beanbag
chairs set in front of the snack-laden coffee table. Dom is
reclining on one of them, and there's a spot next to him.

"You told us," Mads says.

Logan laughs. "Oh, it's way more than that."

Kaden says, "How vintage are we talking here? Early
2000s?"

"Is that vintage?" Joey asks, reaching across Zane to grab

some of my popcorn even though there's a whole pile on the table in front of us.

"Kaden's asking if this is another *Fast and Furious* movie," Zane says, for her benefit alone. The rest of us knew to be afraid.

"No, I said *vintage*," Logan says, waving the remote in the air dramatically. "Not the pinnacle of filmmaking."

Joey laughs. "I saw the latest one. How can every single problem be solved by people driving super fast?"

The entire room takes a breath and looks at Logan.

He's clutching imaginary pearls. "In this house, young lady, we live our lives a quarter mile at a time."

"Ride or die," Mads yells, and Logan nods at her.

"Mads gets it."

Joey is blushing. "I only saw it once."

There's another gasp.

Logan says, "You poor child. We'll have to repair your poor education later. For now I present to you: old white dudes being old and white and dudes. Lights, please, Sky."

He sits down, and there's a taut silence until the movie actually starts and it's *Monty Python and the Holy Grail*. It's not a good movie, but it's not bad, either. I'm laughing before the opening credits are finished. We're all arguing by the time the documentarian buys it. We all say, "Help, help, I'm being repressed," in unison. There are some jokes I simply don't get, and everyone thinks that's the most hilarious thing—even Joey is laughing at me. But everyone knows everyone else's favorite color by the time it's actually over.

Logan looks triumphant as I get a notification of the doorbell on my watch. "Someone's here."

"Pizza! Sky, get the lights!" Logan shouts, jumping up.

"What did you get?" I shout after him as he runs up the stairs, but there's no answer.

"Supreme," Zane says, grumbling.

"He didn't even ask," I say.

Joey says, "Supreme is the best!"

Zane sighs. "It's not pepperoni and pineapple."

"You mean pepperoni and mushroom," I correct him.

Joey just starts giggling.

"She doesn't get it," I say.

Zane says, "You're wrong and you're right, as usual."

Joey looks scandalized. "Oh no, you're not joking, are you?"

"No," Mads says. "They have absolutely no taste."

"You have no idea how many mushrooms I've picked off pizzas," Kaden adds.

Dom says, "He got you pineapple and ham."

"That's not the same thing." Zane sits back, crossing his arms in a pout.

Dom stands over Zane, shaking his head. "Beggars can't be choosers."

Zane, still pouting, says, "This was his idea of a party."

Dom glances at Joey and then me. "And you're grateful."

We hear the door close, but Logan doesn't come down with the pizzas.

"Should we go help him?" Joey asks.

Dom saunters toward the stairs. "I'm on it."

"He's probably getting plates or something," I say.

"Or something," Zane says.

"They're getting pretty close," Mads says, watching Dom disappear upstairs.

"What do you mean?" Joey says, looking at her.

"Just noticing," Mads says, smiling, and Joey throws a Pixy Stix at her. They're getting pretty close, too. When did that happen?

Kaden grabs the Pixy Stix because it's their flavor. "We're all getting kind of close. I mean, look at them," they say, gesturing with the stick at Zane and me.

"There's nothing to look at," I say.

"You've been sitting next to Zane. On a couch," Mads says, stating the obvious. "For hours."

"Actual hours," Kaden says, making another gesture with the now-empty stick.

Fortunately my brother comes down with even more food at that exact moment. "Soup's on! Joey, can you make a spot?"

She gets on her knees and starts consolidating some of the snack containers and crumpling up empty popcorn bags. Zane leans forward to help her. He looks a little red. I'm feeling warm, too.

I adjust the thermostat from my tablet to make the room just a little more comfortable. He doesn't need to know I did it. If he's feeling it, it's probably because there's too many people in one room at the same time. Which means it's not because my traitor brain keeps counting every second we're touching on this couch that I don't remember being quite this small. Dom finally appears with a pile of paper plates tucked under his arm, and in his hands is a tray of what looks like cake. Cake with lit candles on it.

"Happy birthday to you," he's singing, and then we all are, even though I have no idea whose birthday it is until Logan and Dom say "dear Zane" extra loud for all of us, and I notice Zane's frozen like a deer in the headlights.

When we're done and he's blown the candles out, Mads asks, "Why didn't you tell us?"

"It's a need-to-know," Dom says.

"It was supposed to be a secret," Zane says, his cheeks even deeper red than before.

"You're grown now, Zane. Start acting like it!" Logan instructs as the only technical adult in the room.

The pizzas are opened and inside is the supreme we all expected; a vegetarian, which turns out to be Joey's favorite; the promised ham and pineapple; and a plain pepperoni with two little bowls, one containing pineapple and the other mushrooms. "That's as close as you nerdlings get, unless you want to call the store back up and order your own pizza. Humans have to eat this," Logan says, looking at me and Zane.

And I can't help it, I share a look with Zane. Again everyone laughs, and Joey declares, "You both are so pitiful."

"She said it, not me," Dom says, and Logan elbows him.

"What's next?" I ask, taking two slices of pepperoni and

putting my sad, uncooked mushrooms on them because it's at least something.

"Extra vintage for our favorite silver screen throwback," Logan says between bites.

"Should I lower the lights?" I ask, pulling the app back up.

"Yeah," he says, clicking through movies with his remote.

"One moment," Mads says, jumping up. She goes to the linen closet, which is just off the basement hallway, and comes back with a small cache of blankets. "Anyone else getting cold?"

"Oh, me!" Dom says, grabbing one of the bigger blankets and throwing it over his legs and hitting Logan with it.

"You look cold," Mads says to me.

"I'm fine," I say.

She rolls her eyes and drops one of the blankets on my head.

"You got a blanket in my pizza." I'm too busy protecting my food to move the blanket, but Zane frees me.

"This is big enough to share," he says, smiling at me, and I want to tell him to stop. How am I the only one who's way too warm? But just as Logan finds what he's looking for, which turns out to be *Casablanca*, we're all snuggled up, with blankets, on my couch. Still touching. And I've never felt so sure I was about to burst into flames.

Joey ♫

Will you be at the art study session today?

No, Mads would have already hidden my body if I screwed up an art question.

Oh crud.

I wanted to ask you a favor.

Mads will be there.

I don't think she'd help.

Logan will be there, too.

Yeah, no. He doesn't like me.

What?????

Logan likes EVERYBODY.

I mean he's nice.

But . . .

Never mind. I'll be fine.

No, tell me what's up.

I was going to ask if you'd help me with something.

Just ask me.

Worst I could say is no.

I guess . . .

I'd like to ask Zane out for a date on Friday.

Ahh.

That's not a no.

Friday is State.

Oh. Right.

So, the next Friday?

Why don't you just ask him?

I'm still tongue-tied around him.

You seemed fine Saturday.

It's different around people.

Weren't you alone at ScholEx? You had lunch together.

When?

When you came up to the booth.

When?

Right before Pathfinders' Quizposition.

That? No, I met him near the booth. He was looking around or something.

You're both still using the app, right?

Like haven't you been talking there?

We tried talking, but it's only gotten slightly better than the first one.

I have been wanting to ask for your help for a while, but I thought . . . maybe . . .

You thought what?

I wondered if maybe I was missing something with you two.

Joey. You matched with him.

Well, yeah.

Isn't asking him on a date the whole point?

I guess.

But . . .

But what?

Well, he hasn't asked me.

Like, not even coffee.

Maybe he's waiting on you to make the first move.

He's ridiculously polite.

Isn't the chat the move?

Don't ask me!!!!!!!!

But you made it!

Yeah, but this thing's like Frankenstein's monster. It has a life of its own.

Hahaha

Does that make you the real monster?

Mary Shelley jokes?

You should use those on Zane.

You think?

Oh yeah, corny references are his jam.

Didn't you see him at movie night? He knew every famous quote.

I guess. I couldn't hear him well.

Oh yeah, I guess you were by Dad's new speaker. That thing isn't tuned right.

I need to have a look at that . . . you know in my free time . . . HAHAHAHAHAHA 😭 😭 😭

I shouldn't be bothering you.

No, sorry.

There's just a lot going on.

You should ask him.

Worst he can say is no.

That is the actual worst.

I mean, I guess.

There's worse?

Never mind, ignore me.

OK, I'll try.

I'll let you know how it goes.

Cool.

CHAPTER TWENTY-THREE

LATER THAT NIGHT there's a knock at my door while I'm going through my planner app to organize the chaos that my life became while I binged Requite fixes and homework. I'm closing out the English paper I just barely got done in time for class. Fortunately the teacher prefers digital subs. You know, to save paper.

Logan peeks his head around the edge of my door. "You in?"

"Yes." I pull my headphones off. "Just working."

"You're on your bed," he says, opening the door.

"Yeah." I look at my desk. "You can report back to everyone that the last round of fixes went in on time and the HubBub team said they would let me know by tomorrow if there are any other fixes."

"Oh yeah," he says, dropping his school tablet to his side. "How's that all going?"

"Fine."

"When do you think that'll be on the feature page?" He shuffles his feet for a second and then seems to decide he's going to stay, but instead of leaning on my bed like he normally would he takes my computer chair and pulls his tablet up in front of him like he's going to take notes.

"Midnight GMT, which is about seven our time Thursday night but could be later if something gets screwed up," I say, looking back at my own tablet. Whatever he wants, he'll get around to. Eventually. It's probably big if it involves this much small talk.

"Any idea what page you'll be on? Social? Relationships?"

"They cross-categorized us to Relationships and Lifestyle. Which is just ridiculous because all the biggest apps are in Lifestyle." I put my pencil down and look up at him. "I mean, have you seen that feature page lately? It's like not even a promotion anymore, it's just the list of default downloads. I hate being buried for no reason."

"Lifestyle?" His eyebrows go up, and he types something into his tablet. "That's cool."

"Ridiculous," I repeat, looking back at my planner. Crap, tomorrow is the math quiz. I am in no way prepared. I'm pretty sure I've screwed up the last few assignments. I wonder if I can bribe Dom to give me some mnemonics. "You'll see Dom tomorrow, yeah?"

"What?" He stops typing, clearly startled.

I frown at him. "You're in physics together, right? First thing?"

"Oh! Yeah, totally, we have class together. First thing. You remembered. You're so observant."

I roll my eyes. "Could you ask him if there are any good tricks for tangents?"

"Why don't you message him?" He sits forward a little. "You like Dom, don't you?"

"I used to," I mutter, making a note to find him before math.

"Is this the Zane thing?" he asks as if reading my mind, but he looks relieved.

"There's no Zane thing," I say.

"That's because you won't let there be a Zane thing," he says.

"Do you really need to be here?" I ask, looking back up at him, exasperated.

"I just wanted to know more about Requite. Like, how many downloads are you at now?"

I frown at him. "What's this about?"

"Can't an amazing big brother like me be invested in his younger sister's creations?"

"You're the only big brother I have, that's why I'm asking."

"Just humor me."

I pull open DevHub on the admin panel, and Logan rolls closer. The splash page has all the statistics, but I really don't pay much attention to them. I'm about to pass it to Logan so he can gawk, but I frown. "This can't be right."

"What?" He gets off my chair and comes over.

"There's over a hundred thousand downloads."

"There are, aren't there? I wasn't sure if I was reading it right," he says, but I'm drilling down.

The changes I made were to make it easier for the app to be translated into other languages. It was a pain, but Mads got me background buttons as opposed to formatted buttons, and I spent a few backbreaking hours getting the words per-fectly lined up within the box so they worked regardless of the size of the person's device. The new code will even for-mat nicely for tablets.

"My changes went live sometime this morning."

"Is that twenty-five thousand downloads in Korea?" He grabs my tablet from me, and I yell at him.

"Excuse you!"

"Skylar! This is amazing." He looks down at the tablet and starts clicking around. "How long has it even been available there?"

"I don't know time zones! A couple hours?"

"A couple hours?" And then he drops my tablet! I mean, onto my bed and I'm able to catch it, but the doofus actually dropped my baby!

"Get out!"

"Nerdling," he says, quietly, breathy. "What have you done?"

"I just converted some of the menu formatting to CSS so it's easier to translate the text. It's not that big a deal." I put my tablet safely on my bed and get up to start shoving him out.

"How much did the UK downloads go up? Five thousand? Fifty? Do the charts usually shift ranges like that? Oh, wait, they're probably still asleep."

"Get! Out!"

"We haven't talked about HubBub China yet." He's immovable, putting his whole weight against me, and since he's got a few inches on me it works.

"HubBub China has a different approval team, and it's probably still too early there, so it'll be at least morning before it would go live there—now go!"

"Skylar," he says, like he's explaining the universe to me.

"MOM!" I shout in his ear, hopefully stunning him so he moves, but no luck.

"Skylar," he says again. "This is something."

"MOM! LOGAN IS IN MY ROOM, AND HE WON'T LEAVE!"

"Skylar, forget Study Buddy, forget Nationals: It's this."

"Logan!" We both hear Mom and she's closer than the living room.

"I'm going!" he yells, both for me and her.

"Thank you!" I shout in his ear, and finally feel him give.

"I gotta get to work," he says, and zooms for the door, evading my half-hearted kick.

"Just leave. I need to figure out if HubBub's translator works on tickets." This is going to be a nightmare. I have to tell Mads. I have to study for that math quiz. At least I don't have to think about Joey or her date.

LOVELACE ACADEMY'S SCHOLEX HUB

Announcements

STATE LOGISTICS

We are excused from Friday afternoon classes.

Mrs. J will meet us at the lunch table AFTER WE'VE EATEN and we'll go out to the van. The van leaves at EXACTLY noon. NO EXECEPTIONS. If you miss the van, travel arrangements are YOUR PROBLEM. If you NO SHOW at State, the last face you'll see will be MINE.

IT IS A TWO-HOUR DRIVE.

Mrs. James says we're NOT STOPPING, so pee ahead of time and bring APPROPRIATE snacks.

Rooms at Springfield Motor Lodge have two double beds—room assignments are as we agreed in class:

Skylar and Mads
Joey and Mrs. James
Logan and Kaden
Zane and Dom

If you get into a fight with each other before State, you have to make arrangements to swap, but NO dating couples are allowed in each other's rooms on pain of death and possibly suspension from participating in ANY extracurricular activities INCLUDING DEBATE next year. (These are Mrs. James's words, not mine.) (OK, they're mine, but the sentiment is hers.)

After school Thursday (BEFORE THE MUSIC STUDY SESSION), we will be loading the trailer with all our booth stuff.

We'll have access to the Springfield High School gym until about 6 p.m. Friday to set up the booth. We need to make absolutely sure we have EVERYTHING because Springfield doesn't even have a Target!!!!!!!!!!! (Best they have is a Dollar Store, which IS open until 10 p.m.)

Supper Friday will be at the gas station just before town. It has a Taco John's and a Subway. (Or bring your own.)

Breakfast Saturday will be a continental breakfast at the motel. (Doughnuts, it'll be doughnuts.)

Lunch Saturday is boxed lunches. (Mrs. J says last year it was ham, beef, or veggie sandwiches.)

We'll be eating at the Happy's Pizza on Saturday night. (BRING YOUR PENCILS or cash for your own pizza toppings.)

Breakfast Sunday will be at the same gas station. Mrs. J has a budget of $5 for each of us, which is enough for a breakfast sandwich and a drink, so if you want something fancier, bring even more cash.

Van will be back at school by 2 p.m. Sunday.

If you need a ride home from school, my mom will be picking us up in her car, which will fit two more people, and Dom's leaving his car at school, which can fit three. However, Mrs. J says we should get the OK from our parents to ride with Dom because . . . liability.

CHAPTER TWENTY-FOUR

JOEY'S HOUSE SMELLS like cats. No, that's not fair. It probably smells fine, but all I smell are cats. This is one superpower I wish I didn't have. It's not an allergy; it's a migraine trigger. But it's easier to say it's an allergy. People tend to be cool about allergies. They want you to explain migraine triggers, or just not have a headache this time.

Her mom is nice, though—not remotely what I was expecting from a homeschooling mom of a child prodigy. She's accidentally sworn twice while baking cookies for us and keeps wandering through on an old cordless house phone coordinating various things, from cat shelter pickups to her husband's gigs, because he's a musician, too.

The cat itself is watching me. Well, one of them. Joey's family fosters, and the sick ones are sequestered in the basement. We're in the dining room, which is also set up to be a study area for Joey and her younger brother, who keeps forgetting things in the kitchen so he can come look at us.

Logan, Kaden, Zane, Joey, and I are sitting on the world's most uncomfortable wooden chairs listening to music over the speakers they have perched all around the house. If it were our house, Dad would have mounted them into the ceiling eons ago.

"That's a leitmotif," Joey says, pausing the music. "So now listen to this." She plays more music that sounds entirely different from the first and pauses it. "Did you hear it?"

The rest of them are nodding, but I really didn't. The cat was watching me. And the edge of the chair has lodged itself into my thigh.

"Sky, are you okay?" she asks, maybe because I failed to nod.

"The cat is watching me," I say out loud. I want to add that Zane has bumped into me approximately four times and at one point sustained contact for approximately five minutes. But I don't, because I'd have to explain how I know that.

"You gonna make it?" Logan asks.

"Sky hates cats," Kaden says.

"I don't hate cats," I say, stretching my jaw muscles that suddenly feel too tight. It probably looks like a yawn because the cat yawns, and that just confirms he's looking at me.

"She hates music," Zane says.

"I don't hate music," I say. "Just . . . focus."

"Our first violinist says it's just like coding," Joey says, turning the book she's looking at around. "See this? It's the leitmotif I played." She points to a small segment of notes. "Then here is the second segment. See how the first notes are in the second set?"

I nod this time, because I know she wants me to, but the

notes are swimming in my brain. Crap. I don't have time for this. "Like an object."

"What's that?" Joey asks, but I'm too busy rubbing my eyes to answer, so Kaden does.

Kaden used to be as into coding as I was, but that was before debate introduced them to socialism and Mads introduced them to date night. Now Kaden prefers to argue with strangers about the problems in our social systems.

"It's like a leitmotif," they say. "You define an object once—in this case Siegfried's horn—and then you can use it over and over again whenever you need people to think about Siegfried. But didn't Wagner hate leitmotifs? Like, wasn't his thing about how wrong it was to interpret his music that way?"

"Yeah, but that doesn't stop it from being a useful tool. He basically used them everywhere," Joey says with a deep hint of disdain.

"You don't like Wagner?" I ask, shaking through the fuzz to grasp on the first time I remember Joey saying anything remotely negative.

"I hate Wagner," she says, and the whole table gasps. "What? He's intense and funereal and has no idea what to do with a flute. Which is funny because . . ." She picks up her hands and mimics playing while whistling the song brides walk down the aisle to.

"That's Wagner?" Logan says.

Joey nods and then sighs. "Actual worst."

Kaden says, "Truly. He was a socialist, but the worst possible kind. His writing?" They make a gagging sound.

"Joey, honey, we better get going." Joey's mom pokes her head in again, sans phone. She smiles at all of us and says, "I hope you learned something."

We all nod, and I've already got my stuff shoved in my bag, ready to bolt.

"Thank you for having us, Mrs. Harrison," Zane says. He seems to be in as much of a hurry as I am.

"Of course, Zane, we should have had you over earlier. You two make a great team." She winks at her daughter, who groans in embarrassment.

"I didn't realize you had such a nice space to work or we might have come here to do cards instead of Coffee Joe's," he responds, and then to me he says, "Sky, wait up, I need to talk to you."

Joey says, "I was hoping we could talk real quick, Zane."

"Oh, uh, I need to figure something out with Sky. Can I message you later?" I can't hear her response because I'm outside, in the fresh air. It's freezing, but that just makes it even fresher. Logan hadn't even closed his book when I left, so I know he's going to take a while. Plus, we're giving Dom a ride and the two of them don't do anything fast when they're together.

"Sky, wait." Zane is behind me but stops short, realizing I am not full-on running down the street, like I ever would.

"You okay?" he asks, coming around front and blocking the wind. I almost sidestep him, but it's kind of nice. Just warm enough, and he doesn't smell like cat, which is really all I care about.

"No," I say.

"I assume you heard?" he asks, and glances back at the house.

"Heard what?" I ask.

"Joey and I . . ." He trails off.

"Did she finally ask you out?" I say, looking up at him. I'm trying to smile—smiling would be appropriate right now—but all the muscles in my face are resisting, tightening. My teeth feel like they're trying to dig through my sinuses to reach my brain.

"She did."

"Congratulations," I say. I can't look up anymore. I drop my head and start rubbing my temples. I hate these. They're not tension headaches, but they start that way. Everything about my face hurts because my nose decided it smelled something it didn't like. If I don't get home to my injection in ten minutes . . . The cascade failure of missing school, the van, State—all of it is too much to consider.

"You knew?" he asks.

"She needed a lot of help."

"So you helped her." He sounds far away.

"Like her mom said, you two are good together," I say, realizing that the words are almost on autopilot, and if my brain were firing the way it was supposed to, I'd finally understand that this is the worst that could happen. That this migraine is another one that requires hospitalization and I miss State. Study Buddy never takes off. Zane and Joey fall in love, kiss constantly, forget I exist but feel grateful for me about it. That I'd have to pretend for the rest of my life how glad I was to shove them together. Their grandchildren will thank me for intervening when the whole story gets out. One would probably sue me for Requite, saying it was their grandma's idea.

"What?" I say, realizing he's been talking this whole time while everything in my brain crashes like code compiled while still missing a curly bracket.

"You're okay with this," he says again, quieter, closer.

"I mean, you matched on Requite."

"After last week . . ." But he's going too slow. The words, the thoughts. I have to go faster; I have to get home.

"Just have a really good time," I all but shout. I need this over with. I need Logan, and I need to go home. I need Zane to stop being so warm and so close. I need to stop wondering what his curls feel like or what would happen if I just leaned over and kissed him. I can't let him know what it does to me when his arm brushes against mine. He can't know any of that because he's going on a real date with Joey.

I take a chance, looking up at him, to convince him how happy I am about all of this. But the sky swoops and dives as if it's trying to take its name back from me. I can't help it—I stumble a step and almost fall, or would, but he catches me. And it's so much more than a brush of his arm that my traitor brain starts throwing so many error messages it feels like my nerves are on fire.

"Sky, are you okay?"

"Whoa, you two, get a room," Logan says, finally bursting

through the door, Dom and Kaden chattering excitedly behind him.

"Logan, I don't think she's . . ." Zane starts, but I try to pull myself away and stumble again, this time into him. And I can't fight it. I can't run. I just want to be here. I want to rub my head against him, have him hold me there, like somehow he could make it all stop.

"Get her to my car," Logan says, all joking aside. "Bleeping cat."

"We were only in there an hour," Kaden says.

"That's all it takes, I guess," Logan says, "Sky, why didn't you say anything?"

He's beside us, herding like Zane did at the restaurant. Except this time Zane has his arms around me and is holding me against him as he guides me down the few steps to the driveway, where all the cars are waiting.

"You wanna ride with us?" Logan asks Zane as he pulls the door open. "We're going to have to go to the house first, obviously."

"I would, but I've got my mom's car."

"I'll message you later," Logan says, while Zane gently eases me into the back seat.

My mouth starts watering and I have the overwhelming need to be sick right then, so I lean over . . . toward Zane's feet. Whatever happens next, he's definitely going on that date with Joey and never thinking about me again.

I feel his hand on the back of my head and then my pony-tail tightens. "Feel better."

Despite this whole new pain in my head, I just nod and then lie—probably from the outside it looks more like a fall—on the bench of Logan's back seat. I'm definitely on top of breakfast sandwich wrappers and I can feel a Mountain Dew bottle lodged into my lower back like some sort of cheap lumbar support, so I pull it out.

"Just drive," I manage to mumble, and then close my eyes because no day should be this bright.

SkyLessLimits Announces the Launch of Requite

SkyLessLimits is excited to announce our app Requite will be a featured HubBub social app that allows teens with crushes to connect by taking pictures of each other. The app creates a private chat that only the two participants can access.

SkyLessLimits is excited for Requite's international expansion, with translations already taking off in Korean, Chinese, and French. (10,000 downloads in South Korea alone.)

Requite is expected to be featured for the Valentine's Day holiday and has already exceeded 100,000 downloads.

> *"When I added his picture, I never imagined we would match, but my boyfriend and I connected immediately! I never would have gotten the courage to ask him myself before we went off to college, but here we are!"*
>
> *—Logan Collins, client and marketing director for Requite*

SkyLessLimits is the online identity of Skylar Collins, a sixteen-year-old coder who is revolutionizing online spaces with her unusual perspective in social interactions. Started five years ago with the creation of Kitty Katty Colors, a puzzle game for children, Skylar and her partner, Madison Allen (known online as artist LeBrat), continue to develop new and innovative apps for their peers in education, social, and game spaces.

CHAPTER TWENTY-FIVE

I WAKE UP the next morning completely drained. I haven't had a headache this bad in almost ten months, not since I first got the shots. Or I started keeping a trigger diary and avoiding them. I tried to reduce stress. I really did.

My phone is not only silenced, but it's dead beside me, so I grab the cord from the shelf nearby and plug it in. I look around for my tablet, but it's nowhere to be seen. Neither is my backpack. Nor my clothes from yesterday. In fact, my entire room is now spotless, down to the dishes that I left on my desk Tuesday night.

There is one thing that shouldn't be here: a thermal mug that I know will be full of herbal tea and probably still warm. I grab it and move myself very slowly to my desk chair.

My head no longer hurts, but my whole body feels wrung out, like I had the flu or spent the weekend coding and forgot to sleep at any of the right times. I have a stash of protein bars in my desk, and I grab one as I wake my computer up. I could go downstairs and find more substantial food, but that means either doing something or talking to someone. Probably both.

The time says it's noon. My email says it has fifty-eight unread messages and seventeen strangers have tried to create a bubble with me. The admin panel on HubBub has a whole bunch of new charts and graphs on it and about five more tabs than I remember from last time I checked. Mads has sent me forty messages since this morning.

This morning.

When we were supposed to leave for State.

The last one simply says, If you've died without me, I'm coming after you. Do not even think I don't know how.

I send her, I'm alive. And then, Barely. Have you left yet? Tell Mrs. J I'll be there in five minutes.

I'm not remotely ready to be there. But at least I'm packed.

She responds immediately.

GO TO THE MAIN PAGE!!!!!!@!@#!@#!@#!@#!@#!@!!!!!@#!#@!

At that exact moment, my phone wakes up and starts vibrating. It vibrates so hard and so much it falls off the shelf. I run to grab it. Putting my passcode in as I carry it back to my desk, I missed answering whoever was calling, but the app I installed to tell me who anonymous callers are (so I can ignore them) says, "Times Tech Desk."

Not sure what that could mean, I open my phone and it immediately displays the front page to HubBub, a screen I bypass most days, and when I do land there, I barely even register it. It's their sales spam nonsense. I guess someone must look at it, because it keeps the company running.

Right there, in the center, above the scroll, on the primest real estate on the internet, is Mads's Requite icon floating in a field of hearts next to the words "Get real answers on Valentine's Day."

I'm about 90 percent sure I'm still dreaming. And when my phone starts ringing again, I take a risk and answer. "Hello?"

"Finally! Is this Skylar Collins of Skyless Limits?"

"It is," I say, trying to sound as grown-up as possible.

"We received your press release earlier this week and, well, with the attention you're getting on HubBub, we were wondering if we could schedule some time for you to sit down with one of our writers for a piece."

I look at my caller ID app, which says Hearst Communications. And all I can think is that I got that question wrong. "Is this about the *Journal*? Or was it the *World*?"

The woman on the other end says, "No, I'm calling you from *Seventeen*."

"*Seventeen*?" I repeat.

"*Seventeen* magazine, you've heard of it?"

"*Seventeen* magazine . . . wants to talk to me?"

"The sixteen-year-old creator of the Requite app? With . . ." Something rustles and she says, "One hundred thousand downloads and international interest?" She laughs. "Well, that data's clearly old. Isn't it funny how press releases can go out of date in a second nowadays?"

"Oh yeah. I mean, of course, you want to talk to me." I take a breath and then say, "You know I'm not seventeen." I don't even know what I'm saying right now. I'm just buying my brain time to join the conversation.

"And attend Lovelace Academy, right? Oh! Wait! I have a cousin who went there, he was one of the Munroes. You're about the same age, you probably know him. Nerd school, right?"

I can't answer, I can't even think. Somehow I agree to an interview call for the next day at two because that seems like a reasonable thing, and my phone keeps beeping the entire time. Also Mads is still messaging me constantly.

And then, after I've hung up, I suddenly hear the words she said but didn't register.

Press release.

What did he do?

"MOM!" I yell, grabbing my bag and carrying my still-vibrating phone with me as I rush out of the room. "Mom! I need to get to the tournament."

I rush downstairs to the kitchen, where she's stirring some soup and smiling at me. "You're awake!"

"Today is State. They're leaving and I'm here."

"They left already," she says, as if that makes it better instead of worse. "Logan said he'd message you. Didn't you get it? You were so sick we decided it was better to let you rest. Did that lady get ahold of you?"

I look at her, not processing that my friends and brother really left without me, for my own tournament. "Lady? You mean from *Seventeen*?"

"I thought she said she was from the *New York Times*." This, somehow, doesn't seem weird to her. "She called my line, so I gave her your number. Is this for your booth thing?"

"I'm late for my booth thing! Why did you let me sleep?"

"You need your rest. That was a real bad one. We almost took you to the hospital."

"They left without me!" I know I'm repeating myself, but it can't be real.

"Honey, you're sick. If you feel better tomorrow, I can drive you up."

"That will be too late." My phone keeps vibrating, and I can't think. "I need to go."

"Logan said it would be fine, that they have enough Achievers without you." Like that's the only possible reason I would want to be with my team at the State competition for ScholEx. "It's really for the best."

I see his keys on the counter and grab them.

"Skylar, you're in your pajamas."

I look down and she's right. "I'm just getting my backpack. I . . . left it in Logan's car."

"Isn't that your bag you're carrying?" Mom asks me, but I'm already out the door.

I race into the street in my slippers. I start driving and then realize I don't know how to get there, so I pull over and get out my phone. I barely make it to the navigation app through all the notifications but manage to enter "Springfield High School." It's a two-hour drive into the middle of the state, but if I hurry, I can probably make it before they're done with booth setup.

CHAPTER TWENTY-SIX

I HAVE TO put my phone on Do Not Disturb because the notifications kept interrupting the driving directions from my map app. The car has just enough gas to get me there, but I stop anyway because I can make a mad dash out of the house, but I've rethought running into the ScholEx setup in my pajamas.

Mrs. J and the map are wrong, it's an hour and a half drive at most.

I start actually thinking about the whole situation as I pull on the jeans that I was going to wear home on Sunday. I'm here in a grungy gas station bathroom because they left without me. The only shoes I have are the dress shoes I was going to wear tomorrow because Logan didn't wake me up this morning. Despite an hour of driving, I am still not really sure what I'm feeling except that there's a lot of it and it is veering ever more in the direction of mad. I just need to be there. That's all I know for sure.

I don't know if I even want to turn my notifications back on as I pull into the Springfield High School parking lot, but I do.

It's a total mess of vans and trailers and teenagers and teachers, but none of them are the traitors I need. My phone starts vibrating the second I turn HubBub back on, and I maneuver through the mess of notifications to get to the ScholEx channel. I know they're using it to coordinate, but eventually I have to give up. My phone is basically a useless buzzing machine of endless interruptive phone calls.

Instead I decide to try to find someone, anyone I know, and the gym is the most likely spot. And there, in the middle of the room, is my so-called best friend and several of the other traitors.

"Sky!" Joey is the first to see me, and she's happy. "You made it!"

"Where's Logan?" I ask coldly. One problem at a time. One betrayal at a time. Not that I even know what to do about them leaving without me. How to rationalize that Mads, of all people, would let them leave me when she knows how important this is to me.

Joey frowns. "Sky, are you okay?"

Mads comes up. "Sky, I've been freaking out. No one has heard from you in hours. Your mom called four times."

"Clearly," I say, gesturing at the half-built booth. My phone is still vibrating, and now I feel like I am, too. Adrenaline is buzzing in my ears. "Where is my brother?"

"He's outside. The table legs fell apart, and he's trying to fix them."

"I'll show you," Joey says, too brightly.

She takes me to a far less busy parking lot, where my brother, Zane, and Dom are trying to hammer the legs back together. Logan looks up and is happy for a second, and then his face falls. "Sky . . . why are you here? You should be at home. Mom and Dad are worried sick."

"You sent a press release?" I shout across the parking lot. "A press release!"

He hands the hammer to Dom and steps forward. "Wait. Did you drive my car all the way here?"

"Why would you do that?" I ask, ignoring his question. "How could you be so thoughtless?"

"Thoughtless?" he asks, closing the distance between us. "I thought you would be happy."

"Happy? Happy about you making more work for me on an app I never wanted to see again? Happy you left me behind? Happy you made Requite so popular I have people calling me from Hearst?"

"I thought the whole point of this was to make you famous." He looks genuinely confused. How is he not getting this?

"It was supposed to be Study Buddy. Not Requite! It would be a controlled release, and Lovelace would adopt it, and then the districts, and then everything would be fine. It wouldn't be weeks of coding until all hours of the night. Study Buddy wouldn't need urgent fixes and last-minute customer service requests. I wouldn't work myself into a migraine and be abandoned just as the most important day of my life happens without me. I have plans, Logan! Those plans do not include Requite! It's a throwaway app. Maybe four people ever were supposed to use it. I just needed Joey on the team. She just needed to find out if Zane liked her. That was it!

The end of it. Then it could be forgotten along with all my other experiments. I wasn't going to help her flirt with him. I wasn't going to stop hating him. I definitely wasn't going to—" I finally hear what I'm saying and stop, horrified. I remember that we're not at home in my room. That Zane's there looking at me . . . and Joey is right beside me.

It occurs to me that I have just ruined that, too. All the hard work and all the plans, and they're both going to hate me as much as I hate myself right now. I shake my head, overwhelmed with the massiveness of the mistake I just made. "I need to go." I turn on my heels, leaving them all there, a little stunned. I can't believe I just did that. I'm walking so fast out of the parking lot, and there's just enough adrenaline blurring my vision that I barrel straight into someone. Fortunately he's not carrying anything breakable. Unfortunately I know him.

"Sky?"

"No," I say to Nate. "No, not you, not today."

I back up and try to go into the building, but the door is locked.

"Sky, where are you going?"

"I need to go fix my booth, or murder my best friend, or something. I don't know."

"You seem upset," he says, running his hand through his hair. There was a time that would have made my heart skip. I don't know why. I make bad choices.

"Can you please go away? I just want to leave."

"You're going the wrong way for that," he says.

"Clearly." I try to push past him, but he puts his hand on my shoulder to stop me.

"What's wrong?" he asks again, and it almost sounds like he gives a crap.

"Nothing that concerns you," I say, and I make it past him. In fact I make it all the way to the parking lot where I left Logan's car when I hear him say, "You know I still care about you, Skylar, but sometimes you're just a bit too much."

"That's garbage." I stop and turn because I finally have someone who actually deserves all this anger that's been building up inside me. "You don't care about me at all. You never actually cared. You made me think you cared. You said it . . . when no one could hear you. But you just like attention. If you actually cared, you'd know me. You'd know my friends. But, no. It's all about you. Again."

He's staring at me, mouth open. No smart comebacks. No smooth words.

"Go away, Nate, I've got nothing for you."

"If you just calmed down, you'd see how important you are, Sky," he says, and my phone is vibrating again in my hand.

I glance at it and shake my head. "Trust me, I know."

"No, you don't understand," he says, trying to put his hand on my shoulder again, and I shrug away from him. "I screwed up last summer. I get that, but it wasn't just me."

"I don't need your mind games anymore, Nate, I have the *Washington Post* blowing up my phone." I hold it up so he can see the caller ID. His eyes go wide, and he just stands there trying to find something that will make him important. But that's the thing—if he were, he wouldn't have to try.

"You were never worth it," I say, more for him than for me, but still, I give him a chance.

When he says nothing, I push past him, leaving him behind to try to think of a comeback or an excuse. When I finally make it to where I left Logan's car, there's already someone there. Waiting. His arms folded in front of him and that hair hanging in his face again, and he says, "We need to talk."

"Not you too, Zane. Go back inside. Forget what I said." I can't look at him. I don't need him to be mad at me right now. I'm mad enough at myself. Instead I grab the door handle that's just next to him and tug it into him but neither budges. "Can you move?"

"What you said back there . . ." He's looking down at me, and I pull some air into my lungs because I need it, badly.

"I was mad at Logan, and I said things I shouldn't have. I'm sorry. Just forget it all."

"Did you set me and Joey up?" he asks, his voice doing that quiet thing again, like I'm the only person in the whole world who can hear him. And I guess I am.

"I didn't make you match with her," I say, finally letting go of the door handle.

"Yes, you did," he says.

"What?" I drop back against the passenger door of a shiny gray Camry. Probably one of the teachers' cars. It's cold and I'm starting to feel it.

"That day at the meet you kept insisting that she liked me, and I didn't believe you. You wouldn't hear me. So I figured the only way to prove it was to use your own app. But then there she was, in the chat. And it was painful, Sky." He looks up at me through his floppy hair. "But you know that, too, don't you?"

"I thought I was helping."

"That was you . . . during break. Not her."

"I forgot to turn the admin controls off."

"Don't you get it? That was perfect. For a second I thought . . ." He shakes his head. "That's why I kept trying. I thought there might be something because you . . ." He tightens, his whole body a pause. Then he says, "You still hate me. No matter what I do."

"I don't hate you," I say weakly, not able to even address the whole truth. But even a half-truth is a lie, and Zane can't hear what I won't tell him.

"I thought things were changing." There's so much sadness, so much weight, and I don't know what to say. I don't know how I'd even say it.

"Why him?" he says, finally looking up, but not at me, at the school. "Why that jerk Nate?"

"He was nice to me."

"I'm nice to you." His voice breaks a little.

"You are," I agree. "But he made me think I mattered. I was sick and alone, and Mads and Kaden had just started dating, and I felt so left out. And I wanted to be important to someone."

"You've always been important to me," he says, but it's a whisper, and I don't know if I really heard it.

"You don't mean that," I say. He can't. It's me. Even without Joey. He couldn't figure things out with her, and she's so smart and so kind and so very talented.

"Don't I?" he asks.

"You can't," I say.

And he reaches into his front pocket and pulls out his phone. He starts flipping through things and holds it out to me.

It's his match page. And right there at the top is his chat with Joey with a picture of her at the very first ScholEx meet. But just below that is another picture next to a timer. The longest timer I've seen and the dying heart Mads thought would be a deliciously morbid addition. She made me a heart icon that starts a bright cherry red and slowly gets darker and darker as the time counts on. Zane's heart is black, and the timer says two months, five days, seven hours, and eight minutes. The picture next to it is me at the lunch table.

"I waited for you," he says, louder and colder. "I waited and waited. And then Logan took pity on me." His laugh is tight and bitter. "Do you know how much I thought New Year's Eve was it? My chance. Our chance? I almost kissed you . . ."

I open my mouth to say something, but he stops me. "No, I get it. You kissed everyone else. I just . . . I wanted you, and you wanted me with Joey." He scuffs his foot on the ground. "It was all about ScholEx and your future. It was never me."

He pushes off the car, and for a second we're close, so close, I think maybe . . . but he holds his hand up like he's going to touch my face, only instead he pulls away entirely. "I can't do this with you anymore, Sky. I can't wait for me to matter to you. I definitely can't keep being this toy you bat around when you're bored."

And he walks away. Toward the school, and he's leaving, and I don't even know what just happened. He liked me. Me. Skylar Collins.

Dom wasn't being delusional. No one was playing with me.

It wasn't Requite that took Zane away, it was me pushing him.

And now it's too late. He's really done with me. I threw away all my chances myself.

My anger and frustration with the press release and being ditched leaks out of me along with my strength, and I slide down until I'm sitting on the ground between the cars. Suddenly there are tears, and then I'm actually crying because any control I thought I had was a lie.

"Sky?" a voice says above me. I wipe the tears away and try to breathe, but it's Mads. "I told Mrs. James you're here and that we're going back to the room."

"You left without me," I say, and the tears come back. I'm not even mad anymore. I'm crushed. I tried to hold everything myself. But something finally broke and everything is coming out. All the loneliness and doubt. All the things I was trying to face alone because she had a new person who wasn't me.

"Your mom said you were sick," she answers.

"My mom always says I'm sick," I say, between gasping breaths. "But you still left."

"We didn't want to forfeit, Sky. This is too important to you," she says.

"You left *me*," I repeat with all the weepy emphasis on the last word so she knows that this is more than just about the van this morning.

"No, Sky." She's on the ground next to me despite her flowing skirts and heeled boots. "You left me."

"I never went anywhere."

"You went into the hospital. And to the doctor. And stopped telling me things."

"You started dating Kaden."

"You had a whole secret crush you didn't tell me about until the last possible second."

"I was alone. And he tried, Mads. He was always there to take whatever I had. And you weren't."

"Do you think I wanted that?" Mads asks, and she doesn't look too far from tears herself. "You stopped talking to me unless it had to do with code."

"You didn't need me for anything else anymore," I say.

And she hits me. Not hard, just a thump on my arm like in slug bug.

"Ow," I say, rubbing my arm.

And she laughs, and I laugh, and she puts her arms around me.

"Sky, we didn't leave you."

"I distinctly remember driving here alone."

"Okay, well, yes, that, but it wasn't to abandon you. You collapsed at Joey's house. The last time you did that . . ." She's suddenly very far away, and I can see how scared she was. "Your mom said you were sick, and when you're sick, there's *nothing* I can do. But I could do this. There's enough of us to win State for you."

"It didn't feel like it was for me."

"That's because you can't let go for five minutes. You *don't* have to be in charge every second of every day. We can be there for you sometimes. We *want* to be there for you." She's actually mad. "You get that, right?"

She's expecting me to argue with her, holding herself with such confidence, but instead the tears come back and I just nod.

"Oh, Mads, I screwed up."

She laughs and hugs me again. "Well, at least you admit it this time."

CHAPTER TWENTY-SEVEN

AFTER ABOUT AN hour it became pretty clear that a cold parking lot was not in any way going to actually solve the problems, so Mads loaded me into the car, found us a diner that had decent fries, and navigated me to the world's creepiest motel.

Her phone buzzes just as much as mine does through the entire ordeal, and we decide to figure out just how far things have gone. Our notifications are a mess: hers because her legion of followers found her connection, mine because the tech community wants to know how I cracked into the dating app market. Hours later as we sit on the tiny bed eating the last of the extra order of french fries we brought with us, she finally asks, "So, why do you really hate this app?"

"It wasn't supposed to be an app," I say, putting my fry down. "It was just to help Joey."

"Help Joey with what?"

"She wouldn't join the team until I helped her with Zane."

She sits up. "Wait, she wanted you to get him to date her?"

"No, just . . ." I wedge myself against the headboard. My years watching *Supernatural* have utterly failed me, because there's nothing cool or retro in this room. There's definitely not a nice table to spread our research out on. There's just a single bedside table and a couple outlets. "She just wanted to know if he liked her. The app was my way of passing the note to find out."

"And does he?" She's wedged against her own headboard and her phone is on her lap. One would expect the goth queen to be wearing flowing black silk, but goth only goes so far when flannel jim-jams with little dancing skeletons on them are an option.

"I thought he did."

"Thought?" she says.

"Um, so, right before you showed up, I found out he only matched with her to prove she didn't like him."

"Prove to who?"

"Me . . ."

"Skylar Myrtle!" She sits up, leaning forward. "He likes you. And I know you like him—don't even try to pretend you don't."

Even though I'm totally cried out, I cover my face with my hands and push them back through my hair. "He liked me. I ruined it."

"But you still like him."

I look at her.

"Sky. If you don't admit it right now, we're going back to fighting and also I'm taking all the fries away from you because I'm that evil."

"Okay, fine. I really like him."

"I knew it! I knew it! I knew it!" She's dancing in place. "And did you tell him?"

"No." My hands hide my face again.

"So let me guess, he told you he's been desperately in love with you for years and you never thought to say, 'I, Skylar, like you, Zane, and we should smash faces and be nerdy little know-it-alls together for the rest of our lives???'" The way she asks it I can hear the excessive punctuation.

So I throw one of my pillows at her, and she catches it.

"You are the actual worst," she says, and sighs. "This is why you need me. To force you to tell him how you feel."

"How could I? I ruined it."

"You didn't try!"

I don't say anything.

"Skylar. Remember how I love you platonically?"

I nod.

"Remember how I said that out loud to your face so you know?"

"It's too late," I say, knowing where she's going with this.

"You can't just say it's too late and throw up your hands. Have you even tried?"

I hate her. "I hate you."

"You love me." She smiles at me and wiggles her head. "Now say it."

My phone buzzes again, and I glance at it. "That one's in Chinese."

"You sure it's not Japanese? We're very big in Japan."

I roll my eyes.

"No distractions. Say it."

"You're my best friend and I love you platonically, even if you keep ditching me for Kaden."

"I knew it!" she says, sitting forward on her bed. "I'm sorry I didn't try harder."

"It's okay."

"No, now you say it."

I roll my eyes.

"Skylar, you're brilliant, and we're about to be super famous, but you have to say this stuff out loud for anyone to know what you're thinking."

"I don't want to be famous," I say, and she stares at me. "But I'm sorry I didn't tell you. I'm sorry I didn't try. I'm sorry if I pushed you away, or left you out, or hid behind my code, or whatever. I'm just . . . sorry."

"You really do want to be famous, and you're forgiven."

"Requite was a mistake. Study Buddy was the plan."

"And plans change." She gets up off her bed and comes to sit cross-legged in front of me on mine. "This master Study Buddy, ScholEx, take-over-the-world plan you have?"

"What about it?"

"It's not the one."

"It could be."

"You're going to throw away a perfectly good, massively popular app that brings love and joy to millions—"

"Five hundred thousand at best!"

"It'll be millions, watch—but you're still going to throw it away for a flash card app?" She pushes my shoulder. "You're being ridiculous."

"It hasn't brought any joy that I can see."

"You're not looking hard enough."

"I ruined everything for Joey."

"Then you should apologize to her."

"I should."

"But probably in the morning because it's already almost two a.m." She gets up and goes back to her bed. "And we're gonna have to do press first thing, too."

"You mean we have to compete at State in the morning."

"Yeah, yeah, we can do that, too."

"Your priorities."

"Like you're one to talk." She throws my pillow back at me. "Go to sleep, Skylar. We're taking over the world tomorrow."

"Good night, Mads," I say, flipping off the light.

"Good night, mini mogul."

CHAPTER TWENTY-EIGHT

EARLY THE NEXT morning, while Mads finishes putting her makeup on in the room, I head to the van where we're all meeting and start working through some of the messages that have been stacking up since yesterday. One of Logan's terrible poems has been shared more than ten thousand times because a reality star thought it was cute and then someone made a meme out of it.

I'm sorting requests into people who want to sell me things and people who want to ask me things when the van door opens and Joey leans in. Her smile freezes and her whole body with it. She's stuck hunched over, not quite in and not quite out of the van.

"Look, Joey, I'm sorry," I say before she can say anything. "I shouldn't have said those things yesterday. And I definitely shouldn't have said them in front of Zane. I didn't want to ruin things for you. I just . . ."

"No, I'm sorry," she says. "I didn't know about you two or all that stuff."

"You have nothing to be sorry for." I scoot over a little in my nest in the very back, and she comes to sit down next to me. She's not actually crying, but the tears are close. "I screwed up, and I screwed your chances up. I really was trying to help you."

"You did help me," she says. "More than anything you helped me, but it just didn't work. I didn't know how to tell you I failed."

"You didn't fail; I failed you."

"No, Sky, when I asked him on that date, I just, we just . . ." She wipes her eye. "It's not a real match."

"I'm sorry, Joey, I didn't . . ."

"He was so nice about it. And you did all that work, but he's right, as pretty as he is, there's just not a connection. Not like . . ." She looks at me, takes a breath, and says, "I'm just going to say it. Sky, I think he might like you."

"I think he did, but not anymore."

"No, Sky, I think he might like you a lot."

"Maybe," I say, putting my tablet down and looking straight at her. "But the last thing I want is to hurt you."

"I know. I know you did all this to help me. That's why as much as this sucks, I can't actually be mad at you." She wipes her eyes and smiles. "But I just want to know one thing."

"What's that?"

"Do you like him?"

Before I can answer, the van door swings wide open, and Logan and Dom appear. "Nerdling?"

"Logan," I say, acknowledging his existence.

"We need to talk," he says, falling into the row in front of Joey and me, with Dom close behind.

"Now? Because I'm talking to Joey, and after that I'll be

juggling these media requests while working the booth. And after that I'll be in Quizposition."

"I was going to follow up on the press releases, I swear."

"You didn't have to."

"Sky, you made it to the main page. The main page! Don't you realize how big of a deal that is?"

"Yes. Geez, Logan, of course I know. My notifications are a mess. And my tickets . . ." I look down at the tablet in my lap, as if they're coming for me. And I'm about to lay into him again when the door opens one more time and it's Zane, and everything in me quits fighting. And it's not just me. The rest of the van goes silent.

"Don't stop on my account," Zane says, choosing to sit in the front row and not looking anywhere near me. The silence is so thick in the small van that the only thing that slices through it is my phone ringing, yet again.

"I have to take this," I say, but I don't. It's not even press. It's an autodial from a company offering outsourced customer management and I'm almost tempted to let them, but they're not the first. The costs at these places are ridiculous, and I still need to pay for college.

As I make noises and pretend I didn't hang up almost instantly, Mads, Kaden, and Mrs. J join us in the van. Mrs. J starts talking to me, but Logan explains I'm on an important call, and I can hear the scoffing noise Zane makes from two rows away.

Mads, who claimed shotgun, turns on the radio, and she and Kaden and Joey start singing along at top volume. And everyone pretends like I haven't ruined this entire team for the five minutes it takes us to get to the high school.

When we arrive, the van empties out like it's on fire, except for my brother and me. "Are you really mad at me?" He's looking at his hands, and he's like a puppy that got caught in a rainstorm.

"I'm not." He perks up. "I was," I say, keeping him from thinking he's off the hook. "But I think maybe I was mad about something else."

"You and Zane?" he asks.

I nod.

"I heard what you said yesterday and then Joey kind of filled in her side."

"I really don't want to talk about this." That feeling like I'm nothing more than empty space to Zane now hurts far worse than Requite ever did. And then, despite myself, I say, "He's never going to speak to me again."

"Are you *that* dense?" he asks.

"Maybe I am. It's been a really long couple of weeks."

"You *are* that dense," he says, and laughs for the first time. It's a weird relief—there's something about Logan's laugh that makes it feel like everything's going to be fine. Even when nothing at all is actually fine. "It's been way longer than a couple of weeks."

"I don't want to talk about that."

"About Zane?"

I nod, but I'm not crying. I did enough of that last night. I've got too much to do today to be crying.

"How about Requite?" he asks.

"Like I have any better control over that." I'm tapping my tablet frantically, but it's just tapping. I accomplish nothing. Something to keep my hands busy.

"Have you updated your page?"

"What?"

"Skylar, you need to update your socials."

"With what? That I wrote an app that ruins lives and have a brother who meddles in things he shouldn't?"

"It doesn't ruin lives." He yanks my tablet out of my hands and pulls up the admin panel. He starts clicking through the marketing metrics like he knows what they're saying.

I try to grab my tablet back, but he's fighting me. "What are you doing?"

"I'm checking your KPI."

"I haven't set up any KPI."

"I know. I did. Last month. I knew you'd never figure it out." He's frowning at the screen. "This is amazing, but it's not sustainable. I'll put up some posts. Who are you going to talk to?"

He's an entirely different Logan. He's not grumpy or faking at being serious, he's just focused.

"Who are you and what did you do with my brother?"

"I didn't just send the press release and hope, Sky. I've been working on this for weeks."

"Why?" I ask, staring back at a page full of obscure graphs that say things I was going to get to eventually. Maybe in a business class or something in a couple years.

"I told you. You made something here." He backs up, looking at me. "You really never saw it?"

"It was a silly app that solved a problem."

"'Solved,'" he says, making air quotes with his fingers.

"Why would you work so hard on something I was trying to throw away?"

"Requite is genius because you're a genius, and if I can do anything that helps you get that much further, I'm going to do it, Sky. Always."

"Why?"

"You're my nerdling. I love you."

I glare at him.

"But more than that I'm proud of you. You know I've been having problems figuring myself out . . ." He sort of trails off and looks back down at the floor.

"Yeah, I live with you."

"Well, it's been hard living with you. Someone who has known you're going to be the next big thing basically from birth," he says, but it doesn't make sense. My confident, strong, outgoing big brother who literally everyone loves can't possibly be jealous of me.

"Logan, that's—"

He cuts me off with a quick "But ever since I saw this app, regardless of what you thought of it, I knew it was *it*, you were finally going to do it, and I just needed to be here to see it happen. Not off at college. I needed this. I started telling people at school about it, and then the tournaments, and you have to have seen the promos by now . . ."

"The poem has been bubbled up over thirty thousand times," I say.

"You're kidding me." He tries to look it up on my tablet, but it's locked, so he drops it back in his lap. "But, you see it, right?"

"See what?" I ask.

"You helped me find my thing."

"You've always had a thing, Logan. People actually like you."

He laughs, almost bitterly, but shakes his head, and says, "No, Sky, you helped me find what I think I want to do. I'm going to go to business school and study marketing."

I kind of frown at him, and he says, "When I know what I'm doing, I can come help you and you don't have to hire some con man."

"But I have to hire you?" I ask, hoping he'll hear the joke of it, and he does.

"I'm riding your coattails, nerdling, just accept it."

I smile at him, and I know he means it.

"So about your other problem," he says with a wicked grin.

"I still don't want to talk about that," I say, grabbing my tablet out of his hands finally.

"Clearly," he says. "Why didn't you tell me?"

"Tell you what?"

"About why you really made the app?"

"Because it wasn't my story to tell. Joey needed help, so I helped her."

"You played with Zane."

"Not intentionally!" I say, looking up at the fabric ceiling of the van. "I thought it was what he wanted."

"It's not."

"They matched."

"You know he likes you."

"I didn't. And not anymore. He said as much last night."

"Did you tell him you like him?"

"Why does everyone keep asking that?"

"Because, Skylar Myrtle Collins, we know you."

"I embarrassed him, manipulated him, confessed everything in front of Joey—whose only crime was liking him. I even vomited on his shoes two days ago. There's not really any point."

"You missed his shoes."

"Oh great." I wave my hands dramatically in the air. "He must have woken up this morning and realized he's made a terrible mistake throwing a prize like me away."

"Skylar, stop."

"What?"

"I've been trying to show you he likes you for months, but evidently you've been trying to get him to date a random girl he doesn't even like. So who's the smart one?"

I say with a sigh, "I know I screwed up."

"Well, at least you know that much," he says in what is clearly a mocking exasperation.

"Babe!" a shout comes from somewhere outside the van, and we both look up, and then I look at my brother.

"Did Dom just shout *babe*?"

Logan flushes.

Dom swings the van door open. "I have been looking all over for you."

"I was right here," Logan says. "Talking down the captain."

"Well, it's almost our shift at the booth," Dom says, and the he kisses my brother on the cheek. And it's not even New Year's.

"Wait . . . what is happening?" I ask.

"Didn't you tell her?" Dom asks.

"Oh yeah." Logan grins at me—a big, goofy, adorable, weird grin that I very much don't like, but also am so glad to see. "I'm not just the Requite marketing manager, I'm also a client. Which you would know if you read my amazing press release."

I look between them, frowning in confusion. And then realization hits. "Logan?" I ask Dom.

Dom shrugs. "He's adorkable, what can I say?"

I shake my head.

Dom adds, "And I hear you finally figured out you're the Katharine Hepburn?"

I hide my face in my hands. "Not you too."

"No, I'm done helping you," Dom says. "You need to help yourself."

"She thinks it's too late," Logan explains.

"Your sister is not too bright," Dom says.

"That's what I keep telling people, but no one listens to me."

"Things aren't looking great for you, Sky, I'll admit, but you could consider, I don't know . . . trying?"

"I don't know what to do," I say.

Dom shakes his head. "Pitiful."

Logan laughs. "If only someone had made an app or something so you could see if someone liked you."

Dom says, "If only . . ."

"I think I need to stay here and help Sky," Logan says.

I frown. "You can't."

"You're clearly out of your depth," Logan says.

"No, the team needs you," I say.

"If you miss the booth, babe, you won't have enough points to rank in the final," Dom points out, agreeing with me.

"Well, someone has to deal with all this . . ." he says, looking at me.

I look back down at my tablet. "Fine, whatever. You go work your shift, I'll be here . . . filling out interview questions for various media outlets, I guess."

"Oh, I have something for that!" Logan pulls his phone out and fiddles with it. "Talking points. Just hit as many of them as you can. Like the booth, it doesn't matter what they ask—answer with one of those."

I pull open my email and they're basic facts about Requite.

"I really don't have time—"

Logan interrupts me. "You have time for this. We will handle ScholEx. You will handle this."

"I'm the captain."

Logan and Dom both jump out of the van and slam the door shut.

"You can't keep me here all day!" I yell after them as they walk away holding hands. "I'll be there when my shift starts!"

They're not listening, and the unread count on my admin email is now up to almost a thousand, and I realize it's not just my future riding on this project, either.

CHAPTER TWENTY-NINE

AS PROMISED, I made it out of the van right before lunch to work my shift for the booth, but Mads had a question and then Logan got an urgent email and what feels like all of a sudden the overhead page announces that Achievers' Quizposition will be starting in fifteen minutes. I've ignored most of the other such pages because, between Mads, Logan, and my admin box, there's never anything that doesn't feel like life or death.

I get up and shake out the cobwebs. I have let Requite distract me.

Even though I never made it to a single booth shift . . .

Even though they came all the way out here without me . . .

I am going to finish this Quizposition round if it kills me.

There's no way I can rank without booth points, but that doesn't mean my Quizposition points are worthless.

My phone starts buzzing, but I ignore it.

I get to the check-in station and stand in what feels like an unending line.

My phone keeps buzzing. I pull it out.

"Hearst Communications," it reads.

"Oh bleep," I say, because there are at least three teachers nearby.

"Is that . . ."

"Skylar!" Logan bellows from down the hall. He is headed toward me at a run, Mads a dark cloud beside him. "Did you agree to an interview?"

"I . . ." I look at my phone. Um, maybe? What did I even say to her? I've talked to so many people since yesterday.

"A woman from *Seventeen* is trying to get ahold of you."

I hear someone repeat *Seventeen*, and half the line turns to look at me.

"I may have," I say.

"She said she's going to press today and she has to talk to you now or never," Logan says, because the line has shrunk and there's only a couple people between me and check-in.

"I have to sign in," I say.

"Do you, though?"

Don't I? Isn't this what they want from me?

"We don't need you," Mads says. "I mean, you know what I mean."

"You mean let Kaden and Dom and Zane handle this?"

Logan just looks at me. He looks sad. No, disappointed.

My phone starts buzzing again, and the woman behind the table says, "Next." And suddenly everything from the past six months comes crashing down on me. Logan and Mom fighting about his future. Joey's earnest need for help. Zane making my stomach flip. New Year's. Studying. Spring rolls. Mads coming to rescue me in the parking lot instead of finishing her booth. My friends being there for me when I was only ever there for my perfect plan.

The woman behind the desk looks as impatient as my phone feels. Logan and Mads beside me, their futures riding more on this call than me ranking. Dom, Kaden, and Zane have this.

ScholEx doesn't need me, but my friends do.

"Tell them they have to win this," I say before answering my phone. "This is Skylar Collins." I step out of line. Logan pumps a fist and Mads grabs my hand, and the line for Quizposition moves on without me.

A half hour later, I've finished with Logan's talking points. I'm actually getting okay at them. I sneak into the back row of the auditorium to watch the end of the Achievers' Quizposition and find a seat next to Joey of all people.

"You're not up there," she whispers at me.

We're far enough back we don't really get shushed. Most of the folks back here are more interested in their phones than what's happening onstage.

"I double-booked."

She looks away from the stage. "*You* double-booked Achievers' Quizposition at State?"

I shrug sheepishly, finding the table with Kaden, Dom, and Zane. "They must hate me."

"They're actually doing okay without you," she says.

And as I look at the stage and the glowing flops of Zane's hair, I realize that answering that call was only the first thing I could do to help the people who have done everything for me.

Because it's not just my team on the stage—it's also the reminder of how horrible it feels to like someone who won't tell you they like you back. Even when they do. Even when you know.

I pull out my phone, open the app to the camera, zoom in, and click.

He must have it on vibrate and not off because he jumps, just a little, but doesn't reach for the pocket with his phone. He's a professional, after all.

When the lightning round is over and everyone is about to start applauding, I stand up, adrenaline buzzing in my ears. Before I can think about it too much, I move to the aisle and close my eyes and yell, "Zane Michaelson, check your Requite messages." And when I make myself open them, he's looking right at me for the first time today. That's when it hits me that everyone is looking at me and not the stage, and I head through the doors behind me, wondering what I just did.

I don't need to see the results. They don't matter anymore. I have a new plan now. One that doesn't throw away the good stuff I find along the way. One that takes more chances.

But as I sneak away to hide in the van, I hear my name being called. I look back and it's Zane. Framed with the perfect glow of a single hall light. Definitely an old movie star.

"I'm sorry," I say. "I know it's too little . . ."

But he doesn't wait for me to finish. He crosses the hall and stands too close. Close like on Joey's front stoop. Close like New Year's.

"You weren't onstage," he says.

"I had an interview," I say.

"And you weren't at the booth," he says.

"I had to make a choice," I say. "I made Requite for all the wrong reasons, and I hate that I hurt you, but it's important now. Logan—"

"You missed ScholEx for your brother?"

"I knew you had this."

"And that match?" He holds up his phone, his hand brushing my arm on the way and sending tingles down my spine.

"I know you hate me. You should hate me. But I didn't play with you. I really did think I was helping. I thought you liked Joey. And that's all I know how to do to help—make apps and stay out of the way. But you were always there and you were so close and . . . I never really hated you. I wanted you to be happy."

"And you never once thought that being with you would make me happy?"

"It never occurred to me that I wasn't the only one who felt like this."

"What? I didn't hear that."

I take a deep breath. "I like you. Like, so much it hurts. I know every time you were close, every single thing you've ever said to me. I like you so much I wanted you to date someone else."

"You like me," he says, and smiles at me so the whole world glows with it. "Finally." And unlike New Year's, unlike that bathroom hallway, unlike a million tiny moments over the last few months, this time I don't pull away. Instead I lean in and kiss him. Just a little. But then it becomes a lot, and he's warm and soft like his curls. My edgy nerves give way to this floating joy that reaches all the way to my toes. And while we're kissing, time loses all meaning, so whether it's a second or an hour it's not nearly enough. But the one thing I know for sure is that I am not giving this up—not giving him up.

Because it's not just this one epic kiss. It's knowing he likes me the same way I do him. That he's never been afraid of people knowing he liked me. That I'm not too much.

CHAPTER THIRTY

WHEN ALL IS said and done at State, we land in a very respectable second place. There will be no Nationals. No grand win at State. No real future for Study Buddy—not that I have the time for that app to take off right now. Our team got really close, and if the winners from Springfield High can't field a whole team, we might get to go instead. Not that any of us are hoping for that anymore.

If this had happened at Regionals, I would have been absolutely devastated. But . . . well . . . sitting at this tiny little pizza place with my friends while some ancient video game tries to lure us in and too-loud pop music tries to drown us out, I realize that I definitely didn't lose.

I'm not at the end of the table but in the middle. Zane is next to me on one side and Mads on the other. Zane's close, like touching close again, but this time that is very much not a problem. Every so often he moves and brushes against me and there's this smile he has that I've never seen before—it's confident and borderline ecstatic at the same time.

Logan is across from me with Joey on one side and Dom on the other, and he has a similar joy despite his face being in its accustomed smile. Everyone's talking all at once.

Laughing, throwing napkins. Constantly shuffling the Parmesan and hot pepper flake bottles so there's room for whatever they're showing one another.

Joey and Mrs. James are deep in conversation about music while Kaden and Zane are arguing across Mads and me about whether the photos in the Requite app constitute an invasion of privacy.

The pizzas come, and the waitress asks, "Are you all on that app, too?"

The table grows silent, and my marketing manager answers, "You could say that. Are you?"

She laughs. "No, but my daughter and all her friends have talked about nothing else for the last month, I swear. I had to make her uninstall it; it was getting ridiculous."

"How old are they?" Logan asks, sounding very grown-up while we all look at each other awkwardly.

"Thirteen," she says. "Now who had the pepperoni?"

"Them," the whole table says together, pointing at Zane and me.

The waitress laughs. "It's not the weirdest pizza I made today, but it's close." She puts down the pepperoni with half mushroom and half pineapple in front of us.

"What's the weirdest?" Joey asks.

"We do a black olive and pineapple for game days that people actually order."

The whole table bursts into another cacophony of opinions on the toppings, but Zane leans over and whispers in my ear, "We're not weird."

I laugh and say back, "We're totally weird."

He nudges me with his elbow and I nudge him back, and Logan makes a gagging noise, so I throw my napkin at him. "Pass the pepper flakes."

"Stop being so cute and I will."

Mrs. James says, "Wait, are you two dating?" And the entire table bursts into another round of laughter. But she presses on. "When did this happen?"

"About an hour ago," I say, and can feel myself blushing.

"He finally wore you down?" she asks to even further uproar.

"Mrs. James!" I say.

But Zane says, "Yes, ma'am. It only took six years."

"You know, you all could have warned me," Joey says.

Logan says, "Look, they needed a whole lot of help."

And under the table I finally take Zane's hand in mine, closing any distance between us. "No, all we needed was an app."

ACKNOWLEDGMENTS

I am so grateful to be in a position to thank people for a second book.

This story isn't real, but that doesn't mean it wasn't inspired by real events, and the found family we created from trying really hard to beat Urbandale (for reasons) my senior year meant more to me than they'll ever know. To the friends who invaded my lunch table, made me watch old movies, and never had anything appropriate to say about Pixy Stix in Mountain Dew, thank you ... and I'm sorry about prom. (But I DID promise memories that would last a lifetime.) Also, Perman, if you ever read this, you know you're the exception to Urbandale's villainy.

Thanks also go to my agent, Bridget Smith, and the team at JABberwocky. You are all the best kind of nerds.

Extra thanks to everyone at Scholastic, especially Jody Corbett for making me give people faces and clothes and stuff, but also more feelings. These nerds wouldn't shine half as brightly without you. To designer Baily Crawford for all I have put you through—thanks especially for going above and beyond to even make the narrative pretty! To Josh Berlowitz, Jael Fogle, and Janell Harris for making it fit inside the pages. (I tried harder this time!) And to the talented folks at @IReadYA, especially Rachel Feld and Shannon Pender, and the rest of the team, particularly Erin Berger, Lizette Serrano, Emily Heddleson, Danielle Yadao, and my publicist, Elisabeth Ferrari. More thanks go to the sales team, who always make sure my books find their readers!

I have the great fortune to be surrounded by talented and clever writers who have supported and educated me in the ways of publishing. I honestly wouldn't be where I am without the amazing, wonderful, kind, and talented Adib Khorram. Your support through writing, querying, debuting, and especially this trash year went so far above and beyond the call of duty, I'm eternally grateful I get to call you my friend.

A very special thanks to Natalie C. Parker, whose wisdom and kindness always inspire me to share and help others grow. Also the whole team at MadCap. Thank you for creating a space where I can feel like a real author.

Mason Deaver and Nafiza Azad! Thank you for all the screaming! I'm so glad publishing brought our weird selves together. Joel Roth and Adana Washington, thank you for never making my obsessive process stuff feel out of place. Michelle Hulse and Mary, thank you for sticking with me.

I also want to shout out the folks who have been such amazing supporters of my books! The *Speak for Yourself* street team: Chloe, Cibele, Gretal, Jordan, Natalia, Christy, Ellie, Iris, and Mel! Your excitement has been so heartwarming. And Cody Roecker, who will always be my favorite moderator—thank you for introducing me to scones!